Third to Tumble

Moonlight Rogues, Volume 3

Alexa Whitewolf

Published by Luna Imprints, 2019.

THIRD TO TUMBLE

First edition. June 21, 2019.

Copyright © 2019 Alexa Whitewolf.

ISBN: 978-1-989384-01-5

Written by Alexa Whitewolf.

"It often occurs to me that we love most what makes us miserable. In my opinion, the damned are damned because they enjoy being damned."
—Patrick Kavanagh—

Author's Note & Acknowledgements

A lot of me goes into my books. With each one of these installments for **Moonlight Rogues**, I've discovered new things, and Finn's story was no different. I first travelled to Ireland in September 2017, then again in October 2018, and again planning to later in 2019. I've fallen in love with the country and culture, and I think a lot of it is because it reminds me of Romania growing up – beautiful mountains, gorgeous lakes, and lovely people. So, it should come as no surprise that Finn's journey as a Celtic wolf expanded ☺

Once more, in *Third to Tumble* you'll see some characters you've already fallen in love with, and get to see how Dom & Luz, Tristan & Dani are getting along. You'll also be introduced to new ones – some, not so likeable.

I hope you enjoy, and you'll consider leaving a review at the end ☺ If you do and send me a screenshot at info.author@alexawhitewolf.com, you'll automatically get the next book for free!

As usual, a huge thanks to my husband, my mom and furbabies for helping me through this! And the team behind this book who helped edit, design the cover, encourage me— you guys rock and I'm surprised all of my craziness you put up with!! All credits for the cover go to Y. Nikolova with

1

Ammonia Book Covers,[1] who outdid herself with this cover!

And to my readers, you guys rock. Your reviews make me all warm and gooey inside, so thank you!

Happy readings,

Alexa

---

1. https://www.facebook.com/groups/1031687487003253/

∞ ∞ ∞

CHAPTER ONE

∞ Tine ∞

"Words are only painted fire; a look is the <u>fire</u> itself."

–Australian Aboriginal Proverb–

Elisandra

The darned delivery truck had to crap out on us – again. Grandmama had a hard enough time with Grandpapa gone and now... *Ugh*.

And of course there's only one darn mechanic shop in this town, and *he* happens to work there. I wish it didn't make a difference. That he didn't cause my pulse to race, my heart beat fast, nor create butterflies in my stomach. I wish I didn't think of him naked whenever I see him. I wish to hell I was indifferent.

Only, I'm not.

Finn McConnell. Tall, lean, eyes the color of the lush emerald landscape he's from, a jaw I could trace time and time again. And that Irish lilt that melted me to pudding the first time I heard it.

I never had a chance.

Oh, I've seen him around. Since he showed up in town a year ago, I've *seen* him – and the guys he hangs out with, each hotter than the last. You'd think after a year of blushing around him, I'd finally make a move. Only, it's not in my best interests, for various reasons. Plus, Finn doesn't even know I exist.

Which is why it's even harder driving the rusted delivery van to Claws Auto Shop, and making my way inside. A reception desk is set up independent of the garage, but connected with glass doors that allow a view of everything inside.

Behind the desk, a familiar redhead is typing furiously, while the new girl in town stands chatting animatedly. They're dating two of Finn's best friends – Dom, and Tristan. And no, I'm not a stalker. I just...see.

They both look up when I enter, and I hesitate, shifting from foot to foot. "Do you have room for one more appointment?" I don't tell them it's urgent. That my grandmama's business depends on this. I can't appear *that* desperate.

As they share a look, a loud clatter startles me. It's coming from the garage, drawing my attention and completely drowning out Daniela's response. And then I feel *his* eyes on me.

Don't look. Don't look. Don't —

I look. It's impossible not to. Like a darn magnet, my gaze travels through the transparent door and collides with Finn's emerald stare. Burning, intense, each molecule in my body responds when he quickly takes me in, before returning back to my eyes. A faint flush creeps up his neck, then he picks up the tool he dropped and returns his focus on the car, bending over to reach under the hood.

Great. Now my eyes are glued to his corded back, showcased in a dirty white shirt over equally dirty jeans. As he messes with something in the engine, his muscles tense and release, and my mouth goes dry. *He's screwing something there.*

Wish he'd screw us.

I jump at the voice. *This* is why I can't be around Finn. *She* always shows up, without a fault, and I'm having a harder time keeping a rein on her.

It's not that I'm possessed. But, there's something wrong with me, alright. 'Cause that voice in my head, it's me – only a nastier version. And it's been taking over my thoughts, and sometimes more. Grandmama doesn't know. Hell, no one knows. Because I'll be damned if I get locked up in the looney bin like my mom.

Just one bite. Look at that ass.

Did I mention she's also a sluttier version?

No, I scowl, noticing my reflection on the glass pane darkening. It's not the first time I've had full conversations in my head, but I try to force myself to look at Lucrezia and Daniela instead. Sometimes, distractions make her shut up. And it's then I notice they've been awfully quiet, observing me with mirroring expressions of interest.

"Sorry, I'm a bit scattered today. Um, so, do you?"

Lucrezia nods and grins. "Absolutely! What's the issue?"

"Transmission crapped out on me." I hate asking, but it's a must-know at this point. Grandmama's business isn't in top shape, and since her stroke scare, it's gotten worse. Only, I can't tell her how bad, else she'll come back from her sabbatical with her friend, and I can't do that to her.

So I bite back my pride and say, "Any idea how much it'll cost?"

Lucrezia types something in, then shakes her head. "No, but once Finn checks it out he can give you an estimate."

I dig my nails into my palms, refusing to surrender to the temptation of looking his way. "Is there anyone else who could do the job?"

She glances up with a small frown. "I...maybe?"

Daniela, quiet up until then, says, "We can probably rope one of the other guys in, but it may take longer."

Just my luck.

Yummy luck!

Shut up.

Sighing, I nod. "Never mind, then. Anyone will do, but I need this fixed ASAP. We have a baked goods delivery for a wedding out of town and....it's important nothing delays it, Lucrezia."

A small frown creases her features. "Of course. And I told you to call me Luz, everyone else does." When I only answer with a weak smile, she gets up. "We'll do our best, I promise. I'll go get Finn so he can take a peek right away."

"No, stay," Dani smirks. "I'll go." A few steps, and she's by my side, extending her hand in greeting. "I'm Dani, by the way."

I shake it, grateful the presence of another female seems to have silenced the annoying voice in my head. She's not a doppelganger, nor my evil twin, so I don't really know what to call her. She's just there, my mental alter – and not likely to leave anytime soon.

Another heavy breath expels from my lungs. I stare after Dani, envying her confidence as she struts up to Finn.

Finn

This makes three.

Three times I've made a complete fool of myself around this girl – Elle.

Elisandra Worthington. I know because I've made it my business to know. Not that it helps. This is one bird I can't figure out for the life of me. She's shy as all sights, but handles an entire bakery by herself – her granny hasn't been around these last few weeks.

And no, I'm not a stalker. Elle just tends to draw my attention, and this town is too damn small to hide from its few occupants. And while I can't explain my interest in her, I'm also oblivious to why my wolf has suddenly decided it wants to stake his claim on her. Fiercely so.

I want to blame Dom and Tristan. These blokes were first to fall and now here I am, feckin' tumbling head first into something I'm nowhere ready for. So maybe my faoladh blood is partly to blame, demanding I'm mated by the time I'm thirty, but I've still got a few years left to get there. Or, I should.

Jerking at the machinery that just won't give today, I try to direct my thoughts elsewhere. It's impossible, at least while she's in the same building. There's something about Elle, yeah. And the way her burning stare is glued to my ass right now, focus flies out the window – as does the wrench in my hand. Again.

"Look who's all clumsy today."

The breathy voice takes me by surprise. I'm not usually this unaware, especially with females around me. It's with a sigh that I turn to Dani. "No more than usual."

She cocks a hip against the car I'm fixing and smirks. "Yeah? So, it's got nothing to do with the beleza who just walked in?"

My treacherous eyes shift again to Elle. *Beauty, all right.* She's squirming, uncomfortable in whatever conversation she's having with Luz. It doesn't take my special gifts to realize something's up. "What did you two say to her?"

The words come out more cross than I'd intended and Dani's smirk widens. "Não, meu amigo. We said nothing. Seems sweet Elle is just as much of a mess around you."

Damn.

It's a chore to pull my eyes from her, but I do, narrowing them instead on Dani. "You could act touch less smug, you know?" Turning my back on temptation, I pick up a smaller wrench and bend over the engine again.

"She's here for you."

Clatter. I scowl at the engine, and the gap I just dropped yet another tool through. *Is this car trying to piss me off on purpose?*

Dani's chuckle pulls me out of my thoughts, and my scowl lands on her. "What do you want, Dani?"

She steps closer, her eyes full of mischief. Amusement dances in the air between us, and I roll my eyes. "Payback. You want payback for me interfering with you and Tristan, don't you?"

The grin grows wider. "I wouldn't say you interfered, but *sim*. Payback would be very nice, *meu amigo*. In the meantime, I meant to say Elle is here for a job. One that you could do for her."

Images of *all* I could do for Elle populate my brain with scary accuracy. My body tenses more, and a faint groan escapes me. *Feckin' hell and Lord almighty, I'm so done for.*

My gaze moves to Elle again. Our eyes lock across the distance and a zing goes through me like I've been electrocuted.

Yummy.

The word rings in my head as clear as if she'd spoken. Elle's eyes widen, and I catch a whiff of her irrational fear. A drop of conflict, then she shakes her head, mutters something to Luz and takes off.

Get her! I can't deny my wolf his chase any more than I can stop breathing.

"Finn, wait!" Dani's voice echoes behind me, but I'm already gone.

Don't let her leave, or you may not see her again. The impulse is strong – too impossible to resist. That's the problem with faoladh blood – my kind of werewolf. We're logical and rational, until the wolf takes over. Then it's all instinct.

Like a crazed man, I burst through the side garage door and intercept Elle as she tries to flee. "Running off, love?"

I hope to high hell and beyond she doesn't see through the front I'm putting up. Because I'm nowhere as confident as I sound, not when my heart is beating so hard it's about to jump out of my chest.

Elle looks at me then, her lips parted. A current runs when our gazes collide, enough to make my breath hitch in my lungs. The moment lengthens, impossibly so. I taste her interest, mixed with something else. It's everywhere in the air. And it's such a sweet invitation, I'm about to take it despite myself – until her eyes flash.

And it's enough to make me pause.

The short moment of awareness mellows my wolf, and confuses the hell out of me. Then I realize she's talking to me. "Sorry, what?"

Elle crosses her arms over her chest then, scowling at me. "I said I wasn't *running*, you just seemed busy." A pause, then, "Lucrezia said you might have room for one more appointment."

I follow her gaze to the delivery van parked near the auto shop. It looks like it's seen its last breath, but before I make assumptions I ask, "What's wrong with it?"

"Transmission, I think."

Elle's voice is soft now, less edgy than before. Her emotions are too chaotic to place, but one thing I'm sure of – this attraction isn't one–sided.

Which is why my feckin' mouth runs off without me and says, "I'll have a look."

Elisandra

Yum.

Ugh, she really won't shut up. And I'm probably not helping by checking Finn out every two minutes. And why do I have the feeling he heard her earlier? It shouldn't be possible. I mean, there's no way he did, but his reaction...

A hot flush runs through me, and I get to my feet, unable to sit still and more than a little sore. A glance at my wristwatch confirms it's been an hour since Finn finished up the other car he was working on, and drove my van inside.

No wonder my legs are cramped.

Glancing at the receptionist desk, I'm surprised to see only Lucrezia there. "Where is Daniela?"

She glances up, but her fingers continue to hit the keyboard for whatever she's working on, "Went out to meet Dom and Tristan. They're coming from a pat—" She stops typing, biting her lip. "Coming back from a job, I mean."

I nod, wondering at her weird expression. "Is there a washroom I could use real quick?"

Lucrezia points behind her. "In the hallway, past the kitchen."

On way shakier legs than I should have, I head over and handle business. As I wash my hands, I throw some water on my face in a vague attempt to pull myself together. For the first time, I notice the bird's nest on top of my head – my frizzy brown hair. Scowling, I pull this way and that, trying to braid the tangled mess before giving up and tying it into a loose bun.

As I shuffle back to the reception area, one thought keeps going on a loop in my head. *What the hell possessed me to stick around?*

Grandmama's business, that's what. She and Grandpapa took care of me after Dad died, and Mom got locked up. And now, well, somehow it seems only fair I help out since there's only Grandmama left.

My eyes are drawn again to the garage the moment I sit back down. Finn looks too damn good bustling around my ugly, old van.

Double yum.

"Ugh, would you shut up?"

Lucrezia looks up. "Sorry?"

"No, not you." I cringe. "Can't really say I've got a voice in my head that only comes out when Finn's around, can I?"

Her eyes go wide. My stomach sinks.

"I didn't just…"

"Say that out loud?" She grins. "You so did."

"Crap." I bury my head in my hands, taking a deep breath through my fingers. *Could this day get any worse?*

Lucrezia comes and sits next to me, rubbing my shoulder.

I peek out from between my hands. "Please don't say anything, Lucrezia. I swear I'm not a lunatic."

"Of course not!" Lucrezia shakes her head. "But... Do you have something against him? I mean, why are you fighting something that could potentially be everything? I've seen the way he looks at you."

"I... He doesn't..." Shaking my head, I mutter, "I'm not usually this scattered."

Lucrezia smiles. Then her eyes slip over my shoulder and that small tweak of her lips turns into something blinding. I envy that joy, and the soft welcome in her voice when she says, "Hey."

"Draga mea."

The deep voice – I know it. It's Dominic, her boyfriend. I've seen them enough times around town to know they're an item now.

Lucrezia stands and goes to him, burying herself in his embrace. It's not long before Tristan and Daniela walk in, interrupting the moment with their loud bickering.

"I said não, beleza, why won't you listen?"

"Because Lucas is already impossible and you know I can help! If I've got this ma—"

Lucrezia clears her throat noisily and Daniela stops mid–sentence. Her eyes fall on me. "Elle! Still around?"

It's not said in a mean way, but I still get defensive. "Just waiting on a quote, Daniela."

"Call me Dani." She cranes her neck around Tristan and grins at Finn. "Taking his sweet time, I see."

It's then I'm aware of both Dominic and Tristan's heavy gazes on me. They share a look, and Dominic gives a small shrug, as if answering a silent question. Then he kisses Lucrezia. "We can't stay long, just wanted to check on you."

Tristan rolls his eyes. "Wouldn't shut up about it." Dani elbows him in the ribs and he stops with a grunt.

"I'm fine, though. Lucas is at the back, and Finn's always around." Something about Lucrezia's words makes me think there's more to it than what she's saying with me around.

Dominic looks around the area once more, tightens his jaw and nods. "All right." He nuzzles her neck and whispers something, then straightens up and jerks his head at Tristan. "I'm good. Let's go back."

Dani kisses her guy too, then they both take off. I don't hear the sound of a car driving away, which is weird, but then I forget all about it when I'm once more drawn to Finn. His form, his right *everything* moving around...

"Did you know he used to be a lawyer?"

I snap out of my daze at Luz's words.

"Who, Finn?" The way Dani asks it makes it seem like she's overdoing it for my sake.

"Yeah, back when he lived in Ireland."

"Why'd he move here?"

Luz shrugs at my question. "Never did find out. He keeps to himself."

Dani snorts. "Speak for your experience."

A glance passes between them, and I take advantage of it to sneak another glance at Finn. Before we can continue the conversation, another voice draws my attention. "Che diavolo... What the hell is *she* doing here?"

Finn

Shite. This'll cost a pretty penny. And something tells me from the state of this car, it won't be easy for Elle to come up with the funds. Then again, that's not my problem. I shouldn't care. Nor should I care that I've felt her eyes on me the last hour.

Ruckus by the reception area draws my wolf. He's always a bit too damn interested when people exhibit too many emotions. My mouth parts as I taste their scents. See, most wolves focus on their nose, but my ancestry gave me something different. I can taste everything – desire, anger, embarrassment.

It's a skill that comes in handy when you're a lawyer and need to read juries, as well as clients. Not as handy, turns out, when you're in a small town surrounded by way too much temptation. But I've held good, if only because my past is nothing short of complicated, and the girl my wolf decides on will be dragged into it.

See, a faoladh doesn't just mate. They commit for life. And while Dom and Tristan may be able to survive their mate's death, I wouldn't. Her fate, whoever she is, would be intrinsically intertwined with mine, to the point of being unable to ever separate us. So yes, one could say I'm wary of falling in love.

Playing around, I've got no issue with.

Still, my skills have been particularly useful lately. I can see Dom getting ready to punch Lucas before he does, and have been able to avoid that. The rule–follower, they call me. Well, why does it feel like I'm getting closer and closer to my breaking point?

I wipe my hands on a dirty rag, and pick up a clipboard to write up a quote. My thoughts swarm like insects refusing to be quieted, analyzing everything my wolf picks up on.

Like Dani, who's annoyed she's being left behind. Dom and Tristan have been out patrolling the last few days since the fight with the Reapers and her old pack. We don't want to be taken unawares, not that it's helped much. And Dani, naïve in some ways, doesn't understand Lucas is purposefully keeping her in the shop to protect what's here – Lucrezia. As an indoctrinated member of our pack, she's the only human around us. And since the Reapers hate humans, Lucas thinks they might come after her – our weakest link.

Of course, his Italian macho side also wants to keep the women away from whatever terrifying discoveries Dom and Tristan run into on their patrol. With the Reapers power crazy and Cade as their leader, the town itself is changing. It's in the air I taste, and it won't be long before we start seeing the shifts in behavior.

All thoughts of change leave my mind when Lucas shows up next to the girls. I'd feel his anger even without my extrasensory perceptions. *Shite.*

Dropping the clipboard, I make my way to them, pushing past the door separating the garage from the reception area.

"….and Finn's just getting an estimate. Won't be long now."

I walk in at the last of Luz's babbling. "Problem, mate?"

For Elle's sake, we have to try to keep it normal. I can't act like he's my alpha, and his presence here is nowhere near reassuring. Despite my best efforts, Elle still catches on to something, maybe subconsciously, because I can taste her wariness and sense of doing wrong.

Get her out of here.

Lucas' voice is loud in my head – demanding. It's an order if I ever heard one, and I'm usually pretty good at listening. After all, it was my diplomacy that held this pack together when Dom and Lucas were going at it. Not that it matters much now, since they're back to being at war – again.

Instead of lingering on things I can't control, I focus on Lucas' glare. "It'll be a complicated job, but I've got room."

Lucas looks to Elle, dismissing me. "Afraid we're capped out for the week." He doesn't sound the least bit apologetic.

Elle's face falls. "Are you sure? What if I pay double?"

Something tells me it's a bluff. Not that it changes Lucas' mind. "Scusi, but it's a hard *no*." Without so much as an explanation, the heartless bastard walks off.

Elle looks ready to burst into tears, and my reaction gets the best of me again. I step closer to her, touching her shoulder. She jumps as if jolted, and I pull my hand back, frowning at it. *Yeah, I definitely sensed that zap again.* Despite my confusion, I whisper, "Don't fuss about it. We'll do it, just give me a wee bit of time to sort the schedule out with Lucas."

Ignoring the gratefulness in her eyes, I stalk after Lucas. "Why are you being so nutty today?"

Lucas throws me a glare over his shoulder. "Not you, too. I need at least one wolf with a clear head!"

My steps slow down. "Have I ever disappointed?"

Lucas stops moving away, and sighs rather dramatically. Pinching the bridge of his nose, he turns to me and stares, not saying anything.

He doesn't have to. When Dom finally admitted his feelings, he broke all the rules – and then some – all to claim Lucrezia. When it was Tristan's turn, he fell so hard and so fast for Dani, he didn't even see it coming. Nor did he know what to do with it – other than challenge his alpha at the most idiotic of times. And as for me…

I'm not there yet. Nor do I plan to be.

My wolf growls his displeasure, but it doesn't stop me saying the words I know will get Lucas to budge. "She's just a girl. An inconsequential nobody, Lucas. Let me do the job, and she'll be out of our hair."

His onyx eyes glitter, assessing my determination. There's almost resignation in his tone when he says, "It's not a simple job, is it?"

"No. But I'll pay it out of pocket if I have to." *Shite.* Way to go for showing him I'm not interested in this girl.

"That won't be necessary."

Feckin' hell, but today is not my day!

I turn and sure enough, there's Elle behind me, arms crossed and frowning.

How much did she hear?

The hurt I taste in the air tells me she caught more than enough.

∞ ∞ ∞

CHAPTER TWO

∞ Leithscéal ∞

"An <u>apology</u> is a lovely perfume, it can transform the clumsiest moment into a gracious gift."

–Margaret Lee Runbeck–

Finn

"Elle, that's–"

She lifts a hand, shutting me up. Those hazel eyes have lost their shine, shifting toward a darker hue, and they stare at me full of ice. "Don't need excuses. Can you fix the car, yes or no?"

"Aye, I can."

She nods then turns and walks away. "No need for me to stick around, in that case. I'll bring the payment when it's done. Lucrezia has my number."

The statement is thrown over a shoulder, with indifference and a hint of anger underneath. Elle's emotions whirl through the air, leaving me staring after her departing form with a slackened jaw.

"Inconsequential, hmm?"

I face my alpha, schooling my expression. No point in throwing fuel on the fire. "What are you so worried about, anyway?"

Lucas uncrosses his arms and takes a step closer to me. He's trying to hide it, but I taste the fear as though it were my own. It's not the first time, either, but it seems to have gotten more pronounced since Dani stole Tristan's heart.

Unsurprisingly, when Lucas speaks, his tone could freeze hell itself. "I've never been quite this clear. But that faoladh blood of yours? Doesn't give you the right to impinge on your alpha's emotions."

"Wow. I've touched a nerve, haven't I?"

Lucas growls low, putting us nose to nose. "Stand down, Irish. I'm not in the mood."

As abruptly as he snapped, he turns to walk away. Only I recall my other question, and am in no mood to let it go. "Why the reaction to Elle? Is it because you want her?"

It better feckin' not be the case, else we'll have a different kind of trouble on our hands.

Agreed, my wolf growls.

Lucas stops in his tracks and takes a shuddering breath as if to cool himself. "A woman will never get the best of me, Irish. But feel free to let her. Just be wary of who exactly you're taking into your bed."

Before I can deny it, he's gone. I move back to the reception area. Luz and Dani fall silent, both staring at me with concerned expressions. Elle is nowhere to be seen.

"Well. That went well."

I run a hand over my face, then head back to the garage, letting the door slam behind me. Cars, at least, have an easy fix.

∞ ♦ ∞

An hour later, Dom and Tristan come back, to their girlfriends' relief. I sense their uneasiness off the bat – patrol must've been shit again.

I'm about to head back inside the reception area to get Lucas, but he's already stomping our way, barging in the garage. "What happened?"

His gaze travels over Dom, taking him in, then straight to Tristan.

Tristan stands a bit straighter, a habit from his military days. "We patrolled both areas you asked for, and no sign of the Reapers."

Silence descends, as deafening as it is worrisome. Then Lucas speaks, voicing what we're all thinking. "That's not possible. They're always somewhere around here, lurking in the shadows and looking for trouble."

Tristan shares a glance with Dom, who nods. "Nothing. We even checked out the barn Dani knew, and though their scent is there, it's as empty as everywhere else."

"*Imposibile*," Lucas hisses. He meets Dom's gaze. "How do you explain this?"

To everyone's palpable relief, Dom's tone is neutral when he answers – a first, for this week, given they've been starting fights over nothing. "I can't. But we know someone who has a *broader* view, and who might."

A muscle ticks in Lucas' jaw. "Tytus, you mean." Another beat of silence, then he turns to Dani. "Will you find him, and talk to him?"

"Of course," she says. Having trained with Tytus, Dani has more of an inkling of his mind's workings than the rest of us.

"It's not wise she goes alone," Tristan adds. "Let me go with her."

Lucas snorts. "Nice try, amico, but we both know Tytus doesn't have a soft spot for you."

"Finn can go, then."

I glance up from the ground. "Me?"

Lucas mulls it over, then shrugs. "Fine. Can you keep yourself in check around the zmeu, or will I have to leash you, too?"

My eyes narrow. "If you recall, I was perfectly fine keeping a lid on my emotions when you had me guard him. Unlike everyone else."

Lucas rolls his eyes at the murmurs of agreement, then walks out. "Do it your way, but bring me some answers. And lock up when you're done with that junk, will you?"

I glare at his back, biting my tongue so I don't say something I'll regret. The *junk* he's referring to, of course, is Elle's van.

With Lucas gone, Dom turns to me. "What's up with him?"

"Elle," Dani says before I get a chance to tell them to mind their own business. "Sparks are flying more than before between our resident rule–follower and her, and Lucas doesn't like it."

Tristan snorts, looking like he's having a hard time not bursting into laughter. "You too, huh?"

I narrow my eyes on him. "Don't we have Reapers to find, and all that?"

"You're right, we do," Dom says. "Tristan's going to have one more look, then pass the patrol to you in a few hours." On his way out the door with Lucrezia, he adds, "But if I were you, I'd watch myself around Lucas. You know he can be emotional."

I say nothing, instead catching up to Dani and Tristan before they can take off. "Do you even know where to find Tytus?"

Her mischievous eyes meet mine. "I might have an idea."

∞ ♦ ∞

Much like Lucas, I chose a house out of town. When I spend my days around other people's misery, I want my nights quiet.

Not that it helps tonight. My two–story house is empty, cold. Sparsely decorated, it looks like the person living here has no interest to do so. The observation isn't completely off. My heart hasn't been in this country since I got here – not when I spend my nights dreaming of rolling green hills and the smell of the ocean.

The night's chilly, a storm gathering outside, so I walk straight through to my living room and turn on the fireplace. Even with the flames crackling, and heat spreading through the room, I don't take my coat off. Uneasiness has hold of me, and I can't shake off Dom's warning, Lucas' behavior and this whole crap with the Reapers. And above all, Elle's distraught expression. She didn't deserve to be hurt like that.

"Restless, wolf?"

I raise my head from the mantle of the fireplace. The glowing woman in my living room is no stranger, but her presence in my humble abode isn't necessarily a good thing.

"Ileana. How can I help my friend's godmother? Does Dom know you're here?"

Her eyes, shining of the sun's light, are alight with mischief. She glides towards me in a long robe that looks like it was made of flowers. Her unique scent of spring drifts my way. I keep a wary eye on her, recalling how easily she'd slammed me into a wall at our first meeting. Godmother to Dominic, she helped get him on the path to his pack of vrykolakas – hybrid creatures, both wolf and strigoi – and appeared again when Lucas wrongfully accused Tytus. She seems determined to keep us on track and falling in love, though why, I haven't the faintest idea.

"Something troubles you tonight." As usual, she doesn't answer my question, only replies with one of her own. "Or some*one*?"

I look back into the flames. "Would you tell me if you knew why Lucas reacted like that to her?"

"Her, who?" Ileana laughs. "Surely you don't think I spend my days watching over you wolves."

"On the contrary, that's exactly what I think." Her eyes glitter in warning, but she knows I see through it. "Something worries Lucas, and has ever since Dom fell in love, then Tristan. Today, it manifested as extreme rudeness to Elle, and before I go apologize, I'd like to know what exactly I'm getting into."

"Getting into?" Her exotic accent becomes more pronounced as she laughs. "Oh, wolf. The greatest adventure of all, of course – love."

My eyes narrow on her. "I'm not in love with Elle, we barely know each other!"

Ileana tilts her head to the side, her brown hair cascading to one shoulder. "And what makes you think there is a prerequisite to falling in love? Did you not see what happened to Dominic and Tristan?"

"Aye, they lost their heads. It's no wonder Lucas is worried," I mutter.

Ileana snorts. "It is not losing his wolves that scares him, but something else."

"What is it then?" When she remains stubbornly quiet, I press, "Well?"

"Lucas has a problem with Elisandra's, hmm, lineage."

I frown at her odd choice of word. "Lineage?"

Ileana nods, then starts gliding away. "Da. Find that out, and you will have your answer. Now, while your distress pulled me here, I must check on my actual godson. Until we meet again."

She's gone in a whirlwind of flowers, in the blink of an eye. A moment later, my cell phone buzzes. "Yeah?"

"Your turn to patrol."

Elisandra

I've tossed and turned all night, trying to fight the words that cut me deep. They shouldn't have. He's no one. Just someone I've been crushing on since he got into town and I heard him talk.

None of what I tell myself helps.

So I drag my body out of bed, shower and run down the stairs to open the bakery. As I go about the preparations, the phone rings. "Morning, nana."

"Heya, darling!" She's smiling in the phone, I can always tell. "How are things?"

Judging by the chipper tone, she's still having fun with her friend, away from the stress of running a business. That alone reinforces my belief she's better off away, and I table my whining for another day. *Or never.*

"Same as last night," I say instead of the truth.

Grandmama chuckles at my grumble. "Someone woke up on the wrong side of the bed."

"Just a bad night."

Would've been an amazing night if you'd listened to me! Mm, we could've had Finn alllll to ourselves, if you hadn't gotten so mopey over a few words.

It's too early for this, I shoot back, and force myself to ignore her. Instead, I tie an apron around my waist, disinfect my hands and start popping trays filled with goodies in the two ovens. I'd prepared the dough last night in a furious frenzy, thinking I might get ahead of baking the orders today, to prepare them for the weekend.

As if reading my mind, Grandmama says, "You'll be able to make the delivery?"

"I promise, nana. Stop worrying."

"You know I can't. Leaving you there, alone, it's...hard."

I soften my tone, not wanting her to worry. "I know, nana, and I miss you too. But I promise everything is under control, and the delivery will go by without a hitch."

"And you'll tell me, if you need anything?"

"I swear it."

"I love you, sweetie."

"Love you, too." She hangs up, and I lean my head against the oven handle. It's not hot enough to burn, yet – not like it would matter. Fire has always spared me, refusing to mark my skin no matter how many stupid things I do.

The bells above the front door ring, informing me someone just walked in. I cringe, recalling I didn't lock up after throwing out the trash this morning. "We're not open yet."

A silence follows. *Please don't let it be a serial killer.*

"I was hoping you'd make an exception for an eejit?"

I turn around, and there's Finn with two cups of coffee. His emerald green eyes stare at me with contrition, and I gulp. The vulnerability in his expressions melts me, and the way his jet–black hair is all windswept makes my fingers itch to touch him.

"A what?"

He cringes. "Idiot. Slip of the tongue on some old Irish slang, sorry."

Wiping my hands on my apron, I ignore his sheepish tone and take a step closer to the counter. "What do you want?"

"To apologize." He lifts up one of the cups. "I was hoping some caffeine might count for, err, brownie points?"

I shake my head. "If it wasn't for that amazing smell, I'd kick you out of here in a heartbeat." The aroma fills my nostrils, going down my throat with gusto. I hold out a hand. "Gimme."

Grinning, he steps closer and offers me the cup that I practically wrench out of his hands. Closer now, I can smell hints of almond milk and something else – cinnamon. Mouth open, I gape at him. "What... How did you know?"

A faint blush colors his cheeks. "I pay attention."

He's being too endearing, so I dig into the coffee – then nearly choke on it with a realization. *She's* not around. I cough, then take another sip while Finn stares at me like I've grown two heads.

Nope. Nothing. Amazed at the silence in my head, I push the matter aside, for inner pondering later. "Thank you," I whisper, before meeting his gaze once more. "Any progress with the van?"

His smooth expression falters, and he grimaces. "About that... Have you considered getting a new one?"

It's my turn to make a face. "If I had the money, don't you think I would have?"

"I thought as much."

Gut churning, I place my cup back down and focus on arranging a display of freshly baked goods – last night's batch. "Is it that bad?"

Finn takes a seat at the closest table to me and sips his coffee. It's easier to spy his expressions from here, hidden behind rows of goodies and a semi–transparent glass display.

Something about the way he hesitates, then twists the lid off the coffee cup, tells me it's not good news he has. When he speaks, I know he's chosen his words carefully. "Transmission is busted, you were right. But your front and back brakes need changing, and not just the brake pads. We're talking rotors, calipers, the whole thing. And then there's the suspension, pretty much messed up as well."

Nausea wells inside me at the list. Finn seems to catch this, as he stops talking for a moment. "I can fix it, but it won't be an easy one."

"I'll pay it," I whisper, "whatever the cost." He stares at me and I catch the question in his eyes. "I have a massive delivery to do this weekend for a wedding. The money from it will be enough to pay the bills for this place for three months, and I need the business."

Finn frowns through the glass at me. "I can help you make whatever delivery, you know. My truck is equipped for the road."

Shaking my head, I straighten up and dust myself off. "Thank you, but no." Never mind the fact I can't be stuck in a car with him for six hours of a drive. Though the pleasure at being so close tingles through me.

"I mean it." And I know he does. The promise is there, in his gorgeous eyes, but it's also scary. The silence in my head is a one–off, I'm pretty sure of it, and there's just too much at stake. Without me, Grandmama's business won't survive, and I just can't put her through the stress right now.

I don't admit any of that aloud, instead I shake my head. "How long will it take for you to fix it?"

"A week."

A groan escapes me. "The delivery is in three days, Finn, and I can't miss it."

Finn stands then, heading closer, his gaze more intense. "So let me help."

"You're already doing it," I mutter, "I can't ask for more. Is there any way you can work faster instead?"

He hesitates, then nods. "I'll ask Lucas, see if he can lend me Dom or Tristan. Might go faster if there's another person on the job."

I cringe, recalling those cold onyx eyes staring at me the other day. "I'm not sure your boss likes me very much."

Finn opens his mouth as if to dispute it, then seems to think better of it. "I am sorry about yesterday, you know. What I said... Elle, I didn't mean it. My emotions were running high, and I was trying to get Lucas off my back."

He runs a hand through his hair, mutters something in Gaelic, then says, "I'll...talk to him. Don't worry about it." Then he sniffs the air. "Those croissants smell so good."

Laughing, I pull two out of the display and stuff them in a paper bag. When he reaches for his wallet, I shake my head. "On the house. Keep me posted on the van?"

Finn nods, and heads back out the door. "Will do."

Wow. That was almost a normal conversation.

But that sexy voice... Damn!

Ah hell. And she's back now.

Finn

I leave the bakery a bit more at ease than I've been. It's still way early in the morning, and the town's a ghost. Hopefully, it's a sign the Reapers are going to stay off the grid.

Last night was a bust on my end, since I couldn't pick up anything. After giving an early morning report to Lucas, I grabbed a quick nap and headed back in to fix my mistake from yesterday. At least, if nothing else, the evening of patrolling cleared my head.

Today it's Lucas' turn to patrol, but I'm hoping I can convince him to lend me either one of the guys. I wasn't lying to Elle when I said it would be easier as a two person job. Then there's another part of me that doesn't even want to fix the van, if it means she'll be driving alone to that delivery.

She's not my problem.

No. She's ours.

I temper down my wolf. Sure, she's nice. Good–looking, mouth–watering, heart–pounding nice. But that doesn't mean she's mine, or will be mine. At least not the way things are going.

As my feet pass an alley, I catch a whiff of anger. It's all the notice I get before someone grabs my arm and drags me in. Flashes of a similar attack, from long ago, go through my mind. Then the guy's got me by the scruff of my jacket, slamming me against the brick wall.

Only it's not fiery flames I stare into, but stormy grey eyes, and features as cold as granite.

"Tytus. What the shite?"

Something akin to relief courses through me, despite his slamming me against the wall again – hard enough to make my teeth rattle this time. "What were you doing with Elle?"

I glare at him. His grip tightens. He's angry alright, but not like I've sensed from him before. And I've seen him plenty, what with his helping Lucrezia, then Daniela. Seems he's got a thing for helping the females that end up in our pack, which has me even more wary as to his real purpose this close to Elle.

Recalling Lucas' orders to find Tytus and ask him about the Reapers, I get myself in check. No point giving in and starting a fight, not when it'll lead to more issues than not. So I lift a hand atop the one at my neck, letting myself absorb a tiny flick of his anger. Normally, people don't even know I'm doing it. A tiny touch, the emotion courses through me for a bit, and the situation is diffused.

It works this time, too. Just not as I expected.

Tytus lets me go as if scorched, putting more than enough distance between us. His grey eyes reflect shock. "What the hell was that?"

I don't answer, instead straightening my clothes.

"What *are* you?"

Damn, he doesn't give up. A sigh escapes me. "A wolf."

Tytus is already shaking his head at my denial. "No, not like any I've seen before."

I look him in the eye then. "You want the truth? I'm faoladh."

"An Irish wolf?" He frowns as though having just realized something. "That's why you've hated me, isn't it?"

Despite my best efforts to school my expression, he sees right through me. "That's right. You ran into, what, a dragan clan? They're all the rage in that part of the world."

I look away. "This isn't about me."

"Oh, but it is." Tytus laughs, though there's nothing humorous about the situation. "Knowing the dragans and their less than moral ways, they must've done a number on you." His eyes narrow into slits, the grey almost opaque. "Tell me."

Something else courses through me, and I groan against the pull. It's like what I'm able to do, but in reverse. Vibrations rumble through me, and two words are pulled from my lips. "Ciaran Loughey."

Tytus' eyes widen, and his hold on me loosens, his eyes go back to stormy. With it, the sensation goes away, and I shake my head to rid it of the last cobwebs. "If you're going to play, at least play fair," I mutter. "Enough with the magic."

He ignores me, too focused on whatever realization fell upon him. "*You* were the one who dethroned Ciaran?"

"Dethroned?" I snort. "If only. It's me who had to leave the country in exile, after he won a case against a human I defended. He got to keep everything, and I lost it all."

Tytus isn't impressed by my dejected tone. "Fool! Ciaran couldn't have held on to his clan even if he tried, after getting his ass kicked." Something akin to respect reflects in his eyes now. "Interesting indeed..."

I'm too shaken by what he's said to pay attention. If he's right, and Ciaran, the reason for my exile, has lost his hold on my country, then I might be able to return home. *Ireland...* My heart constricts. Visions of emerald green hills, lush mountains and cliffs fill my mind. My gut tightens, the hope almost too much to bear.

Then Tytus' voice gets through. "You've Celt blood in you. How much?"

I shrug. "Does it matter?"

"It does to me. You may prove useful, after all."

He paces around me, assessing me. My wolf growls. "I heard of Celt wolves... Long, long ago. I thought you were wiped out."

"We were. My pack is the last of its kind." I'm still having a hard time understanding what the hell he's trying to get at.

"We've got that in common, then."

Tytus inches closer, and I hold up my hands. "No offense, mate, but keep your distance. I've had enough roughing up for the morning."

As though only now recalling his burst of anger, he says, "Ah."

"You planning to explain that?"

"Sure." He leans against the brick wall. "Soon as you tell me what you were doing with Elle."

"Bringing her coffee to apologize. What's it to you?"

"Apologize for what?"

"No, see, this won't do. I need answers, too."

Tytus shrugs. "I have a particular interest in her."

My wolf growls. But it's not desire I sense off him, it's worry. Then Ileana's words come back to me. She confirmed Lucas was afraid of something, something tied to Elle. The only person Lucas hates more in Rockland Creek than the Reapers is Tytus, which means –

"Lineage!"

CHAPTER THREE

∞ Shinsir ∞

"To forget one's <u>ancestors</u> is to be a brook without a source, a tree without a root."

–Chinese proverb–

Finn

Tytus stares at me patiently, waiting for the rest of my thought. Only problem is, I'm having a hard time voicing it.

"She's your descendant, isn't she?" The words are barely more than a whisper. Because of course there has to be another reason why me and Elle could never work out.

A flash of something crosses Tytus' face. For a moment, he seems like he's going to deny it, but then he nods. "Yes."

This explains so much. Only a few days ago, Lucas had imprisoned him. I'd wondered why Tytus had surrendered so easily, but Lucas must have known about his weakness – Elle.

Is she only his *weakness?*

I ignore my wolf as something else strikes me. "Does she know? Does Lucas?"

"What does your alpha have to do with my decision?"

A growl escapes me. "You know damn well what. And it's not like you two are friendly."

Tytus arches an eyebrow. "Speaking of unfriendly... Weren't we talking about Ciaran just now?"

"Nice try to change the subject, zmeu. But that was a long time ago, and not really relevant to what's going on now."

"Which is?"

It's my turn to take a step closer, opening my senses so I can catch anything else he might be hiding. "Since Dani's lobisomens were defeated, we haven't seen hide nor tail of the Reapers. Any thoughts on that?"

Nothing changes in his expression. "Perhaps you aren't looking in the right places."

"Oh, we're looking, all right. And between Tristan's tracking, Dom's strength and my extrasensory perceptions you think we would've found something. Instead, rud ar bith – *nothing*. But I've caught *your* scent more places than I can count while doing my patrols."

Tytus scowls then. "And how much of this does your alpha know?"

My gut churns, but the truth comes out anyway. "None of it."

His eyes widen. "You, the rule follower? Lying to your alpha?"

I refuse to look away in shame like I want to. "Tell me I was wrong. Tell me he doesn't know about Elle and wouldn't have used her as collateral to get whatever he wants out of you."

Tytus grins. "I would've liked to see him try."

"Like last time, you mean?"

The grin slips off, and he sighs. "Very well. I suspect your alpha knows somewhat. He did threaten me with it not that long ago."

Which proves exactly what I'd been thinking about. I run a hand through my hair. "Damn. We need to bring him in. On all of this. And you need to be honest about whatever's happening with the Reapers."

"And why's that?" A dangerous undercurrent is in the air, and I can taste it as easily as everything else. But I'm not about to let Tytus' anger intimidate me. Sure, I've witnessed his zmeu form not so long ago, but bygones be bygones.

"Because we can help. You can't be in two spots at once, and while you're out chasing Reapers and leaving your scent all over the place, Elle is undefended."

His eyes narrow. "Do you honestly think I'd leave her an easy prey?"

"Maybe not, but the only spot I've scented lingering Reapers is near her bakery. Explain that to me."

He shakes his head. "I can't, there's nothing easy about any of this."

"So listen to me, Tytus. Let us step in and protect her. Join forces with us and we can help out. But it has to come from you, an offer to give Lucas something in return for the protection."

Tytus stares for a beat, then says, "What's all this to you, Celt? Why are you so invested?"

There's no answer to such a complicated question, so I don't bother. "You know why," I mutter and walk out of the alley back to the auto shop.

Not like I can force Tytus to follow, but maybe he'll see the value in having us on his side. When his footsteps echo behind me, I hold back a relieved exhale. Within moments, I step into Claws Auto Shop, and the zmeu follows me in.

Elisandra

She's gone now... Thankfully. The stuff I had to listen to until Finn finally took off is enough to make a sailor blush.

So rather than focus on Finn's appearance in my store, I try to draw my attention towards making baked goods and finishing the order for the wedding. They've asked for all kinds of complicated stuff, but luckily Grandmama left me her recipe book and I'm a natural in the kitchen.

Or, I was. Today, not only do I mess up recipes, but I also burn the ones I do manage to fix. Within three hours, I'm staring at the last batch of éclairs in the oven. If these don't come out the way they're supposed to, I give up.

Another five minutes left on the timer.

My thoughts wander, and when my gaze lands on the empty coffee cup, I groan out loud. "Can't even throw the cup away, Elle? Seriously..." Forcing my feet to move, I pick it up and hold it above the garbage can. Only, my fingers won't let go.

With a pitiful sigh, I rinse it under water, and leave it to dry. It's a memento of a nice gift, I try to tell myself.

Gift? Puh–lease. He wants in bed with you.

Another groan escapes me. "Why won't you leave me alone?"

Alone? Now why would you get such an idea in your head? I'm here to help you, silly.

Rolling my eyes, I move back to the oven. It's what she's always said, since she turned up in my head on my sixteenth birthday. Six years later, she's only gotten louder.

The timer rings, as if on cue. Without thinking, I put my hand to the burning oven and open it. A waft of hot air hits me in the face, and I reach for the tray. It's searing, but not to my touch. All I feel is a tingle.

I let it cool on the counter, too late realizing my mistake. A sizzle and burnt plastic smell fills the air, clueing me in to the fact I've just burnt Grandmama's new laminate countertops.

"Dammit!"

In my haste to try and move the tray, I drop it to the ground, sending the éclairs clattering everywhere. One beat, two... Then I drop to the ground, tears falling down my cheeks. None of today has worked properly, and I feel like I'm losing my mind.

It doesn't help that I'm here, alone –

But you're not alone.

I stare at my reflection in the oven window. "You. Are. Not. Real. Go away!"

Only silence answers me, but it's no comfort. If this keeps going, I'll be in looney bin next to my mom soon enough. Sighing, I pick myself off the ground, dust myself and fix my apron.

"Enough being a crybaby, Elle. Time to fix this mess."

Finn

I taste Luz's confusion in the air the moment we step inside the shop. She offers a hesitant smile to Tytus, but drops it when she catches sight of our faces.

"Could you get Lucas, please?"

She glances at Tytus, then nods and heads to the back. When she returns with Dani and Lucas, I'm not surprised.

Despite the extra help, there's nothing satisfied in his expression. Lucas' narrowed gaze lands on Tytus, and the distaste lingers in the air.

"Ty!" Dani grins, and takes a step forward. Lucas grabs her wrist in his, and I sense, more than hear, his growl.

Dani glances between him and Tytus, then rolls her eyes. "Meu Deus, you two still have a bone to pick?"

I throw her a look.

Tytus grunts under his breath. "Let's take it in an open space, shall we? Your alpha seems ready to snap."

We all head into the garage, me leading the group. Two massive pickups take up almost all the space, but I find a semi-clear area and head for it. Dom and Tristan stop their work on one of the beat-up trucks, and join us. Unsurprisingly, they stand by their mates, while Lucas moves apart. He now has a direct view of me and Tytus, and his eyes narrow even further. His anger is palpable, turning the air too ashy for my taste.

"What the hell is this all about, Finn?" Lucas growls.

"Take a breath, mate. I didn't go outside the lines, nor did I not listen. Just yesterday you gave us orders to find out what Tytus knows about the Reapers, right?"

Lucas says nothing, only glaring back. I shrug and say, "Well, it so happens I ran into him today."

"Ran into him? Come se per caso?" A cold laugh escapes Lucas.

"Matter of fact, it *was* by chance," I reply to his Italian question. "I was visiting Elle to apologize for yesterday's mishap, as well as your rudeness, mate. And then I took my chance to speak to Tytus." I step aside, leaving Tytus in the spotlight. "He'll tell you the rest."

Lucas' eyes stay on mine for a beat, then he meets Tytus' gaze. "Go on, then. Sorprendemi."

Surprise me. I roll my eyes, thinking he's got a definite surprise coming. But not even I was prepared for the full extent of it.

Tytus stares back, and I sense a measuring test taking place. Dom and Tristan glance at me for confirmation, and I nod as subtly as I can. Yeah, this could get out of hand, and fast. So I clear my throat, trying to attract Tytus' attention.

He doesn't change his stance, but something in the air tells me he senses my impatience. Without wasting a beat, he takes a step closer to Lucas. "What is your problem with me, wolf?"

Side by side, Tytus is a couple inches taller than Lucas. Not that it makes my alpha back down. He crosses his arms, widens his stance, and tilts his chin up. "Are you going to keep wasting my time, zmeu, or get to the point *un giorno* this century?"

Tytus doesn't budge, but the air becomes thicker. Dom and Tristan shift their stances, moving enough to put themselves in front of Luz and Dani, as if expecting a blowout. I don't blame them. And not for the first time, my thoughts go to Elle – is *she* being protected right now?

"Well? Andiamo, I don't have all day."

Lucas' sharp tones pull me into focus. A faint rumble comes from Tytus' chest, and Lucas grins as if Christmas came early.

The door to the garage blows open, a gust of wind blowing in. It's chillier than it's supposed to be this time of the year, and something about it makes my skin crawl. Then Tytus tilts his head, and lifts his hand. A rune dances in the air just above his palm. Satisfaction oozes from his pores, and I know he's showing off for Lucas.

"Oh, for crying out loud!" To everyone's surprise, Lucrezia moves from under Dom's arm and before he can hold her back, stalks over between the two alphas. "Tytus, enough! You came here to say something, right? So get on with it. None of these games are making the situation any easier."

I'm fully prepared for him to blow her off, as is Dom. Instead, Tytus shakes his head and gently pushes her back a few steps. "Not your fight, Red. Not right now." Then he returns to his previous position. "Very well, wolf. You found out my secret, the one thing that keeps me tied in this crap of a town rather than the majestic mountains I belong to. And I will tell you exactly what you wish to know, with one caveat. Explain your distaste of me."

Lucas snorts. "I'm not the only one with issues. Look around, zmeu. They're aplenty. Dom knows your kind better than most, since you come from the same region. Tristan's dealt with all types of creatures, and Finn himself has suffered the brunt of a zmeu's deceit."

I clear my throat at that. "To be particularly fair, that's not one hundred percent true."

Lucas' eyes narrow. "Come again?"

Tristan speaks then. "Tytus isn't a dragon – a dragan, like what Finn faced in the past. He's a zmeu."

"They both got wings, don't they?" Lucas shrugs. "Stessa differenza."

Same difference. It's like he's purposefully trying to provoke him.

"Not quite," Tytus says. "A zmeu – or zmei clan – influences weather, and can channel it for magic with runes. We are first and foremost humans who turn to zmeu form. Whereas my shape is similar to a dragon, the difference is even in primitive form I retain my full capacity. A dragon does not, only knows the monster's power."

"Not to mention they're greedy as all bastards," I add. "And have no moral compass whatsoever."

"And Tytus does?"

A silence reigns for a second, then Dani whispers, "He helped me, didn't he? Without Tytus' help, I wouldn't be here, able to master the magic forced upon me."

Lucas shuts his eyes as if in physical pain. Then, miracle of miracles, he nods. "Point taken. Get to it, zmeu. What is so important you think I need to know?"

"To put it plainly, Elle is my descendant. As my entire race has been wiped out, you can imagine it was a surprise for me to find her. Bottom line is, she is not to be touched. But she is in danger, and the Reapers seem to have developed an interest in her."

"And this is our problem, how?"

Tytus grunts again. "Hate me all you want, wolf, but Elle is an innocent. Moreover, following your fight with the lobisomens, you should have realized the Reapers are after something."

"And what's that?"

"If I tell you, I want your assurance you'll put a wolf on my girl. I need her watched, protected."

Lucas' expression darkens even further, if that's possible. His voice is pure steel when he speaks. "My wolves are not up for hire."

"Then we have nothing to talk about."

Tytus turns to walk away, and I intervene before I can think better of it. "I'll do it."

Lucas growls. "Stand down."

"No. You know we have a connection, I'm the easiest choice."

Lucas' eyes narrow on me. Tytus is watching us, as is everyone else. Then Luz speaks. "Maybe it's not such a bad idea. Elle's sweet, and if the Reapers get to her..." She frowns. "Ty... What, exactly, would be the problem? Aside from the obvious fact, that they can turn her into a werewolf."

Tytus sighs. "Red, it's more than that. Elle inherited powers I have... If the Reapers get to her, it's not just her who's in danger, but this entire town."

"Why?" Dani asks. "Can't you teach her to control them?"

"It's not as easy as your magic, little wolf. Elle is part human, part zmeu. She... Her personality reacts differently to the powers."

His admission rings alarm bells in my head. I've seen that in Elle, in the way she's hot and cold, changing... *Could that be it?* I ask before I lose my nerve. "What are you getting at, mate?"

"I mean she's gone without knowing for too long. I'm not sure telling her is best, at this point... But the Reapers seem determined to get to her and she has to be protected."

"I still fail to see how this benefits my pack," Lucas' drawl cuts in.

A spike of fury from Tytus scorches the air, reminding me of Ciaran not that long ago. Then it's gone just as easily. When he speaks, no one else picks up on the fact he's on his last rope.

"Protect Elle, and I'll work with you to find the Reapers. I'll also tell you everything I know."

Lucas stares at him for so long, I fear he might decline.

"Fine," he finally says and turns that glare to me. "Finn, she's your responsibility from now on. I trust you can split your time between her and the shop easily enough."

I nod, but he's not done. He steps closer, lowering his voice. "Let's make one thing clear. You're on your last rope with me, Irish. Make sure you don't follow into the *wrong* footsteps."

With a last accusing look to Dom, he strides away.

On his way out the door, he throws a warning to Tytus over his shoulder. "Your girl gets protection when you stop fucking around and tell us everything. Not a moment before."

I turn to my beta, running a hand through my hair. "I've got the parts to fix Elle's car. Can you and Tristan give me a hand for the next hours?"

If nothing else, I can rely on these guys. So as Tytus watches over us, assessing his options, we go to work.

Elisandra

Running errands without a car isn't as easy as I thought. After multiple trips to the grocery store, I'm finally heading back to the bakery with my last purchase – a massive bag of flour.

"Talk about exercise."

I can't really see where I'm heading, which is why I run smack into someone not even a block away from the bakery. Strong hands go around me to steady me, then move to take the bag from my grip. The face that greets me makes my heart stop. Ebony skin, piercing onyx eyes and a smile as dazzling as the sun, the guy's ripped. And not cold, judging by the meager jacket he's wearing over jeans and not much else.

"Need some help?"

I nod wordlessly, and he grins wider. "A beautiful girl like you shouldn't be hauling things about."

A shrug lifts my shoulders. "I'm used to it."

He helps me carry the flour back to the store, then lingers about as I put all the groceries away. "Thank you so much for your help," I say finally.

His eyes aren't on me, per se. He's raking them up and down my body, blatantly checking me out. I open my mouth to tell him off, but it's not polite words that come out of my mouth. Quite the opposite.

"See something you like?"

Those onyx eyes meet mine, and he grins. "As a matter of fact, I do. What's your name, darlin'?"

My feet move closer. I'm trying to apologize, to take it back, but instead all that comes out is, "Elisandra." I swear it's more a purr than actual talking.

A flush burns my cheeks as his eyes trail down my body again. I want to be infuriated, but she's the one speaking through me – and I've got no way to stop her. "And yours, handsome?"

"Cade," he grins and holds out a hand.

I watch in amazement as mine drops in his, and he squeezes gently before letting go. His eyes trail over the displayed baked goods. "I'll have to come back here for sure. You've definitely whet my appetite."

"Thanks," my mouth moves in a seductive smile. "Come on by anytime. And thanks for the help!"

"It was my pleasure, darlin.'"

With a salute, he's gone, leaving me and my shaking knees. I drop to the ground, holding onto its coolness, praying that what just happened, didn't.

"What was that?"

That, my dear, is how it's done. You're welcome.

"How the hell did you take over my body!"

Nothing answers me. Nothing but silence and a growing dread in the pit of my stomach. I'm losing control of her at an alarming rate.

The phone rings, startling me. After a hesitation, I crawl over and whisper, "Yes?"

"It's me," a voice like warm whiskey says. "The car's fixed, if you want to come and pick it up."

"I'm on my way."

∞ ♦ ∞

At Claws Auto Shop, I pull out my wallet, but Lucrezia waves me off. "It's already taken care of."

"What? By whom?"

She doesn't say, but her eyes slide to Finn. There's another guy next to him, tall and dark haired with grey eyes, but it's on Finn my glare settles.

He looks up, grinning my way. He's by no way checking me out like Cade had, but my helplessness at the situation causes me to overreact. Rather than smile and thank him, I march over to him. "Why would you pay it?"

Confusion fills his features, a faint frown. "Seemed the right thing to do. I'm sorry, did I—"

"I *don't* need charity, Finn."

"It's not –"

Shaking my head, I walk away, heading to the car. The guy next to him makes a move as if to follow, but Finn beats him to it. "Elle, wait."

I don't listen, instead opening the car door and hopping in the driver's seat. Hoping like hell he actually fixed it, and not something else.

Being around him isn't good. It won't be long until she shows up, and I can't afford another episode like with Cade. Especially not around Finn.

"Elle, wait!"

Out of the corner of my eye, I see the dark–haired guy staring from a distance. There's something disturbing about the way he's following Finn's every move, as if ready to pounce on him.

Something nags at the back of my head, as if I've seen him before... Then my hand shakes around the ignition, struggling to fit the key in.

Finn pushes between the door and me, and he's close. Too close.

"Would you wait already? I didn't mean to offend you. Elle, I was trying to help."

His voice is – shit, I've hurt him. I look up, meaning to apologize for overreacting, for forgetting myself, for being horrible to him when all he means is to help. But the apology dies on my lips.

All I see are his green eyes, all I smell is his after shave, all I feel is his heat radiating in the small space between us. Between one breath and the other, I forget how to get air in my lungs.

My eyes drift to his lips, and before I know it I'm kissing him – or he's kissing me. It's hard to tell. All I know is I'm half out of my seat, or he's half over me, and I'm breathing him in, he's kissing me back, his hand cupping my cheek, his body under my touch...

Hard. So damn hard. Muscles I wouldn't have pegged on him, but I feel them now, filled with tension. And still his lips move against mine, taking what I'm willingly giving.

Sinful.

The satisfied voice is enough to make me freeze, 'cause it's not mine.

The second after, Finn is ripped from my arms, and something akin to a snarl echoes behind him. I take a deep breath, am vaguely aware of a, "What the shite, Tytus!"

Then the dark–haired man is there, his grey eyes searching mine, widening at whatever they find. I can't take it anymore. I push him away – more like kick – shut the door of the car in his face, and turn to the steering wheel.

With trembling hands, I manage to get the ignition key in and the engine – bless it – purrs to life. One shift of the stick, and I'm pulling out of there as fast as I can, escaping that emerald gaze and the warring emotions within.

∞ ∞ ∞

CHAPTER FOUR

∞ Marcáilte ∞

"Men are <u>marked</u> from the moment of birth to rule or be ruled."

–Aristotle–

Finn

That night, as I'm walking home, I can still taste Elle's lips, feel her sweet surrender – then her fear. Whatever's going on with her, I need to get to the bottom of it. She's my responsibility now, and Tytus and his meddling self can go to hell.

It took Dom and Tristan to keep him from kicking my ass for kissing Elle, not that I would've minded – it was well worth it. Then Lucas got back inside, attracted by all the fuss. It was his word, in the end, that sent Tytus packing, upon pain of nullifying the agreement between them.

Knowing I need to give Elle some space, I force myself to stay away from the bakery. Or at least, I try to. Before I can redirect my footsteps, I'm heading down the street. Just one look, I tell myself, to make sure she's all right.

But when I turn the corner to her street, I'm not the only one standing watch. At first I can't catch sight of him, but I taste that same mix of emotions from back at the shop. Scanning far and wide, I finally hear a flutter of wings and look upwards. Shadows and wings disappear behind the clouds, until all that's left is the moonlight and a hint of what's hidden up there.

Not for the first time, I wonder how a zmeu can hide without humans seeing him. It's been on my mind since we first realized there was one of his kind in this tiny town, and Tytus himself has never given an inkling as to how he's doing it. Then again, I've lived long enough among humans to know they only notice what they want. After all, wasn't that how Ciaran got away?

Thoughts of the man responsible for my exile dampen my spirits. Before today, I was sure in my purpose here – keeping the peace, helping my pack, helping humans in a different way than before. Now, there's only confusion in my head, not the least helped by the little vixen hidden between those four walls.

I glance at Elle's bakery again. All lights are out, and if Tytus is comfortable getting a distance, so should I. Technically.

Yet with each step away from her, it feels like my soul is being stretched thin. The sensation is new, like there's a physical tie from me to Elle, and it's worrisome. I've stayed away knowing I couldn't possibly have something that lasts, not with a price over my head from the past. Now that I've received confirmation it's gone, could it be I can actually live life, rather than merely facilitate it for others?

And there is another option... Even with Lucas' protection, the fact of the matter is my life ended when I left Ireland, and what I've been living is a poor version of it. If Tytus is right though, that means there's hope. I could go back home, have what I haven't so far, and regain my own pack.

Will I willingly take it, is the answer? Especially now when I might have a shot with Elle?

My treacherous eyes go back to the bakery. I've barely moved a few meters away, like something's telling me to stay. Yet I've been roaming these streets in human form for a while, with no sign of the Reapers.

Tytus is right, much as I don't want to admit it. They shouldn't be this quiet. They haven't been in the entire year since I've been here. So what would cause it now? *If only he'd talk, already.* What with our skirmish, he didn't get a chance to hold his end of the deal and tell us everything he knows.

"Maybe he's having better luck tracking in the clouds." A snort escapes me, and I shake my head. I promised Lucas I'd behave, and since I'm on his last nerve, might as well.

Something ripples in the air, and I whirl around. "What the..."

From the darkness of the street, I see two red, gleaming eyes first. Then the rest of its body comes out – a jet black mustang. I stare, unable to grasp what I'm seeing.

He's got to be the finest beast I've seen in awhile, if not for those unnerving red eyes. Black mane blowing in the breeze, muscles rippling with each step, hooves heavy and sure on the pavement...

Sure enough, the horse throws its head back, neighing, and steps closer. *Maybe he escaped from a farm nearby?* If only I could be so lucky. With each step, I sense its power, confirming this is no normal beast. It's enough to make me back away, attempting to put some distance between us.

"My, my, you really are perceptive."

The voice is dark, filled with malice, and most surprising of all it speaks to me in Gaelic. I frown at the horse. He doesn't move its mouth, but the tone reverberates in the air, like the wind is speaking for him. This image, in a place like this, doesn't fit.

Despite myself, my feet move forward. It's been so long I heard my native tongue, that I have a hard time ungluing my tongue from the roof of my mouth.

A hard gulp later, and I manage a soft, "You... What are you?"

"Take a ride with me, and I'll tell you."

One glance around my surroundings proves I'm alone. It shouldn't scare me, but something about this creature does. Yet the same thing also intrigues me, pulling me in.

A few more steps, and I'm near it. The horse drops to his front knees, and I hold out a hand to touch its mane. Rough under my fingertips, he doesn't move, as though aware doing so would scare me off.

Inch by inch, the creature turns its head to me. I'm staring into red eyes, glowing in the moonlight. What I thought was malice in its voice comes across as haughtiness this time around. "Afraid, wolf?"

That makes me hesitate more. "You know what I am?"

"Aye." Its breath puffs across my face as it snorts. A hesitation later, I hop onto its back. At the back of my logical, lawyer, rational mind, I'm aware there's nothing normal about this. And yet, the actions are no longer mine.

Between my thighs, the horse's muscles bunch as it straightens, then it tosses its head back. A second later, it takes off at a gallop – and I try to hold on. Wind rushes through my hair as it does death–defying leaps in the air, taking me further and further away from town.

I could let go, but when I try to, the horse – or whatever the devil it is – shifts its course and makes sure I can't get off.

"Who are you?" I scream again, my voice hoarse in the night.

Something nags at the back of my head. Through the fog of the ride, the thrill of it, an old story comes forth. A childish nightmare, of a creature that roamed the land, a trickster looking for people to fool. A malicious shapeshifter who always appeared at night.

"You're a púca!"

The horse snorts. "Very well, wolf. Now let's see if you survive this night." Speed increasing, it pushes forth into the night. And this time, I'm holding on not because I can't let go – but because it's a link to my homeland, to something I never thought I'd have again.

Maybe it's a sign that I can finally go home.

By the time dawn comes, the púca finally throws me off its back. I slam into a tree, then slump to the ground, panting and a mess of sweat. Those red eyes look at me, unblinking.

"Why...." I wheeze, trying to gather another breath. I feel dizzy, removed of strength, like my entire energy has been sapped. Considering I've horse ridden before, I know it has nothing to do with the exercise, but with the creature itself.

"What did you do...to me?"

For a moment, it almost looks like the púca smiles. I close my eyes, and when I open them, it's gone.

"What the hell..."

I try to reach in my pocket for a phone to dial for help, but can't find it. Exhausted, I drop back to the grass and pass out.

Elisandra

"Finn!"

I jerk out of bed, hand to my chest, panting like I've run a million miles. That dream... On shaky legs, I make my way to the bathroom and fill a glass with water. It helps my parched throat, but does nothing for my fast–beating heart.

What was that? *Why would I wake up screaming Finn's name?*

You know full well why.

Shut up. This has nothing to do with sex, it's bigger than that. Hesitant at first, then growing more and more sure, I head downstairs to the bakery store and dial Finn's number. He'd called me off it to announce the car was done, so luckily caller ID has it stored.

I don't bother to think what it will look like, me calling him in the early hours of the morning, after running away from a kiss. I need to know he's okay, if nothing else.

The line rings and rings... And it takes me a second to realize an echoing trilling outside of my store. In a half daze, I unlock the door and step outside. The air is chilly, and I'm only in my house flippers and pajamas. Glancing around, I try to find the source of the noise. A faint light in the middle of the street draws my gaze.

On legs growing more unsteady by the minute, I inch closer and pick the phone up. Its screen has a crack from hitting the cement, and a couple missed calls show from a Lucas B. *I take it that's his boss.*

Yet there is no trace of Finn anywhere. What would he have been doing here? I turn around, coming in full view of my bakery. It's the most likely explanation, but... *Was he here for me?*

I pocket the phone and head back inside, trying to figure out what this all means. Before I can dwell too much on it, his phone rings again. And this time, it's another number – Dom K.

This, I can deal with. Hand shaking, I swipe the screen.

"Finn, where the hell are you? Lucas was blowing up my phone all night, saying it's your turn to patrol and thanks to my wonderful example now you're set to rise against him, too. What's going on?"

Patrol? I gulp, then whisper, "Dom, it's Elle."

There's a telling pause at the other end, then Dom says, "Why do you have Finn's phone, Elle?"

"Because it was outside my shop. And I haven't seen him since yesterday afternoon when I picked up my car."

He says a few words in another language that sound suspiciously like cursing. In the background, I hear Lucrezia, and she must have snatched the phone away from him because next thing I know, she's on. "Elle? Are you alright?"

"I'm fine, but I don't know where Finn is. Dominic doesn't seem to, either."

"Where are you right now?"

"At my store."

"Don't move. We'll be there in a bit." She hangs up before I can ask why the rush. Then I glance down at my less than inviting attire and shake my head. Since I can't meet Finn's friends in ratty pajamas, I figure it's about time I go get changed.

Finn

I wake up with a pounding head. It takes me forever to shift to wolf form, and even longer to get home. By the time I do and shower, it's past dawn – and time to head back to town.

Given I left my car at the shop, it's back to four paws again. This time, the run doesn't clear my mind. I can't wrap my head around the bizarre encounter. What the hell would a púca be doing here? And what did it do to me? More importantly, why?

As I'm walking through the last woods, I hear sounds of a fight. Curious, I shift to human and head over – only to find Tytus engaged in a brawl with a Reaper.

"And tell – your – fucking – leader – to – stay – away – from the bakery!"

Each word is punctuated by a punch, until the shifter is bleeding and barely hanging on. That doesn't stop him from grinning like a madman, and trying to aim in return. Tytus' hand reaches for his neck, grasps it, and throws the wolf into a tree. They go at it again, and again. Five minutes of clashing bodies and increasingly harder punches lead to an easy victory for the zmeu.

By the time the man's all bloody, Tytus turns to me. "Enjoying the show?"

With one last glare to the Reaper, he walks away. I quicken my step to keep up with him. "Why were you fighting him?"

"Trying to get a message through in hopes their leader gets it through his head that Elle is off limits."

I snort at the idea. "Weirder things have happened than Cade and his pack coming to their senses."

Tytus stops in his tracks, narrowing his eyes on me. "This is as much your fault as it is mine. Cade was already following Elisandra, but it was our scents around her spot that clued him in to being right. And make no mistake, wolf. Just because you're watching over her does not make us friends. I know your goal, and it's not happening."

"No idea what you're getting at."

I try to push past him, but he grabs my bicep. A faint zap of electricity runs through me, and I taste his anger in the air. "You want to play that game with me?"

"Fine. Say I'm interested. Say I've finally gotten my head outta my feckin' ass and want to give it a shot because I've got no price on me anymore, according to you. Who are you to stand between us?"

"Someone who knows you've got no clue what you're getting into."

When I make no move indicating I'm hearing him, Tytus digs his fingers into my arm. That same electricity runs into me, but a second later he pushes me away, his expression halfway between shock and anger. "What the hell? What was that creature?"

"What creature?"

"The horse–like entity that sucked up all your energy last night."

"It...what?"

Tytus shakes his head. "You're marked, fool."

"Marked?"

Tytus rips my shirt to the side, exposing my right shoulder and the crescent moon I've had since birth. Only, rather than the usual white it is, it's now blood red.

"Marked," he repeats.

"The púca…"

"The what?"

Seeing no reason not to, I describe to him what I saw, and my nightly adventure. Tytus' expression grows darker with each passing moment.

Elisandra

By the time I head back downstairs, there's a shape outside my door. With the foggy glass, I can't figure out who it is so I open the door, thinking it might be Dominic, or Lucrezia. Or Finn.

Instead, it's the guy from the other time – Cade. He grins when he sees me, raking his eyes up and down my body. Luckily, my alter seems to be quiet for the day.

"You again."

My less than excited tone clues him in. "What, not happy to see me?"

I roll my eyes and step back inside. "Not really. And if you're here to ogle me some more, then you can just walk right back out."

Cade's silence tells me I hit a nerve. When I turn around to face him, he's quiet. I think angry for a second, but then no, he smiles. "You didn't seem to mind it last time."

And we so, so didn't.

Shut up!

Determined not to let her take control of me again, I place my hands on my hips. "That wasn't me. I wasn't feeling well, and I'm sorry for the mixed feelings, but I don't appreciate being stared at like a piece of meat."

Oh, but I do.

Ignoring her, I keep my eyes level with his. Emotions run through his face too fast for me to grasp them, so I don't bother. Then Cade smiles. "Noted. Let me apologize...profusely."

The door to the bakery opens again, and this time it's the dark–haired man I'd seen with Finn that steps through. His expression is stormy when he notices who I'm with, but all he does is step inside and grab a seat by a corner. He gestures as if to say *'carry on'* and I try to focus back on Cade.

"I'm sorry, what?" Not for the first time, I wish controlling blushes was a thing. Grandmama always makes fun of me, but there's nothing more embarrassing.

The onyx–eyed man in front of me grins, and it's shiny enough to blind me. There's something about his hard jaw, the ebony skin and the muscles on display that has me feeling all kinds of wrong things.

Wrong, but so, so good.

I realize he's been speaking this entire time, and I haven't heard a thing because I'm too busy trying to bridge the gap between my thoughts and my alter's. *And* attempting to avoid another fiasco like last time. "Sorry," I mutter, avoiding his distracting gaze. "You'll have to repeat that – again."

"Grab a drink with me later?"

The stranger in a corner clears his throat, and stands up. Walking over, his eyes are on me, but he's talking to Cade. "The lady doesn't seem much interested. Maybe go try your luck elsewhere, yeah?"

Cade turns to him. I can't catch the expression on his face, only the periphery, but the air feels more tense. Or maybe it's just me. Grandmama will kill me if there's a brawl here – we don't have nearly the right insurance to cover damages.

"Leave while you can," the stranger says.

"Or what? She's not taken, that I know of."

"And she's not yours *to* take."

It's like they're speaking in code. Then the stranger lifts one hand, and Cade takes a step back. He seems afraid of what the other man is doing – drawing something in the air.

Before they can go at it, I step around the counter and straight between them. "Okay, enough. Are you actually here to buy anything?"

Cade looks at me, smirking. "Maybe."

Rolling my eyes again, I point towards the door. "Out. You're causing trouble for me, and I'm not in the mood."

"Are you sure I can't tempt you for drinks?"

Oh yes, please!

"I..." My decisive tone is gone. She's trying to gain ground again, and it's about to land me into serious trouble. I press my lips together in an effort to stop further words from escaping.

Before I can answer, the door behind him opens. And the guy who walks in steals my breath away – literally. Until he opens his mouth and speaks.

"Get the feckin' hell away from her, Cade."

CHAPTER FIVE

∞ Pionós ∞

"If people are good only because they fear <u>punishment</u>, and hope for reward, then we are a sorry lot indeed."

–Albert Einstein–

Finn

Breaking rules is not my thing. Anyone who knows me will attest to that. Being a lawyer, the eldest in a family, and the only one with a brain not ruled by hormones in this pack – well, it weighs on a person.

Which is why this isn't me.

Barging into a bakery? Not me.

Clenching my fists so I don't smash Cade's pretty face into a bloody pulp? Not me either.

Wanting to claim the girl behind the counter so bad it leaves me breathless? Yup, that's *definitely* all me. And when my eyes land on Cade, an intense rage fills me. I've only ever felt it once – when I pummeled Ciaran into the ground.

And look how well that turned out, my rational mind tries to warn me – too late.

"Ah, hell no!" Elle steps in front of me, palms held up and fury in her eyes. "You're not about to start something in my grandmama's shop, I've barely gotten these two to settle!"

"Two?"

She looks at me like I'm slow, and I snap out of my head enough to take in my surroundings. Tytus arches an eyebrow my way, as if asking what took me so long.

In my defense, after arguing with him about the púca's good or bad intentions, I needed to cool off. Had I known he was heading here first, I would've come with him.

As it stands, the zmeu's amusement tinges the air. As does Cade's ready–to–snap attitude. The moment I realize it, I grab Elle's wrist and tug her behind me.

Cade smirks, and something tells me I've played right into his hands. "You'll impinge on another alpha's turf?"

Elle's confusion clouds my head, as does her vanilla scent so close to me. *Feckin' hell.* I shake my head, glancing at Tytus for help. All he does is step by my side, providing an additional layer of protection for Elle.

"Isn't it you who is on Lucas' land, mate?" Fists clenched, I lift my chin in a movement he'll hopefully understand – to back the feck off. Instead, Cade smirks and widens his stance.

"Hardly. Here I was, attracted to this gorgeous lady you're hiding behind you. And now you, a mere pup, intervenes? Tsk. Does your alpha know what you're up to?"

Rough nails dig into my palm, and I inhale sharply. Last time I broke the rules, it didn't go so well for me. But there's no way I'm letting this progress further than it already has, and putting Elle in danger.

"Good call," Tytus mutters out of the corner of his mouth. And I'm glad at least I don't have to fight him, too. He may think I'm marked, but he obviously has no issue with me protecting Elle.

So long as I keep from claiming here, I assume.

Elle is suspiciously quiet behind us, but I'm not about to get distracted again. Instead, I offer Cade a smirk of my own. "How about you bite me, Cade? Go crying back to your pack and see what they do."

Nostrils flaring, he's in my face the moment after. Elle makes a noise, but Tytus glances her way. His harsh expression is enough to keep her silent. It also draws Cade's attention.

Rather than cower as he should – if he's smart, he should feel at least part of Tytus' power – the fool only sneers at him. "Mark my words, dragon. You ain't seen nothing yet."

His icy glare moves to Elle, then he taps an index to his lips and walks off. The minute he's finally gone, I realize everything we've just said in front of Elle, and throw a look at Tytus. He's focused on the little fireball behind us, and by the air I can taste, she's about to spit flames.

Elisandra

Pup? Dragon? Alpha? I don't know what the hell just went down in my bakery, but I'm ready to tear into these two with an anger that surprises me.

Yes.... Show them what we're made of!

Her egging me on doesn't help. But it's Finn's emerald gaze, watching me patiently – as if knowing I'm about to blow up – that calms me down. So rather than rip him a new one, I take a deep breath and push past him and Tytus.

Their massive forms in front of me were enough to make me claustrophobic. Safe, yes, but too damn cornered to like it. Away from them, I rub between my eyes, trying – and failing – to focus on something else.

"What just happened here?"

Somehow, even without turning to them, I know they're sharing a look, and it just makes me angrier. I shift my gaze to the ceiling, feeling my hair fall out of its messy bun and swipe my lower back.

"Anytime now."

Another ominous silence answers me, then someone clears their throat. Not Finn, the voice is deeper, graver. "My apologies for the, ah, misunderstanding."

"Misunder..." I take another deep breath. Do these guys take me for a fool?

Maybe they wouldn't if you listened to me every once in a while!

"Elle, if you'd just listen–"

His whiskey voice rumbles my insides, and combined with her annoying prodding, does the trick – I snap. Whirling around, hair up in my face, I point an accusing finger his way. "You. Don't. Talk. First you say I'm inconsequential, then I fall for your pathetic serenade. Next thing I know, you're paying my mechanic bills and trying to decide who gets to leer at me? Hell. To. The. *No*."

To his credit, Finn has the grace to look sheepish – and then I can't stare in that face anymore. I turn to the stranger. "And *you*! What the hell are you playing at, nearly starting a fight in Grandmama's store? I don't need some mystery stranger protecting me. I'm no one's little girl, nor fool!"

Is it me, or do his grey eyes flash lightning for a second? The air feels chillier in here, but that's probably my imagination, too. Clenching my teeth, I add one more thing. "I want you to leave. Both of you. Now."

They share a look at that, and the stranger says, "No can do, my dear."

"And why not?"

"Because," Finn takes a step forward, "Tytus isn't a stranger or some random lad who just walked into your store. He's your ancestor. And I know this is going to sound insane, but you need to hear us out."

"Us?" I glance between them. "You know this guy?"

Finn sighs, looking as weary as I've ever seen him. "Yeah, I do. And he knows you, too. And, gorgeous, Cade isn't as innocent as you may think."

Before he can explain his cryptic statement, the door to my bakery store blows open and in walk Dominic and Lucrezia. They take one look around the store, and Dom lifts his head to take a long inhale.

His expression is odd when he meets Finn's. "Reaper?"

"Yeah."

Dom's blue eyes turn to me, but his question is obviously to Finn. "How much does she know?"

I glare at him. "*She* doesn't know anything because people keep barging in here like it's their own place!"

Lucrezia snorts by his side. Her amusement dampens my spirits, but it seems to ease up Dom as he grins. "Right. We'll, uh, go brief Lucas in the meantime. Good luck."

The minute they're gone, I turn back to Finn and Tytus. "All right. You've got five minutes, then I'm calling the cops."

Something in Tytus' expression implies he'd love to see me try, but I ignore him. Finn does the same, instead taking a seat and gesturing for me to do the same. I listen, if only to give my feet a rest.

"I'll start with the easiest. Cade comes from the wrong side of the tracks, so to speak. You must recall a while back, some guys dressed like him had it in for Lucrezia?"

That does ring a bell. Not so long ago, they stormed into the bakery because they'd seen her, and delivered a rather icy message for Dom. "And if I do?"

"Their leader is dead, and Cade is his replacement. These...aren't good people, Elle."

I snort. "And who are you to judge?"

Finn shakes his head. "Back in Ireland, I used to be a lawyer. I know lost causes when I see them, and Cade's people are it. At the present time, there's a bit of a feud between his people and us."

"Over what, a mechanic job gone wrong?"

Tytus tries to cover his laugh with a cough, but I'm nowhere as amused.

"Something like that," Finn says with a side glance to Tytus. "They're pretty vengeful. They've seen us coming in here, and that's why Cade is trying to get friendly with you. To rile you up."

Sadly, that makes more sense than him actually being interested in me. Finn frowns, concern sparking in his eyes. I'm not sure what could've caused it, but I wave him to go on.

"I spoke to Lucas, and he agreed to offer you protection from us."

"Protection?" I laugh out loud at that. 'What are you guys going to do, shadow my every move?"

"If they have to, yes." Tytus' tone is dark drawing my attention to him.

"And why would you? I don't work for Lucas, or Cade's people. I'm just another regular person in this town. If I want protection, I can call the cops."

Finn shakes his head. "It won't work with these guys, Elle. Please believe me."

I cross my arms over my chest, mulling over everything he said so far. According to him, these guys were after Lucrezia, and now she's safe and sound – and loved – with Dominic. Dani has Tristan, and something tells me there's a similar story there from the way he watches over her. Would it really be so bad, accepting their protection, whatever that entails?

Hell, yes! Bring on the hotness.

Ignoring her, I focus on the last piece of the puzzle and narrow my eyes on Tytus. "And what's your story?"

Finn clears his throat before Tytus can speak. "I know you're here only with your grandma, and that she raised you. But you've had another family member this entire time, Elle. Tytus is it."

I look at the dark–haired man, seeing nothing of myself in him. "As if!"

Tytus grins. "I accept the challenge." He moves away from Finn and heads behind the counter, drawing both me and Finn after him.

Under my bemused gaze, he stops straight in front of the oven. "This thing on?"

"Yeah, it's burning hot tho–"

As if I haven't spoken, Tytus reaches for the handle same as I did, and opens it. A waft of hot air surrounds him, then he sticks his hand inside, touching the burning hot grid. "Stop!" I rush towards him before he ends up with first–degree burns, but to my surprise he pulls his hand out – completely unharmed.

He turns it this way and that, showcasing for me the taut, tanned skin, with no traces of burns or blisters. Same like...me. I look up into his face then. "How did you do that?"

Tytus opens his mouth to say something, then stops. "A genetic trait, darling. Fire doesn't harm us."

I notice his stare go behind me, and turn from my surprise to Finn. He's tilting his head to the side, as if listening to some music only he can hear. After another beat, he sighs. "Don't want o interrupt, but Lucas is waiting."

Finn

Fucked doesn't begin to describe the mess I just got myself into. Not to mention Elle still only knows a fraction of the danger courting her... *Bollocks*. I eye Tytus as we escort her out of the bakery and to Claws Auto Shop.

He shakes his head, then mutters, "We have time later."

"Time for what?" Elle asks.

Since there's no easy way to answer that, I change the subject. "Lucas may be a tad angry when we get in. So, whatever you do, don't egg him on and let me deal with it. That goes for you too, Tytus."

Elle rolls her eyes, but follows in silence. I love the little pucker of her lips as she concentrates, though I keep tasting mixed emotions off her. Tytus is easier to read. He's angry we had to hide most of the truth, but relieved we've got her with us.

You and me both, mate.

Once we reach the mechanic shop, I pause for a brief second. Lucas' rage wafts through the walls, it's that strong. And for the first time, I regret that I've already tested his patience by taking Dom and Tristan's sides in the past. Maybe, if I hadn't...

Shaking the thought off, I turn the handle and step inside. *Yep, scorching hell would feel more welcoming than this.*

Tytus and Elle follow in my footsteps. Lucas' anger must be strong enough even for them to sense it, as their demeanour changes.

"In here."

Thankfully, my alpha chose to turn the garage into a meeting place again. When I enter, he takes in Elle and Tytus, then his eyes meet mine. Iciness fills my blood at the lack of emotion he portrays.

"Will you give me a chance to explain before you kick me out?" I'm already resigned to it, but trying is worth a shot. The alpha blood in me demands as much.

Lucas presses his lips in a thin line, and gestures for me to speak. "Certo. But first, let's get everyone else in, shall we?"

He whistles and Dom walks in, followed by Lucrezia, Dani and Tristan. The latter two throw me an interested look, but I sense their distraction. Dani, especially, seems eager to talk to Tytus about something.

"Cade was in Elle's shop," I start, but grow distracted again by their palpable excitement. *Maybe it's something that'll mellow Lucas.* Tilting my head to the side, I turn to Tristan. "You two found something, didn't you?"

Dani nods, practically jumping on the balls of her feet. Ignoring Lucas' growl, she steps closer to me. "I told them to let me go with for the last few days and they finally did. I was able to use a tracker spell and find the Reapers, or at least their latest hideout. I think we can find them tonight, but I'll need Tytus to fly in for backup."

Ah, shite.

Dani stares at me for a beat, then Elle, and her eyes widen. "Not again. Merda, Finn, how many times are you going to let me run my mouth!"

Much the same thing happened a few weeks ago when Dani accidentally told Luz a tidbit about Tytus, without realizing she wasn't up to date. As this seems to be a trend, I simply roll my eyes and throw a look over my shoulder to Elle. She looks petrified next to Tytus, and has slowly backed herself into a corner. I try to catch her eye, sensing her confusion.

Instead, Tytus jerks his head to Lucas. I know what he means – handle my business first. So it's with a heavier heart I turn to Lucas.

"Tytus could go with them tonight. I'll take Elle home."

"You can't." It's Dani again. I'm getting concerned with how quiet Lucas is, especially as I'm not picking up nearly enough off him as I should.

"Why not?"

With an apologetic glance to Elle, Dani says, "Because Cade is furious and he wants her – tonight. We overheard two Reapers yap about it as we got into town. After what happened in the bakery, Cade took it as a personal affront and he's calling an all out war."

Tristan adds, "You need to leave town, meu amigo. Let us cool off the waters, and if not, you can come back and help us fight. But first, get your girl somewhere safe."

Elle starts to say something, but Tytus whispers furiously to her, and she settles down. Then before I can intervene, Lucas draws my attention.

"Hey, Irish?"

I turn around – big mistake. His right fist catches me under the jaw, sending me stumbling backwards. Between no sleep and the freaking púca, my reflexes are slow, but not that slow.

Ducking his next hit, I retaliate with a punch to the gut. Lucas takes it in stride and rams his head in my gut, throwing me off balance. My forehead smacks the side of a car, and I see stars for a second.

Elisandra

"Stop it," Tytus hisses in my ear. "I know you don't agree and that you've grown in a world where a woman speaks her mind. But there are things going on here you don't yet understand. Give Finn a chance to explain before you write both of us off."

I turn to glare at him, but he seems unimpressed. Those stormy eyes dance with amusement. "Done yet, micuță?"

"What does that mean?" He says it like *me–kuh–tzuh*.

Tytus grins. "Little one."

I'm about to retort when grunting noises draw my attention. Lucas or Finn threw the first punch and now they're going at it with a brutality that stuns me.

Finn gets up off the floor, bleeding all over the ground from the head. I take a step closer but Tytus puts a hand out to stop me. "Don't, Elisandra."

"Is this part of what I don't understand?"

Tytus nods. Then Finn gets hit again and this time I wince. I feel physically sick with each blow he takes.

Tytus notices it, and his expression changes. From speculative, it grows to panic, and finally resolution. Leaving me behind, he throws himself between Lucas, grasping him by the throat. "Enough."

His growl vibrates the ground, and the sky outside seems to darken. I'm finally starting to understand there's something else going on here. Something beyond my understanding, and maybe not completely normal. I can't focus on it, though, not when it looks like this situation is ready to spin out of control.

Lucas' expression is murderous. "You *dare* interfere?"

He lifts a hand and grasps the one Tytus has on his neck. Something flashes in his expression and next thing I know, the walls are shaking. I step towards Finn, who's leaning on Tristan, wiping at the side of his face with the bottom of his shirt.

Dani catches my eye. "He'll be okay, it looks worse than it is."

I shake my head. "Lucas is a barbarian."

Dani doesn't seem to agree, but she also doesn't say anything. Then Finn lifts his head, his eyes more clear than I would have imagined given the hit to the head.

"Are you okay?"

Lucrezia comes with ice wrapped in a clean cloth and holds it out for me. I help Finn place it to the side of his head to stop the bleeding, and he smiles feebly.

"Sorry."

"For what?" I ask, bemused.

"I know you've got questions."

I think about it. "Just one that matters right now: am I really in danger?"

"Aye, gorgeous. And we need to leave tonight."

I think back to the business, and what I committed to. "Fine. The delivery is in two days, and with my van fixed, I've already got everything ready to go. You can come with me, I guess, to hand off everything... And we can talk more about all of this."

Finn nods and turns to Lucas and Tytus. While we've been whispering, there's an entire contest taking place between those two. From my standpoint I see Lucas, and I swear his eyes change for a second as if rimmed with red. Then I blink and it's gone, and I'm thinking it's probably a trick or the imagination.

I turn to Finn to see if he noticed it, and he's frowning their way. Then I grin to myself – *she* hasn't made herself known yet, a small miracle.

On the heels of that realization, Tytus and Lucas break apart. In synchronized paces, they circle each other until Lucas points to the exit. "Get the fuck out of here, Tytus, while you still can. Dani, Tristan, go find out what you can and return to me." To Tytus he adds, "Our agreement is null and void."

Tytus smirks. "Not quite. Your cub made a promise and this would make two oaths broken to me. A third has dire consequences, so I wouldn't test me. Let Finn protect Elle, and we'll call us even."

Lucas glares at him. "Esci!"

Which, I take to mean some Italian version of, *Get out.* Tytus looks our way one more time, then salutes and takes off, followed by Tristan and Dani. I glance at Dom, who's been keeping to the side, eyes narrowed on Lucas.

When it seems like Lucas is heading back to Finn to finish what he started, Dom steps between them. He tosses a set of keys to Finn. "Take my car and get out of here. Make sure she's safe and watch your back." A glance to me. "And you watch over him, too."

Mm, maybe he'll get us on our back.

I groan. The silence was fun while it lasted.

Finn's quiet in the passenger seat next to me, and it's making me uneasy. He has a way of looking at me like he sees right through me, and now that he's not saying anything, I'm almost edgy. We left Dom's truck in front of the bakery, after quickly piling everything in the van and taking off.

It's been about thirty minutes of a drive so far, meaning we're out of Rockland Creek and on our way to the destination – no trouble on the horizon.

I glance at him out of the corner of my eye, noticing Finn's got his eyes closed. "Are you sleeping?"

He snorts. "Not likely. I'm supposed to watch over you, remember?"

Dom's words echo in my ears. Then I recall the mess we left behind. "What was that, back there? With Dom and Lucas?"

Finn opens his eyes, but he's staring out the window rather than at me. "They've got issues, those two. Too bullheaded to make it work."

"And with Tytus?"

Finn hesitates, then says, "Same thing, more or less."

It makes sense, given what I've seen so far. But something still rankles me. "Why did Dom say to keep an eye out for me?"

Finn sighs and finally looks my way. It's a good thing I'm focused on the road, else I have a feeling I'd be a little more unnerved by his emerald gaze.

"Because Cade seems to have developed a keen interest in you – more than normal, like he wants something specific."

"And how is that your problem?"

Finn taps his fingers against his knee, then mutters under his breath. "It's not like they said I couldn't tell you." Louder, he says, "You may want to pull over for this."

My back tightens. "I think I made it clear I'm done taking orders."

"Have it your way." A sigh, followed by words that rock my world and topple it sideways. "I don't suppose you ever realized you live in a town full of werewolves?"

My foot slips off the gas pedal and I almost swerve out of control. Last minute, I right the van in place. Gripping the wheel, I pull onto a dead–beat road and turn to meet Finn's amused expression. "*What* did you just say?"

"You heard me, precious. Rockland Creek is full of wolves, and you're caught in a battle of wills between Lucas' pack – us – and Cade's – the Reapers."

My mouth opens and closes as I try to figure out if he's lost his mind – or if I have.

CHAPTER SIX

∞ Caite ∞

"If we open a quarrel between <u>past</u> and present, we shall find that we have lost the future."

–Winston Churchill–

Finn

Elle's hazel eyes are wide and settled on me. Yep, she definitely thinks I've lost it now. And judging by the way she's curling towards the driver's door, she's about to hop out of the car.

I slowly move my hands, palms up, in a gesture of peace. "Before you bolt, hear me out."

"Wolves... Werewolves aren't *real*."

Panic tinges her voice, and I can't help laughing. This only sets Elle's pulse racing, which gets my wolf in anxious mode, so I stop.

"I'm glad my logic amuses you."

Ignoring her dry tone, I say, "I was only laughing because your reaction is a hell of a lot more normal than Lucrezia's when she found out."

This grabs her interest. "Luz...knows?"

I nod. "Has for a while now. But unlike us, she's human."

With each soft statement, I thank my lucky stars she's still in the car, rather than bolting down the dirt road. "We all – me, Dom, Tristan and Lucas – landed in Rockland Creek from all corners of the earth. Because we each used to have a pack, but were now rogue wolves in a town full of humans, we banded together under one leader."

Elle frowns, then her expression eases as she lands on one name. "Lucas."

"Yep. And he makes the rules – *our* rules." Everything's coming out like word vomit, and I know I'm overloading her with information. But each second she's with me is a second won, and the best way she can prepare – and protect herself – is with knowledge. So I keep going. "The Reapers have Cade in charge, and they hate humans. Look down upon them as food rather than actual beings. We've been keeping things in check here, trying to make sure they don't end up in control of this town. It's kind of hard when their bite turns humans to werewolf."

Elle gulps, and fear flashes in her eyes again, dirtying the air around us. "And can your bite...?"

"Turn? No." I debate how much I should tell her, and opt not to scare her further. Instead, I add, "There's been loads happening these last few weeks, especially since Dani came into town."

"Is she...?"

"Yeah, she's a wolf. But she's a lobisomem, as is Tristan, versus me being a faoladh."

Panic gives way to confusion in the air, so I sigh. "Okay. Unlike books and movies, there's not just one type of wolf in the world. We're all werewolves, but with different abilities. I'm a faoladh, which is an Irish wolf. My people are blessed with an ability to, shall we say, read people. And emotions. We can take away their pain, too."

Elle frowns at that. Then she seems to think of something, and all color drains out of her. "So you can hear my thoughts?"

"No! I'd never infringe on your privacy like that. It's more of a... Your emotions, I can taste them in the air around you. Like now, you're panicked because of everything I'm saying, but also a tiny bit curious to learn more."

The admission seems to have the desired effect – or so I think. The second after, Elle shakes her head and gets out of the car. I go to follow, and she says, "I'm not running away. I just need a minute."

Watching her walk away takes more out of me than I'm willing to admit. Hands dug into my jeans' pockets, I force my wolf to relax, to breathe and let her be. It's not easy when all I want is to tell her everything else she doesn't know.

About twenty minutes later, Elle heads back to me. Her emotions are less all over the place, though a trace of wariness still remains. "All right. I'm not yet ready to get back in a car with you, but you're right. I'm curious to hear more."

I search her expression, more in an effort to make sure she's not bluffing. Satisfied, I say, "Good." A pause. "What should I elaborate on?"

"Well, you mentioned you're all different. What about Dom and the rest of them?"

"Dominic is a vârcolac, so he's a Romanian wolf. He has extra strength at certain times of the month, and silver hurts him. Tristan and Dani are lobisomens, a type of Brazilian wolf. They're the only ones able to do magic – though Dani's the one who can do that. And they can also increase or decrease their wolf's size."

Elle gulps. "And Lucas?"

Hell if I know.

Rather than give her that unhelpful answer, I say, "He's a bit of a complicated case. I'm not even fully sure what his *lupo mannaro* abilities are – he's Italian. But I know he's got a flair for harnessing all our strengths."

I give her a minute to absorb all this. "Anything else you want to know?"

Elle shakes her head, as if at a loss. "How could I not have known? You guys have been in my store a million times!"

"We're good at hiding, love."

A faint blush paints her cheeks at the endearment, which slipped off my tongue much too easily. "What about Tytus? Is he a wolf?"

I think back to him sticking his hand in the oven. "Nope. Wolves get burned by fire, same like all other furry creatures." *Not the scaly ones.*

I don't say that out loud either. What's the point of scaring her further? Plus, Tytus wouldn't be too pleased if I stole his thunder.

Gesturing to the car, I watch her carefully. Elle glances between the vehicle and me, then walks over to the passenger side. "You can drive for a bit."

Satisfied she's finally comfortable enough to get in, I don't waste any time to start the car. No sooner are we off, that Elle adds more questions.

"Do you only turn on a full moon?"

"Nope, we're shifters so we can turn whenever."

"Is your diet different?"

"Only when in wolf form – I'll eat anything, raw or cooked."

Her nails scrape at the door handle in agitation. "You said silver hurts Dom. What about you?"

"Why, you planning to kill me?"

Elle throws me a look implying I'm nowhere near funny. "I just...would like to know what to worry about."

"It's cute that you're worried. But no, I don't get hurt easily." Unless you count dragon venom – but I don't tell her that either. Yeah, I'm really doing a bang–up job with this being honest crap.

"I have another question." Something about the way she says it raises the hairs at the back of my neck, but I wait patiently. "Did something happen to you last night?"

I think back to the púca and my less than delightful nightly adventures. "Err, I had a rough night. Bad luck seems to be following me lately, and the pack. Why do you ask?"

"Because I woke up in the middle of the night and tried to reach you. Something told me you'd been harmed, and then I found your cell phone outside the bakery."

Surprise hits me straight in the gut. She was worried about me? In the middle of the night?

"I... must've dropped it. Sorry for upsetting you."

Elle says nothing, instead turning to stare out the window. *I take it question period is done for now.*

Elisandra

"I don't believe it," I whisper a few moments later.

Finn glances at me out of the corner of his eye. "It's a lot to take in, I know. For some weird reason, Lucrezia hopped on board, but take your time coming to terms with this. I can only imagine the shock of learning all of this, especially given you're not exactly human yourself."

"*What?*"

Finn cringes as if he wasn't supposed to have said anything. "Maybe I'll leave Tytus to explain this." Then he glances at me, and his eyes widen. "Or...maybe not. Elle, love, take a breath."

I don't understand his panicked tone until I smell smoke. And I glance down to see I've burned a hole in my jeans – but my skin in unmarred.

"What the..."

For the second time that day, we pull over. I turn my hand one way and the other, but there's no trace of fire. Yet there's a massive hole on my thigh now, the size of my palm, right where the jeans use to be. The edges are blackened, as if burned. When I stare up at Finn, he's got a weird expression on his face.

"What did you mean that I'm not exactly human? And screw Tytus, he just showed up in my life out of nowhere. You've known me for the better part of a year now, so if anyone's to tell me something, it should be you."

Finn sighs. "All right. I didn't lie, earlier, I just didn't want to overload you with information. Tytus isn't a wolf, but he's not human either. He's a zmeu. Basically, a type of Romanian dragon that can do magic and control the weather."

I gape at him. Then start laughing hysterically. By the time I calm down, he's staring at me like I've lost my head. "A *dragon*? That guy?"

"A zmeu, aye." Finn nods. "I know how impossible this sounds, but as his descendant, you carry some of his powers. It's just...complicated because you're female. Listen, we can call Tytus once we stop, but it's getting dark and we should find a spot to sleep in."

I stop questioning him and curl up in the seat as he drives off again. Another forty minutes later, we're halfway to the delivery spot when Finn slows down. I glance at him, noticing his frown and intense concentration. It's not the first time I've seen that look.

"What's going on?"

He glances at me, as if coming out of a daze. "Don't freak out, okay?"

It's my turn to frown. "Freak out about what?"

Finn hits the brakes, jerking my attention back to the front of the car.

"That."

A midnight horse is blocking the way, eyes glowing red. They slide over me and stop on Finn, and I could've sworn the beast smiles. "Hello again."

It should be impossible, as nothing about the mustang moves, but I hear its voice as clear as if it was coming through speakers. A faint Irish accent tinges its tone, much like Finn's. Only, unlike the warmth I feel when he speaks, it's dread that fills my stomach.

Finn clenches his teeth, and unbuckles his seatbelt. Panic rises within me. "What are you doing?"

"Finishing something. Stay inside."

He opens the door and is out in the next moment. And I'm tempted to listen, if only because the creature, whatever the hell it is, looks dangerous. But *she* has other ideas.

This looks like fun.

No, it doesn't. We should let Finn handle it.

Mm, fun as it is watching that ass, I don't think so. Move.

Despite wanting to resist it, my hand reaches for the handle, and the door pops open. My feet carry me out of the car, and I'm left a spectator in my own body, much like when she spoke to Cade.

Finn

"What do you want, púca? What's your deal with me?"

"If you haven't figured it out yet, why should I spoil the surprise?" The horse neighs as if it's snickering, then kicks its front legs towards me.

I'm blasted backwards a few steps, until I come into contact with something. A vanilla scent drifts in the air, and soft arms wrap around my waist from behind. A warm breath whispers, "Yum."

It's a shock to my system when those same hands rake up and down my stomach, as if tracing my abs. A purr in my ear tells me that's exactly what she's doing, and I taste the satisfaction – and desire – in the air.

"Elle, what the hell?"

She lets go of me and walks around to face me. There's a different tilt to her chin, and those eyes are stormy–grey, like when she kissed me. Her lips are turned in a wicked smile. "Let me handle this, dearie."

As if I'm a child, she turns her back to me and walks to the púca.

"Elle, wait!"

The horse is watching her, head tilted to the side. And I taste something else in the air – curiosity, but also uneasiness. "What *are* you?"

Elle whispers something, and I inch closer. Her hand lifts in the air, drawing something I've seen Dani do before – a rune. A storm of sparks hits the horse, making it shake its head. The red eyes glow almost burgundy, and the púca takes a step forward, emitting something close to snarl.

To my surprise, Elle doesn't even flinch. She tosses her hair back, tilting her chin up. "Not had enough? Alrighty, then!" Her hand comes up once more.

While she's drawing another rune, the púca takes one look at me. "This is not over." Then it disappears.

Elle sways in the air, then drops to the ground. I run to her in time to stop her head from cracking open on a rock. A breath later, her eyelids flutter, and it's the regular hazel gaze staring into mine. "What happened?"

"You don't remember?"

She shakes her head. "No, only that you stopped for that...creature."

I help her up, muttering, "It's a púca, a trickster from my country."

"A púca?"

I think back to the stories I grew up with. "The story goes, they're fairy folk. Tricksters who can take any from they wish. They've been seen as deformed goblins, boogeymen, giant eagles... The malicious black horse is another of its incarnations. They always have golden or red eyes, and can wield human speech."

Elle's intent gaze stays on me. "And what do they want?"

A shrug lifts my shoulders. "Talk, provide advice... Sometimes they disappear without a word. Sometimes they expect a share of farm crops, otherwise they'll destroy the area."

Elle's silent for a bit. "So, did you forget to pay the thing a couple years back, or something?"

"No..." It's my turn to frown. "But it's after something, all right. And I seem to have incited its worst phase – the horse that deliberately takes you on a wary path. The hardest to get rid of, or tame. Unless you're the last Irish High King, and we're pretty much out of those."

"Huh?"

"Legend has it that there was a púca, eons ago, that wouldn't stop with mischief in Ireland. Only the High King of Ireland was able to tame it, and it was never seen again."

Elle glances where the púca had been. "I don't suppose said legend tells you how to do that, too?"

"I wish, but naw." I hesitate to bring it up. "You seemed to handle it just fine, though."

"What do you mean?"

"Well, you... I don't know, Elle. You just walked up to it and did some magic shit."

She snorts. "I don't do magic." When my serious expression doesn't change, her mouth opens in surprise. "Are you serious?"

"Aye, love."

She looks around, as though expecting some camera crew to pop out of nowhere. A deep sigh escapes her. "I... That's all got to do with Tytus, then. And whatever I inherited from him."

"Maybe... Or maybe it's got to do with whoever just took control of your body."

Her panic tinges the air again, and I back off. "Never mind. The middle of the road is not the place to have this conversation, not when we may have Reapers on our trail. Let's just find a motel or somewhere to spend the night."

As we walk back to the car, Elle whispers, "And you really don't know why it's here?"

"I've no clue why it appeared, nor why it seems to be following me everywhere."

"Can it be killed?"

"Silver's supposed to burn through it, but hell if I know."

I wait until she's back in the passenger seat, with the seatbelt buckled, before taking off again. Then I spend the next twenty minutes trying to come up with a strategy to get through to her, and find out whatever's really going on under Elisandra Worthington's skin.

∞ ◆ ∞

We exit the car and I'm about to go in the antiquated motel to get us a room, when the air changes. Already wired from the encounter with the puca, I'm not in the mood for more games, though I'm well familiar with this particular energy.

Grasping Elle's hand in mine, I turn on my heel and put myself between her and the immortal. "What are you doing here, Ileana?"

I glance around, trying to make sure no one else notices us. The lack of lights inside this roadside inn tells me all the humans within are probably fast asleep, otherwise they'd be getting an eyeful.

Unconcerned of them, Ileana smiles, and her gaze shifts behind me. "Move out of the way, wolf."

"No."

Those iridescent eyes meet mine, and one pale hand lifts in the air. Like I'm nothing but a curtain, she moves me to the side, leaving Elle to her view. They stare at each other, and Ileana smiles. "You have a lot of Tytus in you, child."

Elle glances at me, and I taste her confusion. "This is Ileana Cosânzeana, Dominic's godmother. She's... Well, she helps out the pack. She won't hurt you...I think."

Ileana's tinkling laugh echoes around us. "Of course not. I merely came to see if it was true, that a zmeu's line had produced a female last offspring."

"What?"

Reading Elle's confusion, Ileana says, "A zmeu, my dear, is inherently male. As is his line, his offspring, and heirs."

"And why's that?"

Ileana tilts her head to the side, and her hair flows over her shoulder. "Do you really not know?"

The way she stresses the question has Elle shift uncomfortably. She glances at me, and I read the panic flaring in her eyes.

"Ileana..." Her name is a warning on my lips, but the witch ignores me.

"Have you not felt her inside you, pushing you aside?"

Elle's gaze snaps to Ileana's. And with sudden clarity, I remember those stormy grey eyes, the shift in her attitude, something I've seen many times since knowing her. Tytus' words about the powers affecting her differently also ring in my ears.

"She *is* you, child. Only, the wild part of you. The zmeu part of you. By ignoring things you have been able to do, you have forced her to show up as a separate personality."

"I didn't..." Elle's denial is weak.

Ileana steps closer, reaching with a hand. I taste the magic in the air, and I'm a second too late in yelling, "No, don't!"

Elisandra

It's the weirdest sensation, like water running through me. Then I feel *her*, only rather than being at the back of my mind, she comes to the front. Speaks for me. I'm able to hear her – myself – but not stop her.

"What do you want, witch?"

"To prove a point," Ileana says. "And warn you. You cannot take over this one's body. Neither I nor her ancestor will allow it."

The feisty me snorts, then crosses her arms over her chest. Her – my – eyes shift to Finn, and she – I – we – grin. "Heya, handsome. What say you to getting out of here?" It's a hell of a confusion, even more so than with Cade.

Finn's staring in shock, then glances at Ileana. "Is Elle...?"

"She is fine," Ileana says. "Only thrown to the back while this one takes over."

"Uh, *hello*? Right here." I hate the sound of her voice. *My* voice. Snotty and full of...malice.

"Not for long," Ileana says.

"As if you can banish me!"

Ileana's eyes take on an unnatural hue, and her smile goes icy. "I could, but I will not. Because this girl deserves to be her full, complete self. And you cannot stop her."

She – I – glares back, but says nothing.

"You have been warned. Elle may not have been aware of her lineage, but she is now. And you do not need to take over, she will willingly embrace her powers."

Then Ileana touches my forehead again, and I'm inhaling air as if I was underwater. "Crap." There's a slight throbbing on the side of my head, then I open my eyes and it's my voice I hear.

Ileana smiles. "Now, do you understand?"

Tears gather in my eyes. "No! Why is she there? Am I going crazy, like my mom?" Pleading, I look at the one person with the answers – this insanely beautiful woman who looks like she belongs in a fairytale novel.

"No, dear one." She lifts a hand to touch my cheek, but Finn's there, pulling me in his arms – and away from her.

Yummy, she says, as if nothing happened.

Shut up.

"Please... Tell me."

Ileana looks from me to Finn, and her expression softens. "A female zmeu, as she grows to an age of marriage – which at the time was in the teenager years – develops an alter. Normally, this is the primal part of her that takes over when she shifts into her zmeu form."

"Like my wolf," Finn whispers, rubbing circles in my lower back. Somehow, the admission makes me feel less alone.

Ileana nods, her expression somber. "The problem is, you cannot shift to full zmeu form, because you have more human in you than zmeu. Which means the alter is there, and has nowhere to go, nowhere to take over."

"Except my life," I whisper miserable, and more tears run down my cheeks. She laughs in my head, but I forcefully ignore her.

"Yes," Ileana admits. "So there is but one way to get rid of her. You have to claim her – and your full powers, by learning magic – before she claims you."

My throat closes, and I bury my head in Finn's chest. "I'm not ready for this. A few hours ago, I was a human, and now I'm some freaking psychotic bipolar monster... I can't!"

Finn speaks above my head. "That's enough for today, Ileana. Elle needs sleep – as do I."

His harsh tone must do the trick, because when I next look up, Ileana is gone. Finn's arms tighten around me, but not even the safe bubble he has me in is enough to lessen my fears this time. What will I do, if I can't achieve what Ileana says I must? Will she simply take over...everything?

∞ ∞ ∞

CHAPTER SEVEN

∞ Pearsantacht ∞

"**Personality** is an unbroken series of successful gestures."

–F. Scott Fitzgerald–

Elisandra

Weakened, I let Finn lead us into the motel, and lean against the wall as he grabs us a room. Ileana's magic – whatever she did to me – still courses through my veins, and I'm more aware than ever of *her*.

Only, rather than her talking *to* me, it seems my voice is now just as strong. And for the first time, maybe because of everything Finn revealed or maybe because at least now I know I'm not losing it like Mom, I'm less afraid of her.

Is what Ileana said true?

I'm thinking this, but it's another thought that answers me. *Yep.* A pause follows, then she says, *Now do you get it?*

A quick glance at the counter confirms Finn is busy arguing with the clerk, so I pretend to be picking at the gaping hole in my jeans. *Not really. Supposedly I'm not human, and that's what's causing me to hear voices in my head? Doesn't compute.*

Something akin to a sigh rings in my head. *You're not hearing voices, silly. Just me. And I'm you. So, really, you're as sane as one can be.*

Somehow, that doesn't really reassure me.

Well, we wouldn't be in this dilemma if you hadn't ignored your powers for so long.

"As if I knew I had them!"

Out of the corner of my eye, I catch Finn turning to me. His expression shifts as he takes me in. Whatever emotion he catches from me must be bad, because he rushes the clerk – yet he's not quick enough. She still gets the last word in.

Did you ever ask?

Then Finn's there, frowning at me. "You all right, love?"

"Just peachy." I hold my hand out for the room key, and he gets that sheepish look on his face again.

"I swear it's not what it looks like."

Ah, drat.

∞ ◆ ∞

Just my luck they only had the one room. With twin beds. As if that's going to make me less aware of the sexy man sleeping next to me.

Double drat.

What are you complaining about? You get to look at that *all night long.*

I glance out of the corner of my eye to see Finn shed one shirt for another. He left the van parked under our room window so we can keep an eye on it, given the food we're delivering, but grabbed our bags. Hopefully, as it's pretty cool outside, the stuff we left inside won't go bad.

As Finn changes, my mouth waters at the sight of his corded back muscles. Then my stomach grumbles, and he faces me with a disarming grin. "Hungry?"

"Starved."

He picks up his wallet from the pile of clothes, and points to the door. "I'm going to find us some food, but lock the door behind me. Don't open unless it's me."

Rolling my eyes, I grumble under my breath. Yet the moment he leaves, I do as he asked and lock it. Then my feet take me back to his shirt, discarded on the floor. Daintily, I pick it up and clench it in my fist. There's something comforting about his scent, like sandalwood and cloves mixed together with an ocean breeze. Before I know it, I'm taking a deep whiff.

Wow. Desperate much?

I frown at the floor, thrown off by her again. "What you said earlier, fine," I say aloud. "Maybe it's my fault for not asking more questions, but I was trying to live a normal human life."

And you doomed us both.

"Don't play innocent." Recalling Ileana's words to her, I add, "You're just trying to make nice now because of what that woman said."

As if!

Shaking my head, I sit on the corner of the bed and stare at the ceiling. Her muttering in my head lulls me to sleep, and before long I'm closing my eyes and drifting off.

The smell of pizza wakes me up, and I wake up practically drooling. Finn's seated on his twin bed, munching on a slice and going through his phone. I must've made some noise – or it's his extrasensory perceptions – but he meets my gaze.

"You looked so peaceful, I figured you at needed a wee bit of a nap." He holds up the box of pizza. "Want a slice?"

"Or five," I mutter and get to an upright position. It's only then I realize I still have his shirt crumpled in my hand. Finn's gaze lingers on it, too, his expression full of questions. "Um... It, I dunno, smelled like you."

He bites a corner of his lip as though he's trying not to smile. Instead of making fun of me like I fear, he stands and places the pizza box on my bed instead. "Eat, you'll feel better."

"Tempting, but I need a shower first. Save me a few slices." I take off with a change of clothes to the bathroom, and wash up in record time. Nothing like a grumbling stomach to light a fire under my ass.

Though cheap, the soap and shampoo do the trick, and I walk out in sweatpants and a new shirt, hair still damp, and feeling like a new woman. The pizza is still untouched on the bed, so I head for it.

Finn's by the window, staring outside. Something about his profile, the concentration on his face, makes me think of him as a lawyer. *He must've made a damn imposing one.*

Sensing my gaze on him, he turns around. I'm pretty sure he's reliving the kiss we shared not too long ago, given the way his emerald gaze zeroes in on my lips. A real magnetic pull vibrates in the air surrounding us. The intensity scares me, and I try to break it.

"Do you miss it?" He throws me a confused stare. "Ireland, I mean."

His expression clears and he smiles, but his eyes are sad. "Aye, I do. Every day."

"You said before, and the girls mentioned it too, that you used to be a lawyer. Why didn't you try to do that here, too?"

Finn shrugs, taking a seat on the corner of my bed. His proximity makes me almost choke on the slice I'm nibbling, but I manage to swallow.

"After the way I left, let's just say some of the shine was gone from the job. Plus, the road just naturally led me to Rockland Creek, and I ended up staying there."

I think back to his camaraderie with Dominic and Tristan, even Lucas – before me, that is. I finish my slice, then venture out with another question. "Have I caused a lot of issues with your, um, pack?"

Finn smiles at my use of the word. "Aye, you have. But nothing I can't handle. Lucas will get over all this, you'll see."

"Why does he have a problem with me? I mean before, I thought it was because he saw me as an inconvenience. Now that I know the rest... What's his deal?"

He grabs a slice at the same I do, and our hands brush against each other. The moment freezes, as we do, just lingering and extending it. Then Finn pulls back, takes a big bite and bides his time chewing. Finally, he says, "Lucas and Tytus don't get along because they're both equals. Alphas and whatnot. Technically Tytus is stronger than him, given his bulk and magic he can wield. Lucas doesn't like that."

"And since Tytus is my ancestor, he doesn't like me, either. Got it." I nod, but my thoughts are carried elsewhere. "Umm, so, what Ileana said..."

Finn smiles as if he knows exactly what I'm doing. Then he takes another bite, and shrugs. "What about it?"

"Did you know? About the alter in my head?"

Finn tilts his head to the side. "Aye, of sorts."

"Right, the whole reading emotions." Curiosity sparks my next question. "What, exactly, were you feeling when she was around?"

"At first, just your panic whenever it happened. Then I realized your eyes change color – like Tytus. It's hard to explain." He pauses. "Was it her again, in your head earlier? In the lobby, I mean."

I look away. "Yeah."

"Why the... I don't know. The shame, with it? The panic?"

For a moment, I debate on how much I want to tell him. Unluckily for me, Finn realizes that, too.

"I hear you on not knowing whether to trust me or not. I mean, a few hours ago I was telling you my best friends are werewolves and revealing a ton of information you weren't necessarily ready for. But...." He stands, running a hand through his messy hair. "I wasn't doing it to hurt you, and I promise you'll find no judgement here."

What's up with that tone in his voice, like... "Why do you even care, Finn? All of it. The car help, the paying my bill, keeping Cade away."

He pushes the pizza box away and leans forward so we're almost nose to nose. "Have you really not figured it out yet?" The green in his eyes turns dark with something else, and my breath hitches in my throat.

"Maybe. But I want to hear you say it."

He smiles at my direct tone and moves closer still. One hand cups my cheek, his thumb resting on my bottom lip. "I like you, Elle. Feckin' hell, it's way more powerful than that to put into words. The best I can say is, I've felt out of place since I had to leave my country. And I've seen you around before... But a couple weeks back, I really *saw* you. And I haven't been able to get you out of my head."

"I..."

"And now I'm going to kiss you." He gives me a second to figure out if I want it, then his lips meet mine and nothing else matters.

This is different than the kiss in the garage. Finn takes his sweet time, tasting my lips at first, then nibbling on my lower one until I open on a gasp. Using the hand on my cheek, he angles my head and delves deeper, making my toes curl and my heartbeat quicken.

When he pulls away, she shows up in my head again. *Damnnnnnn. That. Was. Hot.*

Finn frowns, as if picking up on my craziness all over again. "Now that's settled, will you answer me? About the shame?"

I take a step back, needing space for what I'm about to tell him. "My grandparents didn't just take me in because I was an orphan. I still have a mother... But she's locked up in a mental institution. When I was nine and came back home, police were around my house. Daddy was dead, and Mom was.... I don't know. She wasn't herself. So they took her away and locked her up in an asylum. Which, until recently, is exactly where I thought I'd end up."

Finn looks into my eyes for a long moment, then nods. "That explains a lot. It's also why you haven't told anyone about this, isn't it? Not even your grandmother?"

"Yeah."

The second after my admission, he pulls me into a hug. It's so unexpected that I freeze, but then he rubs the sides of my arms. Delicious shivers run up and down my skin, and I lean closer still. Wrapped in a cocoon of heat and safety, I have no choice but to give in, fully melting.

"You really meant it, huh? The whole no judgement thing."

Finn grins. "Of course."

It's enough to reassure me I'm doing the right thing by prying. "This thing between us... You said it makes you feel like you belong. But why were you forced to leave Ireland?"

The grin slips off his face. "Because I was arrogant. Back then I was a lawyer, and I took to court a powerful man. Long story short, I lost the case, he was pissed and wouldn't let it go, so I had to leave."

My heart bleeds for him. I can't ever imagine living somewhere other than here. For Finn to leave his family and country behind must have been agonizing. The memory seems to overwhelm him, as he turns and walks to the small window. Hand on the wall, he stares outside with a lost expression and I want nothing more than to take away his pain.

Too bad you're too chicken to do anything.

The taunt echoes in my head....

Echoes....

Echoes....

And then I'm moving towards Finn. I reach out for his back and he whirls around, catching my raised hand. His green eyes are a sea of confusion, staring at me as if trying to both devour and learn my very soul.

His touch is hot on my wrist. Lips parted, I have trouble swallowing or speaking through my parchment-like throat. "I need...."

My gaze drops to his mouth, remembering that kiss, the intensity. It's throbbing on my lips and I reach my free hand to touch them. Finn intercepts my movement with his, and still never leaving my gaze, draws that hand to his mouth. Kisses my fingertips, one by one. With each touch, my breath leaves more, and more.

And then he moves against me. Just one step, and we're chest to chest. My forehead to his chin. His heat all around me.

Rough, calloused fingers go under my chin, forcing my gaze upright. "Is this what you want?"

"Yes."

He drops his mouth to mine, and I give back everything he allows. Finn's kiss grows more heated, his hands dig into my waist, and then he picks me up. Kissing me like the world is ending and like we have all the time in the world, all at once, to the point I feel it in my core.

And then we're on one of the beds, and I'm straddling him, and his hand is under my shirt, making my skin burn and my breath come out in gasping little pants.

"Finn..."

I throw my head back. He does something, some kind of caress to my skin that forces my attention back on him. His gaze is too burning to hold, but when I try, he cups my cheek so I'm forced to look at him.

"Is this what *you* want?" He asks again.

I frown. "What..."

"Or is it what your alter wants?"

It's like he's thrown a cold shower over me. I scramble off him, but Finn grabs my hips so I can't move, and shifts us so he's on top. He lets me retreat to the headboard, but the way his arms are spread tells me he's ready to catch me if I try to run any further.

"What are you talking about?"

His gaze is hot on me, but the clenching of his jaw tells me he's serious – and slightly on edge. "You know what. I won't play games, Elle. Especially games this advanced. When I take you, it's your eyes I want on me. Not hers."

"Hers who?"

"The part of you that you refuse to accept."

I go to shake my head, but the ring of a cell interrupts us.

Finn reaches for it off the bedside table and answers his. When his gaze returns to mine, I know something bad happened.

Finn

"Cade burned down the bakery."

My body is too hard–wired, too tense with what almost happened, for me to absorb Dom's words at first. When they sink in, the last remnants of desire are washed away by a chill in the pit of my stomach.

I swallow past my rage, and release one word. "How?"

"Don't know," Dom says. "Me and Tristan were casing the area when we smelled the smoke. He must've been pissed she wasn't around."

"How the hell... Where was Tytus? And wasn't Tristan supposed to be with Dani and him?"

Dom sighs. "Yeah, but she took off with Tytus on some hero quest. Lucas is losing his shit and went after them, leaving me and Tristan to keep an eye on our shop and Elle's." His loaded silence tells me there's more.

"What else?"

"There was a message, too." His rage reaches me over the phone, so I'm slightly prepared when he says, "Signed by Cade. Saying he'll find Elle no matter where she is, because he figured out the truth behind her lineage."

A muscle ticks in my jaw, and no amount of deep breaths will slow down the racing. This, and the púca hot on my tail – Tytus was right, I'm marked. But is Elle, as well?

"You still there?"

"Aye," I mutter, avoiding Elle's curious gaze. "So you're saying here isn't safe anymore."

"I wouldn't think so, no."

"What does Lucas say?"

Dom's silent.

"I see."

"He won't take action on it, not until he speaks with Cade. And right now he's too damn focused trying to find Dani and Tytus."

"Got it." I hang up while he's still talking. Already, Elle is moving out of her crouch.

"What happened? Why isn't here safe anymore?"

The lie is on the tip of my tongue. Then she touches my hand and those eyes bear into mine. The hazel turns to stormy grey, and my vision narrows until it's all I see. An odd feeling spreads through me, like everything's slowing down, my breathing included.

And then I blink, and Elle's gone. I look back at my cell, and twenty minutes have gone by since Dom's call.

"Shite!" *The little minx tapped into her powers and put me under.*

Elisandra

This is a bad idea.

"This is a bad idea," I repeat out loud.

Not that she's listening. And for once, I don't know that I actually want to hold her back. After Finn went in sort of a daze, I saw the texts on his phone from Dom – warning him to stay away, that there's nothing he can do now that the bakery is burned.

They screwed with Grandmama's store, is the bottom line. *They'll pay.*

I just hope Finn's all right. It wasn't my intention to do anything to him – but she took over. I watched her, felt the magic tear into him. Everything got slow motion, then she was moving us through the motel and back to the van.

Still loaded with the baked goods, we've been driving top speed through towns, taking back roads to the back roads to get back to town on time. We make it in half the time it took me and Finn – and then she really takes over.

The van swerves off the road, and I don't even know where I'm going. She does, apparently. My palms warm up, enough to notice I'm burning through the steering wheel. I keep driving, though.

And then I end up in the middle of nowhere, get out of the car... *Keep walking.*

Listening to her is probably a bad idea. *An extremely bad idea.* Then Cade is there, talking to three other men and dressed as scantily as he always is.

Yum, more bad guys.

Shut up, I tell her. *Let me handle this.*

I head on over to them. "Cade!"

He turns slowly to face me, and a smirk lights up his face. "I told you she'd come if provoked. Just in time."

He gestures to the woods and two more Reapers come out of the woods, dragging a lady between them. Her clothes are dirty, her hair white as snow, but violet eyes filled with life meet mine. I think I see regret in there, but then the guys let her go and she stands on her own two feet.

My turn, the other me says.

Before I know it, she's pushed me at the back. Only this time, like when Ileana did it, I see what's going on. I'm lifting my hand, drawing something in the air and it burns bright, before a shield explodes and crawls over me.

"So you went and got yourselves a witch? Tsk... And here I thought you were just bad boys. Now you've made us mad."

Us?

Cade seems to be thinking the same thing, not that I give him a chance to do anything about it. Another rune, and this time a blast of fire hits him, sending him flying backwards. He gets up, cussing under his breath. His clothes are burnt, as is his hair, but his skin remains unmarred.

The witch takes a step closer to us. "Good thing your protection held, Fiona," Cade tells her.

She throws him a look full of hate, which he ignores as one would a fly. Then the air vibrates, and we all look up – to see a massive dragon flapping his wings.

"What the f—" Cade's expletives are lost on me.

"Hey, ancestor!" The other me grins and waves at the dragon. He spits out a ball of fire, drawing a line between me and the wolves.

Perilous flames burn bright and hot between us. Cade glares from the other side, flanked by Fiona and his Reapers. Then he turns to the witch, gesturing wildly to the flames. She shakes her head, taking a step back – and the last thing I see is him backhanding her. She falls to the ground, but still won't use her magic to make the flames disappear.

Then Tytus lands, causing the ground to shake. It's the stuff of movies, really. His scales are massive, his head the size of a small house, canines look fit to rip through anything... A shudder runs through me, and if she hadn't been in charge of my body at the time, I'm pretty sure I would've lost it.

As it is, my alter grins at him. "Took your sweet time."

In one fell swoop, he's back to the dark–haired man I met before. His stormy eyes glitter, settling on the wolves. Then Tytus tilts his head and I have the odd feeling he's sizing me up. Step by slow step – considering on the other side of the flames we got wolves ready to pounce – he inches closer, his gaze never wavering from mine.

"You're not Elisandra."

"Oh, but I am."

His glare shifts over my shoulder, going from Cade to the witch on the ground. Hissing, he moves past me. "So that's where you've been hiding, is it?"

She glares at him with enough heat to char him, but all I see is Tytus's back from where I'm standing. His voice, however, is icy when he speaks to Cade. "You've got no business with the likes of her, fool. Release her in my care."

"I think not," Cade smirks. "She may be a helluva spitfire to tame, but I'm quite enjoying it." He pauses for dramatic break. "Plus, she has proven herself useful, you know."

His taunt gets Tytus riled up. But I'm more interested in the way he's palming something, a necklace of sorts. "She's a witch. What use would she have to you beyond magic, which you evidently cannot control?"

Cade throws his head back, and raucous laughter escapes him. "Wouldn't you like to know."

Tytus shifts, turning to me. Grabbing my hand in his, he pulls me away. Cade yells something in the background, but I can't make it out.

My ancestor seems determined to drag me to the other edge of the forest. Yet even as we're nearing it, the flames behind us burn higher, and his eyes are busy scanning. One more stride and he freezes, causing me to run into his back.

"You're late," he says.

I peer around his shoulder. A white wolf steps between to massive pine trees, and I recognize the emerald green eyes. He has a crescent moon on one shoulder. "Finn?"

He nods, and steps closer, his eyes on Tytus. Whatever they communicate, Tytus shakes his head, then turns to me with a clenched jaw. "No, you had your chance. It's my turn to protect her now."

One-handed, he draws something in the air, even as his hold on me tightens. One blink of my eyes later, I'm no longer in the forest, but standing in front of a mansion.

∞ ∞ ∞

CHAPTER EIGHT

∞ Deacair ∞

"Our <u>separation</u> of each other is an optical illusion of consciousness."

–Albert Einstein–

Elisandra

Dropping my hand, Tytus walks ahead and opens the door. I take a step to follow him robotically, but the moment after I'm on my knees, heaving. My gut clenches repeatedly as if I need to vomit, but nothing comes out.

"Using magic you don't understand will do that to you." His unconcerned voice rankles me. Wiping my mouth, I stand and glare at him.

"That your idea of protecting me?"

He arches an eyebrow, leaning against the door. "Ah, so you're back to normal then. She's gone?"

I don't answer anything, instead mirroring his pose and crossing my arms.

"You might as well speak. There's nowhere you can run."

For the first time, I look away from him and take in my surroundings. There is nothing, and I mean *nothing*, around. It's like we're smack in the middle of a mountain, surrounded by high, metal fences. Intricate, pretty...but fences nonetheless.

I whirl back to him. "What the heck?"

Tytus isn't there anymore. From within the house, he calls out. "Hungry?"

Well, go on then. Maybe you'll listen to him, if not me.

If only to ignore her, and because my stomach is growling loudly, I head into the house. Mausoleum, more like. By the time I cross the white marble floors, white living room into the charcoal kitchen, Tytus is pulling out something out of the oven. It looks suspiciously like a cooked hare.

He must read my expression, 'cause he grins. "I like my meat plucked fresh."

Serving me a plate, he gestures for me to sit. "I imagine you have a lot of questions. Not the least of which being how much of my powers you've inherited, hmm?"

I nod, stuffing my mouth and trying not to choke as I eat too fast. It doesn't seem important anymore that he teleported us here, practically kidnapping me from my boyfriend.

Ooooh so we're on names now, hmm?

Tytus' fork clatters and his eyes narrow on me. "She'll have to go, mind you."

I gulp past my now dry throat. "I don't know what you mean."

A storm builds in his eyes as he pushes his plate aside and leans across the counter. "I am zmeu, darling. And you are my flesh and blood. I know what's in your head – have for a while now. And it's about time we fix it."

The last of my appetite evaporates. "I met Ileana."

A muscle twitches in his jaw, but he says nothing.

"She, umm, did something to me. And it made the alter in my head come forth. Then she took over when I was with Finn."

Tytus rolls his eyes. "Yes, there is a reason for that. It's also the reason why there are no females left of my race."

I frown. "What's that?"

"Well, they tend to kill their mates. And if they're not properly trained from young, the male they choose will awaken their primal nature – and periodically drive them insane."

My jaw drops, but all Tytus does is hand me a glass of water.

Now *do you get it?*

Yeah. I think I finally do.

Finn

The minute Tytus takes off with Elle, the flames disappear. Which leaves me facing Cade, his wolves and his witch all by myself.

All fine and dandy, considering I'm fuming enough to start a war. So rather than turn around and leave, I step forward.

Cade narrows his eyes on me. "Where did he take her?"

As if I'll tell you.

He sure as hell seems to understand my stance. One glance at his men, and they're surrounding the witch again. The next moment, Cade morphs and lunges at me in wolf form.

I meet him mid-air and we smack into each other, then drop to the grass and roll away. He's the first to get up – I'm too distracted by someone else. Fiona, the witch.

She's not using magic but she's putting out an odd emotion, like a call for help. Cade lunges again, interrupting my train of thought.

You really don't quit, do you? He bares his teeth at me. *Your alpha won't come near me for a reason. He doesn't want a war, which means you can't go starting one. Might as well cut your losses and move on.*

I shake my head and stand. *Elle is with me. So whatever you've got planned, you can forget it.*

There's a mean look in his eyes at my words. *Not going to happen.* He makes as if to jump me, but something stops him. His glare shifts over my shoulder.

Their presence tinges the air, so I don't even turn around to make sure they've got my back. Instead, I take a step closer. Cade moves further away. One more step, and he takes off. The wall of flames goes back up, and the Reapers drag Fiona away with them.

Only once they're gone past the trees does the barrier break down. I make a move to follow, but a voice stops me.

No.

This time, I turn. Lucas in his reddish coat, Dominic in black and Dani in human form are all there.

I bow my head towards Lucas. *Finally decided to do something?*

He stalks to me, his bulk even more massive up close. *You broke the rules first, causing Cade to retaliate. Do not pin this on me, Irish.*

I'm not. But take some damn responsibility about letting this sit a bit too long before acting, will you?

You have no idea why I decide things the way I do, so back the fuck off. His glare moves to where Cade disappeared. *Dominic, take Dani and go after them. Do not engage, I only want to know where they're hiding.*

They listen and disappear, and then it's just us. Lucas paws the ground and asks, *Where is Elle?*

Now you care?

His glare tells me he's in no mood for my antics. *Is she safe?*

She's not with the Reapers, if that's what you're asking. Tytus has her.

Damn it, Finn!

I bow my head and look away. My wolf lets out a whine. *Yeah, I know.*

Elisandra

When Tytus pours me a glass of water, and himself some vodka, I glare at him. "I'm not a child."

His eyes crinkle at the corners like he's laughing at me. "Oh, but you are." Then he turns and pours me a glass of the clear liquid, too.

It burns my throat as I drink it, but I hold out for another. When he arches an eyebrow, I scowl. "You just admitted women like me kill their mates. And considering I happen to like Finn – like *a lot* – that blows. So yeah, I need more."

Tytus shrugs and puts the entire bottle near me. It's my turn to act surprised.

"I'm your ancestor, not your keeper. If you can drink, then drink. I only hope you know your limits."

I don't, but he doesn't have to know that. As I pour myself another glass, I try to keep my voice neutral. "Is this... Her, inside me, is it permanent?"

"No."

"Is it what happened to my mom?"

His eyes narrow. "I'm not familiar with that particular story."

Sipping my glass this time, I quickly go through my childhood drama. When I'm done relating the story, Tytus runs a hand over his face. "Yes. Yes, it's exactly what happened to your mother."

"How come my grandmama is fine?"

"Perhaps the gene doesn't run through her. What did your grandfather do for a living?"

"He was a firefighter."

Tytus laughs aloud this time, and I cringe. "Right. Fire can't hurt us, so his career choice was the best suited to hide his supernatural abilities." The link seems obvious now that I think about it. "So if I can fix it.... Will you show me how?"

"I will."

"And then I can be with Finn?"

Tytus rolls his eyes. "You could have chosen anyone else. Anyone. And you pick a mutt?"

I glare at him. "Yeah. Get over it. What about these powers? There's so much I don't understand."

Tytus sighs and sits back near the island, pouring himself another drink. "So ask me."

Finn

"Maybe it's time to stop chasing your tail with this girl and instead help."

I glance up from my cup of coffee. After Dani and Dom came back empty, we all returned back to the auto shop. Lucas has been on my ass ever since, while Tristan's been arguing with Dani over risks she's taking.

Tuning them out, I struggle to focus on Lucas. There's a pull to the side of my heart that's making it hard to breathe, and it started the minute Tytus and Elle disappeared.

Unable to hold it in, I say something I'm probably going to regret. "If you're so scared of a war, then maybe it's time you stop trying to handle Cade with kid gloves and act like the feckin' alpha you're supposed to be."

Lucas' fury is vibrant enough that everyone else quiets down and stares at us. Dom takes a step forward – maybe to correct my insolence, or support it. Then Lucas snarls over his shoulder, and he stops.

I set my cup down and stand. "You said reading your emotions is none of my business. Well, then I guess you shouldn't have accepted a wolf like me into your pack."

When I turn to leave, Lucas says the one thing that can get me to stop. "Do you want to see her?"

I'm in his face the next second, nostrils flaring. "*Where* is she?"

His eyes narrow. "Who do you think alerted Tytus she got the drop on you?" He lifts his index finger and motions for Dani to come closer. "Tell him where she is. It won't do him much good."

∞ ♦ ∞

Of course he'd live in a freaking mansion by the side of town. Why wouldn't he, he's a damn zmeu. Not quite a *dragan*, but probably has a pile of gold in a massive subterranean cave there anyway.

I get out of my truck and stomp to the door. Forget knocking – I'm pounding on the steel obstacle, feeling each hit reverberate in my arm. The gut–wrenching sensation doesn't leave me for the entire five minutes he keeps me waiting.

Then Tytus answers. He glances behind me, as if expecting a few others. "Yeah?"

"I need to see her."

He leans against the door. "Not sure I get your meaning."

"Don't play games with me, zmeu." I growl, "I need to see Elle."

His eyes flash a stormy grey. "You cannot."

I take another step. "And *you* don't understand. I have to see her. Now."

Tytus doesn't seem impressed by the desperation in my tone. If anything, his gaze grows icier. "No, wolf. Go back home before you really cross me."

Without giving me a chance to explain further, he slams the door in my face.

Elisandra

"Why won't you let him see me?"

Tytus' expression softens when it lands on me. "You know why they recommend addicts not form relationships in their first year of recovery?"

I shake my head, unsure where he's heading with this. *Is he seriously comparing my relationship with Finn to an addict with their vice of choice?*

You've got to admit though, he's a yummy vice, that Irish boy of yours.

I don't get a chance to answer her, because Tytus crosses his arms over his rather massive chest and says, "Because they need to focus on their recovery. And the same is true for you."

"I don't need recovery! What I *need* is to understand what's going on, what these powers are!"

Tytus takes a step towards me, his expression as stone cold as the statues he favors in his house. "And you will learn all there is to learn. However, you also have to take some time away from anything that can make you react. Our strength is easily misused, and it *can* become addictive."

His words ring true, but that doesn't stop the dull ache in my chest, nor the longing to see Finn. I'm surprised she doesn't pop up more to laugh at me, but she's been relatively quiet since Tytus showed up.

Alone in my resolution, I meet his gaze and give a small nod. It feels like a latch has wrapped around my heart, squeezing it ever more.

Finn

The Irish whiskey tastes sour in my mouth. But I drink another one, my gloomy gaze settled on the backyard. *Damn Tytus.*

"You cannot be mad at the zmeu for protecting what is his."

I felt Ileana when she popped up – uninvited – a few moments ago, and I'd been wondering how long it would take her to speak. *Not that long, then.*

"She's not his," I mutter, my nose in my drink. My phone buzzes again. It's Lucas, I can feel it, and this is my fifth call I'm ignoring. I came straight home after failing to see Elle, not in the mood to be around people.

"Elle is a descendant of his. For all intents and purposes, she is Tytus' responsibility."

Seeing that I'm not turning to face her, Ileana walks in front of me. "I thought you, of all the wolves, would be easier to talk to."

"Whatever gave you that idea? The fact I can feel everyone's mood swings?"

She shrugs, and it looks too pretty to watch. My body yearns for Elle. It's a literal burn in my veins, and no amount of drinks can staunch it.

"Speaking of mood swings... You are mad at me."

"Damn straight," I stand then. "Whatever you did at the motel made it worse. That alter of Elle's took over, and did some spell on me. I could've been there, and not needed Tytus to intervene."

Ileana looks at me with pity in her eyes. "That has nothing to do with me. On the contrary, what I did helps Elle see what her alter does. She needs to bridge the gap between them, otherwise she will lose herself, and take down this entire town with her."

"That's gobshite, Ileana. Dani didn't need your help. What the feck makes you think Elle does?"

"Dani is a wolf with magical powers gifted by a witch. Elle is a zmeu descendant who has been ignoring her other half her entire life, and who is prone to human emotions. They are completely different, make no mistake."

I scowl. "Then *help* her."

"I cannot, only you can."

"And how am I supposed to do that? Tytus was clear."

Ileana steps closer. "He is making it harder on purpose, or are you blind? Do you know why you crave to be with her so?"

"Why?"

"It is the beginning of the *legătură* stage. And sooner or later, it will lead to the *împerecheare*, whether Tytus wants it to or not."

The foreign words are enough to make me pause – it sounded like like *leh-guh-tuh-rah* and *ihm-peh-reh-ke-re*. "The what and *what*?"

"Legătură means *link*, in Romanian, and it's the first stage of a zmeu mating. It's a tie between two souls, two people meant to be. You and Elle have that, since you first met each other. Each time you come together, it builds, until the ultimate moment of joining that will lead to the împerecheare. Then, you will be what you wolves call *mated*."

"But mated for us, doesn't lead to this...crave."

"No, it does not." There's amusement in her eyes. "That part is all Elle."

She turns away from me, and I panic at the realization she's leaving. "What am I supposed to do, Ileana? I don't want to act on this, not when her alter is here."

"Then perhaps you had best figure out a way to join the two." She floats away, then stops by my gate. "That púca following you... Be wary. Tytus will not allow anything dangerous near his precious. And you do not want to make a zmeu angry."

∞ ∞ ∞

∞ Buanseasmhacht ∞

"Energy and <u>persistence</u> conquer all things."

–Benjamin Franklin–

Elisandra

It's been a torturous few days of hell. Each day is harder to get out of bed, but Tytus makes me whether I want to, or not.

Each day he pushes my buttons, trying to get her to come to the surface. He's got this cute idea that he can make her leave forever.

That's not what *she's* telling me though. Even as I'm going through my shower routine, she's there like a nasty headache.

You need to find a way to escape.

I wouldn't have to if you'd show yourself and talk to him.

No. He wants to shut me out forever and I'm not going to let that happen. It wouldn't be safe for you.

146

Brushing my teeth, I roll my eyes at my reflection. "He's only trying to help, you know. Stop seeing him as the enemy."

Help, huh? Is that why he's keeping Finn away from you?

I have no answer to that. Each night I dream of him as if I could touch him, and it's the main reason I have such a hard time waking up. Better to dream than live a reality without him.

Turning away from the mirror, I brush my hair and pull it into a ponytail. Tytus made arrangements to have clothes of mine here, and he's made sure I'm way beyond comfortable, even letting me use his phone to call my nana.

Since me and Finn never quite made the delivery – and the baked goods spoiled at the back of my van, probably still in the forest I left it in. Grandmama's been going crazy with worry. I'm half afraid she's going to come here to check on me, and I figure it's as good a time as any to talk to Tytus about it.

You're avoiding thinking of him.

Yeah, I am.

'Cause each time Finn crosses my mind it feels like something is scorching me. Hearing his voice a few days ago didn't help much either. There's something unfinished between us, something we didn't even get a chance to see grow, and it's eating me from the inside out.

We need to get out of here, she says again. *Then you can see him.*

I stare at my reflection. "There's a reason Tytus doesn't want me out there, and it's because I'm dangerous. With you in my head, and what we can do, I won't risk anyone getting injured."

Pulling on some sweatpants and a long–sleeved shirt, I head downstairs. Tytus is waiting with breakfast cooked, and my mouth waters at the smell of bacon. I half-wonder if he cooked it with his zmeu fire, or the regular way, but don't say anything aloud.

As I munch through the food, he watches me with a speculative look on his face. "How did you sleep?"

I shrug. "Fine, I guess."

He leans on the counter as is his habit, tilting his head to the side. "Fine? In that cause, I take it not seeing Finn does not affect you?"

"You know full well it does. Why torture me with this?"

"Because you're not being honest with me."

My fork clatters on the plate as I glare at him. "You want honest? It felt like I was being ripped apart when you shut the door in his face. It only got worse overnight, and since then. But I've got my grandmama to stress about, too. If she comes back because she's worried, she'll be in danger. And don't give me fairy tales about how you can protect her."

Tytus straightens up and says, "I won't. And the last thing I want is for you to suffer. Distance from Finn is inevitable, at least for the time being. But as for your grandmother, will a visit offer her some comfort?"

"Yeah…" I stare back at my plate. "I think it will."

He nods and moves back. "We can leave after you finish eating."

∞ ◆ ∞

Half an hour later, we're on the road in his Hummer. "If you don't work, how do you afford all this? Finn and the others, they work."

Tytus snorts. "Call it inheritance. Millennia–old inheritance."

I stare out the window, mulling his words. What does it feel like, I wonder, to have lived so long and seen so many kingdoms come and go…

"It's wearying, for one."

My head snaps up and I notice his wry smile. "Did I say that out loud?"

"You sure did."

"Sorry."

His eyes shift back on the road, hiding his emotions. "Don't be."

A moment of uncomfortable silence lengthens. Since I've already put my foot in my mouth, I see no point in being quiet. "It must have been lonely, being the last of your race."

"It was."

His crisp answer is not enough to deter me from prying. "I mean, can you.... I dunno, do you have to be with..."

"A female zmeu? No, I do not. I also have not lived as a monk, if that is the purpose of your question. To be perfectly honest, I can take my pleasure anywhere. But true fulfillment from having a mate, I will never know that."

"You can't find a human mate, like Dom?"

Tytus snorts. "That fool does not even realize how lucky he is. To find a human able to accept all parts of you, the good and the beast, and be willing to be thrown into an insane universe, as dangerous as ours? No, I will not subject any human to that. Plus, it wouldn't work."

"Why not?"

"Because while I can sleep around with humans, our mating process requires them to be supernatural in order to survive it."

I gulp. "Why?"

"Because, my dear, when you really mate with someone, you burn them. If they survive, they are your true mate. If they do not, well...."

He reads my silence as horrific – which it is – and turns to me briefly. "You won't have to, with Finn. You are not a full zmeu, and there are...other things already taking place which are testing you."

"Such as?"

He turns to the radio and the sounds of some country song echoes in the car. *I guess we're done talking.*

And just when it was getting interesting, she says.

Grandmama's friend, Violet, owns an old antique store. She has a place right above it, and it's where my grandmama's been staying at.

As soon as Tytus parks, I run inside. She's talking to a customer but the next moment I'm there, engulfing her in a hug.

"Elisandra! What.... What are you doing here, child?"

I can't help it. The tears come unbidden. Used to my craziness, Grandmama just holds me and pats my back. Inch by inch, she moves us away from the bustle of the daily operations, and outside at a nice picnic table set in the backyard.

Her knowing brown eyes settle on me, then Tytus who had followed us. "What's going on, darling? Why didn't you tell me something was wrong?"

Tears threaten again and I try to stop them. "It's been....hard. I... Grandmama, I need you to promise you'll stay here, no matter what."

Worry flashes across her face and she takes my hand in hers. "Why?"

Because some badass wolves want my hide somehow doesn't seem like the right answer. Instead, I breathe in and say, "There's some trouble in Rockland Creek. You remember those guys that used to run with Jared?"

Her wrinkled face scrunches up. "Leather and lots of skin?" When I nod, she says, "Yeah, those boys needed a solid beating as kids, mark my words. Why do you bring them up?"

"They torched the bakery, that's why I couldn't make the delivery. Tytus," I pointed to him, "and the guys at Claws Auto Shop helped me clean it up and I've put in an insurance claim but.... It's bad, nana. It'll be a while before we can get it fixed."

Her eyes fill with tears, but she bravely wipes them away. "That place is just four walls and some oven, darling. I'm just glad you're okay, that's what really matters." Her gaze shifts to Tytus. "Thank you for taking care of her."

He bows his head, but remains oddly quiet.

"I won't come home, if it'll make things easier," she promises. "But what about you? Where are you staying?"

I flush, thinking of Finn. "Right now, Tytus is renting me a room."

Her gaze goes shrewd. "A room?"

"Yeah," I flush. "In his house. He has a big house. But umm, Finn and I..."

Her face clears at that. "Did you finally ask that boy out?"

I feel the red blush creeping on me as clear as the sun. "Grandmama!"

"Oh, but he is *fine*. Mind, you're fine too, Tytus, but not exactly what my granddaughter needs, you know?"

He laughs. "Oh, I do."

We say our goodbyes and then we're back on the road. As I reach for the radio, Tytus stops me. "I'll bring you back to him, I promise."

His tone leaves no doubt as to his honesty. Before I can ask what changed his mind, he goes rigid. The car swerves to the side – luckily the road is deserted.

I manage to grab the wheel, at the same time trying to see what the hell got into him.

But Tytus isn't really responsive. His eyes have gone glassy, almost white, and his fists and jaw are clenched to the point of breaking.

Heaving with effort, I manage to pull on the steering wheel and nudge the car into a ditch.

What's gotten into him?

"I don't have time for you right now," I mutter and take my seat belt off.

Exiting the car, I circle it and open Tytus's door. He's shaking now, and I'm half afraid he's having some kind of seizure, but it's not like any I've seen before.

I check around him and pull a cell phone to call for help – it's dead.

Then his fingers start drawing in the air – runes that take a life of their own. It must last for at least ten minutes, while I stand there not sure what to do, too entranced by the runes. After a few moments, they shine brightly, then drop onto his forearms like rain droplets.

Finally, Tytus inhales sharply, blinks and jerks himself upright. His stormy gaze is dark, taking in our surroundings and the car's precarious position.

"Thank you," he says. It's the last thing I expect to hear, but he still seems shaken.

I kneel next to him, grasping one clammy hand in mine. "Tytus... What was that? Are you alright?"

There's a new kind of sadness in his expression when his eyes land on me. "Nu, micuţă. I'm nowhere alright, and will not be for a while. What you saw, it was a vision. Zmei don't get them often – but when we do, it's never a good thing."

I gulp. "What did you see?"

Tytus is silent for so long that I fear he won't answer. When he finally speaks, it's only two words. "My brother."

Grunting, he then pushes himself out of the driver's seat and into the passenger. With one hand, he draws a rune that pushes the car back onto the road. "Drive, little one. I haven't been able to break through to your alter, but perhaps someone else can. I do believe it is high time we get you back to Finn."

Finn

I've been back at the house every day since Tytus shut it in my face – to no avail. Today, there's a different feel around it. Empty.

Panicking by the second, I try to find a way to get in.

"Don't ruin his fancy mansion," a voice says and I whirl to face them.

Dani's there, tilting her head to the side. "They're gone, but they'll come back."

"How do you know?"

She pulls up a note. "Because Tytus left this taped to the door."

I snatch it out of her hand and read it. *Don't panic, wolf. I'll bring her back. We have to see the grandmother before she worries and becomes Cade's chow food.*

I look back up at Dani. "So what were you doing here?"

"Time for my weekly magical workouts with Tytus."

"Oh."

I taste her pity in the air – something in my expression must've sparked it – and crumple the piece of paper in my hand. "Don't."

Walking past her, I become aware of something else in the air. Some*one* else. But it's not the Reapers. It's....

"Fecking púca!"

Without waiting for Dani, I take off after it. Still in human form, it means I quickly lose its scent and come to a full stop.

A moment later, Dani draws near, watching me with a frown.

"What's gotten into you, meu amigo?"

Aside from Elle, I haven't told anyone about what's going on, least of all my alpha.

Dani must read some of that in me, as she squeezes my shoulder. "I won't tell Lucas, if that's what you're worried about."

I run a hand over my face, but before I can answer, something shifts in the shadows. I hold out my hand to stop Dani. "Don't. Move."

Right. Left. It's running everywhere, a crazy neighing filling the air. Then the púca is there, its red eyes glowing.

"What is that?" Dani asks out of the corner of her mouth.

"My feckin' nightmare," I whisper back.

The mustang stops a few feet feet away from us, its red, glowing eyes shining with malice. "Having trouble finding your mate, wolf?"

I frown. "What's it to you? She's got nothing to do with this."

The horse throws its head back. "As if I would believe that." It's malicious eyes take in Dani. "Interesting mix, wolf–witch."

She hates being called that. In retaliation, she draws a rune in the air and holds off on it. "Just try me."

The púca meets my eyes again. "I don't suppose you've managed to find trace of your precious Reapers either, hmm?"

I blanch at that. "How do you know so much?"

This shouldn't be possible. It shouldn't be.... And then it dawns on me. Our inability to pinpoint the Reapers' locations. The conflicting scents. My own comment that bad luck seems to be following us...

"It was *you*!"

The púca throws back its head again, shaking its midnight mane. "My, you really have grown soft." It turns to leave.

"Wait! Why? *Why* are you doing all this?"

"If you don't know, I won't make it easier for you to find out."

One glance at Dani's magic threatening it, and the púca disappears back through the trees. My friend drops her hand, the rune disintegrating. "Finn... Are you saying *that's* the reason we can't locate the Reapers?"

My shocked gaze meets hers. "Aye. You sure you're not going to tell Lucas now?"

∞ ♦ ∞

After Dani assures me she won't tell Lucas anything, we head back to town. As we walk into the shop, the receptionist desk is empty. It's only once we walk to the back that we find Dom in the kitchen.

He throws us a look, and I taste curiosity in the air – he's thinking we came back from patrol. "Anything?"

"Nada," Dani mutters. "Where's Lucas?"

Dom throws me a side glance, and this time I can't read his emotion, like he's not sure himself of what he feels. "Off on other business with Tristan."

"And Lucrezia?" I ask, jabbing a finger over my shoulder. "I thought you weren't letting her out of your sight."

Before he can answer, a bell rings, signaling the front door is open. I would ignore it, but a scent fills the air – one I haven't felt in too damn long. The vanilla hints have me whirling around and sprinting towards the entrance, where I almost smack into Lucrezia.

"Just in time," she grins.

It's hard to find words, when the reality of that scent envelops me full on. Luz is at the head of the little trio, but she steps to the side, revealing the girl behind.

Elle.

And right next to her, Tytus. My fists clench but Luz is already shaking her head, walking towards me. "He's standing down, Finn. Just let him talk."

I meet Tytus' stormy gaze with one of my own. "So?"

"So." He shifts his stance, nodding to Dani and Dom behind me. "Where's your alpha?"

"On an errand," Dom says. "What's it to you?"

"Need to tell you all something...about the magic here." His gaze drops on Dani again.

"What's going on?" I taste her confusion, as much as everyone else's, in the air.

"Little wolf, I'm sorry," Tytus whispers, low enough that I'm sure only I caught it. Louder, he says, "I lied when I met you. I'm not the only one of my kind left. There is another...only I thought he was dead. His name is Declan, and he's my brother."

Silence descends on everyone, a mix of confusion and anger. Dom steps by my side. "Explain yourself."

Tytus widens his stance, as if prepared to fight off blows. "I apologize in advance, because I should have told you everything. I simply did not think it relevant any longer."

With an introduction like that, I know we're in for a treat – the kind that'll lead to a hell of a reaction. I want to take Elle aside, but Tytus starts talking and his story freezes me.

"Long ago, before this world was fully formed, two races of sky creatures fought for dominance. Dragons... and zmei. As land was split and borders drawn, a Council was established, formed of ten of each of our members. I was on that council. The main rule was not to let humans know of us. We were already hunted by then. Declan, my brother, went against this rule, time and time again."

His tone changes, filling with emotion, and I taste the trace of the past in the air. "We had to move from kingdom to kingdom more than once, until one particular order of knights decided to eradicate us. Their hate was not random, rather it was spurred on by Declan's constant attacks on humans. And while the Council saw what was happening, it was I who called the vote to banish my brother, thinking he would find a quick end. Only instead of destroying him, we imprisoned him. Not knowing that over time, he'd find weaknesses in the protection holding him hostage..."

"I don't follow," Dom interrupts. "Why not kill him outright?"

"There were so few of us left, the Council didn't want to take one more life. It was stupid, and arrogant, to believe Declan could be redeemed at some point. We thought our magic would keep him. Never foresaw that he would be stronger... Nor that he could still reach out and influence a witch...who would then influence an entire wolf pack."

Dani's gasp is the only sound in the room. "You mean, my magic..."

"Yeah." His contrition fills the air. "Fiona is harnessing Declan, and that is where your pack received its powers from. It was all engineered by Declan. He was the cause of all your troubles."

While the new information is overwhelming, and a much-needed piece to know, my mind isn't in it. My wolf is struggling against my hold, wanting only one thing, and I can't hold him back anymore. "Elle."

Her gaze meets mine, and I try to keep my tone neutral. "We need to talk."

She nods, and heads towards me. Tytus watches her go, but says nothing. I leave the rest of my pack behind, uncaring as their voices rise up, asking Tytus question upon question. All I'm focusing on is Elle's hand in mine.

We head to Lucas' office. I step away from her once we're there, my body shaking with need.

"Elle, I —"

She rushes into my arms, as if unable to stand the distance any more. "It was hell being away from you."

A relieved breath escapes me, and I wrap her tightly in my embrace, inhaling the scent of her. "Same, love."

She pulls away slightly. "I know according to Tytus it was needed so I could figure this out, but the truth of the matter is I'm nowhere further along than before. She's still in me, and..." Elle trails off, shaking her head. "I'm sorry for leaving you like I did. I just... I couldn't resist it. What Cade did was horrible!"

"I know, Elle. But if you had waited, I would've come with you." She feels so good in my arms, I don't want to rock the boat. But I know I have to. "Was it her, that led those impulses?"

Elle nods in my chest. "Yes."

I nuzzle her hair, enjoying her sweet vanilla scent. "I know she's part of you, Elle. And I'm more than willing to accept that. But please don't let her get between us."

"I promise I won't."

I push back slightly so I can meet her eyes. There's only one burning question I need an answer to. "Do you want to be with me? Because, love, that's all that matters to me. Girlfriend, mate... I'll be whatever you want, because you're all I need, regardless of what's happening out there."

She smiles tentatively and intertwines our fingers. "Yes. All that, and more... I'm yours, Finn. All yours."

Her submission is the sweetest sound, answering to a part of me I have long thought forgotten. For the first time in ages, my wolf, in all his dominant capacity, pokes his head and takes over.

Ours.

I drop my mouth to hers then, taking all she's willing to offer in the short time we have.

∞ ∞ ∞

CHAPTER TEN

∞ Phian ∞

"We cannot learn without <u>pain</u>."

–Aristotle–

Finn

Much as I'd like nothing better than to stay with Elle, we rejoin the others. Tensions are high, I taste it in the air the minute we walk back in. And it's easy enough to see why.

It's no longer the crowd we left behind. Lucas and Tristan are back from their errand, and Lucas has Tytus by the collar of his shirt – again – and he's all up in his face. Tristan, surprisingly, seems to be trying to hold him back, but Dom is on the sidelines, talking softly to Dani and Luz. I glance between the two groups, trying to figure out where I'm best suited to disarm the situation.

Elle squeezes my hand. "I'll take Tytus, you go to Dani."

After a brief hesitation – they're both way larger than her – I head on to my lobisomem friend. She's shaking her head as I approach. "Não, Dominic. Not even they could take a stand against this."

"They who?"

Dom throws a look over his shoulder, taking in the still–pissed off Lucas a couple feet away. His voice is low when he answers. "My vrykolakas."

My stomach churns at the thought of the creatures he calls pack. Part werewolf, part strigoi – a type of Romanian vampire – they're foul. Or, were, before Dominic became their leader after defeating his cousin. Most of them had left after that, presumably never to be seen again. Yet just a few weeks ago, we ran into a wee bit of a pack that stuck around to protect Lucrezia. The sight of them had been enough to get Lucas all riled up.

Narrowing my eyes on Dom, I point that out. He shrugs. "Lucas always has a stick up his ass one way or the other, acting like he's king, rather alpha. Look where it got us. The Reapers could've been disposed of long ago."

"It's true he took the softer approach, but he also tried to keep in mind that we live in a town full of easily killed humans – no offense, Lucrezia."

"None taken," she whispers, then glances behind Dom. Biting her lip, she says, "Be right back," and takes off. A quick look around explains why – the roles have been reversed and now it's Tytus who has Lucas in his hold, and they look nowhere closer to solving their issue.

"What, exactly, did I miss?"

Dom rolls like eyes. "Lucas flipped his shit when he found out Tytus didn't tell us everything. Started talking about how he's been more than accommodating, but it's time for Tytus to leave the territory."

"Which of course got our zmeu friend fired up, since he's not ready to leave Elle behind, nor my training," Dani adds.

"But if Declan only influenced the witch," I say, "can't we just break that hold, and be done with it?"

"Not quite." Dom's expression darkens. "For one, we can't freaking find her, and two, Lucas is wary about making a move. He wants to protect the humans here."

I shake my head. "We can convince him otherwise, and you know it. But what I don't get is how the heck would a zmeu supposedly entrapped overseas end up linked with a witch *here*, in the Americas?"

They share a look, and Dani whispers. "Because he wasn't punished overseas. Tytus admitted the Council thought it best Declan be removed from all temptations, so they forced him under escort across the ocean, and used elemental magic to trap him here."

"Fecking hell! Seriously?" They both nod, and I groan. *That explains also what else led the púca to me. It must have sensed the power in this earth.*

"Finn, there's more...." Dani trails off, unable to meet my direct gaze, and I taste her hesitation in the air.

Dom, thankfully, gives it to me straight. "Tytus said he's figured out what the Reapers are after now – Elle – because they want to unearth Declan, and free him. If that happens, we're screwed." To Dani, he says, "That's why we should have as much wolf power as possible with us."

Rising voices from behind warn us Lucas and Tytus are nowhere near fixing up their issues. I'm about to join in the efforts to keep them apart, when Dani says, "It wouldn't matter even if you called the vrykolakas, Dom. Aside from being a complete slap in the face for Lucas, they can't really stand against a zmeu now, can they?"

A muscle ticks in Dom's jaw. "There must be something we can do. If only we knew where the Reapers are, we could see how far along in their efforts they are to unearth Declan."

Dani throws me a look, which Dom catches. "What? What is it you know?"

I sigh, rubbing the back of my head. "Not enough. Listen, there may be something we can try, but let's wait until tonight, when things settle down. Can both of you meet me back here around midnight?'

Dom nods, and I can taste his questions in the air. Then a fury like no other fills up the air, and I hear Elle's voice – only, it's not quite hers.

Elisandra

Talk about two pig–headed, stubborn fools! Between Lucas' accusations, Tytus' pride and my own haywire brain, it's a wonder *she* didn't show up sooner.

Then again, I'm almost glad when she does and takes over my body even more smoothly than before. "Are you two boys quite done pissing about?"

Tytus freezes, turning his head halfway to me. Lucas throws me a glare, "Stay out of it."

"Now, lookie here." I step closer, a different swag in my step as I cock a hip and with my index finger tap his forehead. "You may not like me 'cause I'm stealing your golden boy away, but that doesn't mean you can't listen to me."

Lucas glances at Tytus, as if trying to guess what's going on, but she – I – goes on to flick his forehead. "I'm talking to you, boy!"

"Puta merda..." He grits his teeth, and storms out of Tytus' embrace, stalking to me. "I've never had a woman disrespect me, and I'm not about to start now."

I toss my head back, taking him all in, and grin. "Wanna bet, pretty boy?"

He takes another step closer, and Tytus steps between us, facing me. "Just the person I've been trying to get to."

There's a dangerous glint in his eyes, one she seems to pick up on as she recoils. Tytus moves closer. "Are we going to have a problem, little girl?"

I scowl at him. "No."

"You need to leave Elle."

"I've got other plans."

"Then you leave me no choice."

Tytus lifts his hand, but Finn comes between us. "No. Don't do anything that's going to make it worse, Ileana already tried."

My ancestor growls, low and angry. "Ileana does not have my powers. I can remove her alter, once and for all."

Finn shakes his head, and I could kiss him right then. *We both could*. "It's not right, taking away a part of her. I don't like it either, having her torn in two, but it should be Elle's choice in the end."

"She doesn't know her own mind," Tytus hisses. "And with Declan looming over our heads, we cannot afford to have Elisandra become a liability."

Anger simmers under the surface, and I clench my fists.

I told you he doesn't believe in us, she says. It's hard to ignore her when the words sound so right.

"Declan is your problem," Finn says, his voice tight with determination. "Elle is mine to protect, and I plan to do exactly that."

He holds out his hand behind his back and I take it, marveling at how right it feels. She has nothing left to say, and retreats. Relief courses through me at the thought of no longer having to deal with her – for now, at least.

Finn turns to me, and smiles. "Come home with me, gorgeous. It's time you get some actual rest."

Finn

Somehow, against all odds, Tytus and Lucas both let us take off. Dominic promises to keep in touch with updates, so it's without remorse that I leave him to handle our alpha.

The drive to my house is quiet, and I think it's because Elle's dozing off. When I park, however, I find her wide awake and staring at me. "You okay?"

She nods. "Thank you, for back there. Tytus has it right, though. I don't know how much good it's going to do, having her in me like this. Every time she takes over, I feel less and less like myself."

I take her hand in mine, kissing it. "I'm here with you. And I know a thing or two about being plagued by the supernatural, remember?"

Elle grins at the already far-away memory of the púca. "Any updates on that?"

"Yeah... Looks like it may be the reason we can't find the Reapers. But I'm about to remedy that tonight."

Worry tinges the air, and I pull her to me, kissing her temple. "I'll be fine." Then I open the car door for her, and we head inside. "It's not much," I say by guise of introduction, "but you can take my bedroom, if you like."

Elle turns to me, resting a hand on my chest. "Will you join me?"

The invitation is there in her eyes, and I drop my forehead to hers. "Aye, but not as you're asking, little vixen. Tonight, we sleep."

Looking more than a little put out, Elle follows me to the bedroom. I give her a shirt and pair of shorts that she can wear to bed, and she slides into the cotton sheets with a blissful sigh. Other parts of my body wake up, but I shoot them down.

When I climb into bed with her, it feels right. Right enough that I fall asleep immediately, and don't wake up until my alarm rings close to midnight.

I get to Claws Auto Shop in wolf form, and find Dom and Dani already waiting in the shadows. His dark fur blends

in with the night, but Dani, as a sable wolf, is too visible –
much like me.

If we do find them, I tell her, *you'll have to camouflage us or
something.*

She nods. Dom steps ahead, his eyes tinged with startling
blue. *Are you going to elaborate on this plan of yours?*

Bowing my muzzle, I say, A*ye. I think it may be my fault we
can't find the Reapers.* When he's silent, I tell him all about
the púca, while Dani waits, keeping watch.

As I reach the end of my story, Dom only tilts his head to the
side. *And let me guess. You didn't tell Lucas because, as usual,
he'll overreact?*

And probably throw me out of the pack for disobeying, I reckon.

Dom snorts. *It's been known to happen.*

Dani rolls her eyes at our antics and interrupts. *Are we going
to do this, or what?*

Aye.

And what is this, *exactly?* Dom stares between us, and I sense
his trepidation in the air.

Improvising, I say.

Then I take off on a run, and they follow in my footsteps,
equally silent. It really is improvising, because I've got no
clue what I'm actually doing except throwing a hail Mary.

Every few kilometers, I stop and lift my nose in the air, scenting and tasting it.

After about three hours of what feels like going in circles, Dom catches up to me. *Will you fill us in, already?*

The púca is erasing traces of the Reapers' presence, coating it with its own scent. You guys don't know it, and I've only come across it when meeting the púca directly, so it makes sense I can follow it.

And if you find it?

I'm hoping to catch a fresh mark of the púca's presence, ideally leading us to the latest spot the Reapers were at.

Dani joins my other side. *And are we anywhere closer to that?*

Another sniff in the air. *Yep. This way.* Another half an hour later, we end up deep in the mountains. At the bottom of a valley, there's a cabin with a barn nearby. We wait patiently, then something moves.

It worked!

Dani's excitement almost rubs off on me. At least until Dom says, *Yeah, but we've got trouble.*

I look in the direction he's staring at, and the excitement is gone, just like that. Because tied up on something that looks like a wooden cross, is the witch. And surrounding her is Cade, with two of his men. But that's not the sickest part.

No, the worst is Cade drawing runes in the air, and using them to burn the flesh of her bare arms – marking her.

I make a move to help, but Dom steps in my way. *We can't. If we alert them we're here, then it's an automatic loss. Think about it – no way Cade is here alone with only a few Reapers.*

Fiona's raw scream of agony fills the air, and I squeeze my eyes shut. *Then we don't have a minute to lose. Let's get Lucas – and Tytus. Now.*

Dani nods. *You two go. I'll call Tristan, get him to join me, and keep an eye on these bastardos to make sure we don't lose them.*

We run off like hell itself is following us.

Elisandra

"You did *what*!"

I cringe at Lucas' shout. Tytus, by my side, looks less than impressed. He woke me up barely a few hours after I fell asleep and dragged me to another house in the middle of nowhere. It turned out to be Lucas' place, which was soon filled by Dom and Luz, and Finn.

I should've known something was up when he didn't immediately join my side. Then I realized why. Lucas is beyond himself with fury, and my ancestor isn't much better off.

"You should have told me about this the minute it happened," Lucas growls. "And where the hell are Daniela and Tristan?"

"Keeping an eye on the Reapers," Dom says, eyes glittering with warning. "We need to move, Lucas, before it's too late."

He clenches his jaw. "A lot of people are going to die because of this. You're ready to have their marks on your soul?"

Something about the way he says it gives me shivers, but it doesn't affect Dom. "Then it's a good thing we'll keep the fight away from town."

Thick silence lingers between them, until my ancestor breaks it. "Unless you're afraid." He's taunting Lucas with his words, and by the looks of it, it's working. "And if that's the case, you need to get over it." Tytus glances around, ignoring Lucas' snarl, and his gaze falls on Finn.

"You've got one thing right, though. This isn't a fight for everyone. And I've already told you that you're marked, wolf. You shouldn't be around us."

Lucas stares at Finn, nostrils flaring as he assesses the situation. "Is he right?"

Finn doesn't get a chance to answer. An infernal neighing echoes outside, drawing everyone's attention. Lucrezia moves to the windows, but Dominic beats her to it and pulls the curtain aside, revealing the black mustang with red eyes.

"What is that thing?"

Finn sighs, pinching the bridge of his nose. "It's a púca, an Irish trickster meant for legends and myths, not the real life. But it's very much real, and has followed me from my past, to here."

He stares at Lucas, who glares back. Feet width apart, arms crossed, thundering expression, he looks ready to blow. His voice, when he speaks, is surprisingly calm. "How long have you known it was after you?"

"Long enough."

"You should have come to me first thing, not let this get so out of control."

Finn's features harden with determination. "I can fix this."

"Be my guest." Lucas steps to the side, making no other move to help him.

Unable to stand back anymore, I walk to Finn and touch his hand, intertwining our fingers. "You can do this. If I'm able to get my crazy alter in hand, you've got this."

Not exactly true, she's quick to point out.

The only way I've gotten her in hand is when she wants me to, but I need to show Finn some support. Whether or not that's real, is another story altogether.

My fibbing seems to work, as his emerald gaze clears up and he smiles at me. "Right."

Despite my bravado, when he walks out, I fear I'll never see him again. Luz and Dom step by my side in comfort, while Lucas and Tytus glare in the background.

"He'll be okay," Luz says.

"Celtic wolves are known for their resilience," Dom adds.

I appreciate their encouragement, but my stomach still clenches at the thought he's facing the creature alone.

Finn

The púca is pacing impatiently in front of the house. "Back for another ride so soon?" I ask it, forcing an arrogant pitch to my tone.

It neighs, throwing its massive black mane in the air. "Do not push your luck, faoladh. You owe me."

"What's that, precisely?" I move closer with each step, refusing to let the beast get to me again. "Really, tell me. What's so bad you have to chase me across oceans?"

The red eyes glint. I swiftly glance around, ensuring no humans linger. The last thing I want is any innocents getting hurt.

To my surprise, the púca moves towards me. "Do you remember the dragan whose case you prosecuted?"

Not what I expected. My steps falter. "What?"

"Tsk," it says. "You cannot have forgotten."

I didn't. Ciaran Loughey had been charged with negligent manslaughter when his company's faulty security proceedings led to a loss of life. The victim had left behind a family – three kids, a husband – and I'd sued on their behalf, prosecuting him. It was, ultimately, the case that sent me into self–imposed exile.

But what does this púca have to do with it?

"You're right, I didn't forget. Merely put it out of my mind. For the record, I didn't know he was a dragon until I was facing him in that blasted courtroom. Not that it helped. He got away scot–free – justice, my royal arse." Bitterness infuses my words, and I can't hold it back.

The púca stops its infernal neighing, and watches me, its glare unflinching. "If only you'd let it stop there, foolish one."

Surprise makes me silent. For a bit, at least. "How did you know?"

"I was there, wolf. It was I who led the robbers to the jewelry store. It was I who played trickster to you, leading you to the wrong clues."

"And why would you do that?"

"Because the dragan owed me, too. And he promised to pay his due, if I helped him get the insurance money. See, he refused to part with the gold in his own mansion." A snicker. "Tsk, these dragons. Always so selfish." Then its gaze falls on me again. "And I would have gotten my due, if not for your intervening."

I shake my head, refusing to accept blame for a crime I did not do. "Ciaran was still alive when I left him. If you were truly there, you'd have witnessed him overseeing my punishment."

The púca laughs again. "Only after you beat him first. And besides, he was never the same. His reputation was ruined by a faoladh wolf. And he especially never paid me, avoiding me and setting his witchy goons on me."

"So go get your due from him!" I'm missing something, as the story makes no sense. *Why come after me, when Ciaran is the real target?*

The red eyes burn of an inner fire. "Ciaran was killed months ago, foolish one. By his own people. Which means the only one able to give me my due, is you."

It really dawns on me then. As the man responsible for Ciaran's downfall, it now makes sense why the púca came for me. *An eye for an eye.* Out loud, I say, "So you've come to collect."

"Yes."

"If it's money you want, I've got none."

"Then I will settle for your pain."

I refuse to take a step back, knowing what awaits me. But if it means I can pay my due, that I can return to Elle, it'll be worth it. What's one more beating, when I've already had enough?

The púca rears back its head, then lifts both legs up. Its hooves hit me smack in the chest, sending me flying backwards. My lungs rattle in my ribcage, and each breath is agony.

Fight it, my wolf demands.

I can't. If I do, the debt will be unpaid.

A growl escapes me, my wolf pulling from my insides, trying to get out. *If you don't fight, we will both die.* I shake my head, standing up – only to have the púca jam its head in my side, sending me flying again.

Groaning, I try to hold my wolf back – but my vision is already swimming, and still the púca comes at me. When its hooves hit me again, and again, I give in to the pain – to the suffering he demands.

Just before it kills me, the púca bends its head down low and whispers, "I lied. Your suffering is not enough. I want my due payment, or I will take what truly matters to you – your mate."

Darkness tries to claim me, but a moment later Elle is there, crying over me.

Elisandra

"Help me!"

The minute the púca is gone, and Tytus releases me, I run outside and try to get Finn to move. He's a mess of bruises, blood and dust, but I don't care. His heartbeat is strong under my hand, and that's all that matters.

I try my best to hold him up, but in his weakened state, his limber self is heavier than usual. Dom sees my struggle and moves forward, ducking under Finn's other arm and taking most of his weight.

"Thank you," I whisper.

Finn groans, then drags his gaze from the ground to Lucas. His cold onyx eyes are fixated on me, but at the sound, he switches to Finn. "Well? What does the creature want?"

If it wasn't for Finn's weight on me, I'd march there and punch him myself for his indifference. I know Finn wouldn't want me to cause more trouble, which is the only reason I stay silent.

A second later, Finn breathes out, "Payment."

"For what?"

"Dues accumulated in the life I left behind."

Lucas frowns. "You told me that was in the past. That your self–imposed exile would never interfere with this pack."

I sense Finn's shaking, and it takes me a moment to realize he's angry. "And it hasn't, has it? I fought the púca myself, and intend to keep doing so. As for your other statement, aye, I did say that. But I didn't possess all the facts at the time. The púca was waiting to collect from the dragan I chased after. And despite my family demanding a replacement as alpha, and leaving them behind, none of it helped. It has come to collect, and because I don't have the money, it intends to collect in pain, and suffering. Until I'm dead, or driven insane."

I shiver at his admission. Having seen the creature itself, sensed it malice, it shouldn't come as a surprise. But this is the first I hear the defeat in Finn's voice – like he's done fighting whatever punishment is coming his way.

He's yummier by the second.

Shut up, I tell my alter.

But he's a bad boy! Dragans and exile? Yum!

I don't respond, instead trying to emit as much support as I can, hoping Finn will be able to taste that in the air around him.

After another beat, Lucas says, "How much does it expect?"

Finn rattles of a sum that makes my jaw drop, but Lucas doesn't even flinch. "Is there a reason this creature acts like some mafioso out to collect?"

I'd been wondering the same thing. Finn turns his head to the side and coughs. Blood spatters on the ground, but still he doesn't make an attempt to sit or stop talking.

"A púca does collect money, but no one really knows what it does with it. Some say it redistributes it among the poor.

Others claim that it lives in a cave made of gold, like a dragon." His voice drops a few octaves and I strain to hear the rest. "My mum always said that it transports the money to a different land of fairies and goblins, where the greed coins bring is turned into something good."

Lucas snorts at that. "Fairytales, then. That is what you bring me?"

Finn says nothing. Not for the first time, I wish I had some of his abilities, so I could figure out what he's feeling. He squeezes my shoulder a bit, as if sensing my worry, and I try to temper it down. For once, he needs to focus on his internal battles, not mine.

After a heavy silence, Lucas says, "And if this creature gets the money – the sum you mentioned – it will leave you alone?"

"So it says."

Lucas nods. "Then consider it done. I'll have it tomorrow, and you can put an end to this."

Shock reverberates through Finn, into me.

"Why?" he asks.

Nothing in Lucas' expression changes as he shrugs. "Because you're my pack, my family. And we have bigger things to worry about than some trickster who wants payment." Then he looks at me. "Take care of his wounds, and make sure he's back in tomorrow."

I nod, and Dom helps me carry Finn to his truck. He drives us home in silence, and helps me bring Finn inside. As Finn lounges on the sofa, Dom nods towards a corner, and I follow him.

"Will you be okay with him?"

"Yeah," I whisper, "but what's this about an exile, and him being an alpha?" Finn had mentioned leaving Ireland, sure, but I'm starting to think it was only half the story.

Dom glances between us, then rubs the back of his neck. "No offense, but it's probably best you get him to explain that."

I watch him leave, then turn a mystified stare towards my boyfriend. *Just who, exactly, is Finn McConnell?*

∞ Damhsa ∞

"If you cannot get rid of the family skeleton, you may as well make it <u>dance</u>."

–George Bernard Shaw–

Elisandra

I'm debating how much to pester my new boyfriend, when he throws his head back on the couch and waves me over weakly. I rush to his side, but hesitate, afraid I'll hurt him more. "Is there anything I can do? How bad does it hurt?"

Finn grimaces, his emerald gaze filled with pain. "Like I got run over by an angry horse – which, I was."

"Isn't there something that can be done? I mean, you're a werewolf..." I trail off, not wanting to say something stupid.

"My system's not like Dom's or Tristan's," Finn says. "They have healing already in their body. All Dom has to do is shift from one form to another, and it takes care of his wounds.

185

Tristan's saliva, on the other hand, can close any cut in the blink of an eye."

"And you?" I'm kind of afraid to hear the answer, but I perch on the edge of the sofa nonetheless, careful not to rattle him.

"I heal like a regular human if away from home. The only thing that can speed it up is magic or a full moon."

Biting my lip, I ask, "Should I call Dani?"

"Naw, just stay with me."

He opens his arms and I go in willingly, resting my head on his chest. He takes a deep inhale, then asks, "What's on your mind?"

There's no point in denying it, when he can read me so easily. "You mentioned home... And earlier, an exile. What happened?"

Finn sighs, and it feels like the entirety of his body releases pent up tension. Then he coughs, winces and shifts a bit, before settling back. "A lifetime ago, I was a lawyer in Ireland – to humans. I left behind my pack, of which I was alpha, to chase justice for humans."

"That's admirable. What pushed you to it?"

"Many things, chief among all was the childhood I had. The neighbourhood I grew up in was strictly faoladh, which was great for creating long lasting relationship and growing up fully aware of my powers. Then, when I was but a teenager, a government raid took most of the people away. I later found out they'd been surveilling us for months, and imprisoned my kin to run experiments on them. The rest of my pack went into hiding, far from human cities, and chose seclusion so that we could survive."

I bite my lip, hesitating. "So... How, exactly, did that make you want to be a knight in shining armor for humans?"

Finn laughs – a dry, humorless chuckle. "It didn't. On the contrary, I wanted revenge, and worked towards it with all my might. As part of my plan, I used to go at night in human neighbourhoods and wreak havoc. Key cars, puncture tires, scare people, the like. And then, my damn faoladh senses got in the way."

"How so?"

"Despite my thirst for vengeance, and my back–then hate for humans, I started catching whiffs of their emotions. Their pain, loss, love... It changed my perception of them. My nightly inquisitions turned into curiosity and I spied on them, learning all that I could. More than once, I intervened in muggings or situations about to go wrong, because my nature wouldn't let someone suffer – couldn't."

He shrugs, completely unaware of how amazing that is to hear. "In the end, I went from thinking humans were the scum of the earth to seeing them as a weaker species, in dire need of protecting."

I tilt my head back to give him a look. "That hasn't changed much."

Finn has the grace to look sheepish. "I didn't mean to come across as overprotective, love. It just... You bring it out in me, more than most."

I snuggle closer, breathing in his scent. "It's okay." A beat later, I ask, "And the exile?"

Finn snorts. "I was young, had graduated with flying colors and didn't give a shit about money or whose feathers I ruffled. Turns out, I stepped on someone's rather scaly toes."

I think back to Tytus and some of the things he told me when we were at his mansion, about other creatures that exist. "Do you mean a dragon?"

"Yeah, we call them *dragan* back home. Well, this particular one – Ciaran Loughey – was a tycoon with money. I butted heads with him over a case, and when it didn't go my way, I followed my own type of justice."

There's an underlying pain in his words that makes me think it's not as easy as he just summarized. So I tilt my head back, meeting his gaze, and wait. After a beat, Finn whispers the full story.

"He owned this jewelry chain, see, and decided to use a cheap security company. I later found out it was because he planned to have an easy burglary, in order to get the insurance money. See, dragans love gold. Ciaran, more than most. He didn't care who got hurt in the process. One day, there was a heist, and this lady was killed. She left behind a husband, three kids. It was her case I took."

He pauses. "I involved my pack, too, and Ciaran went after them – my beta, specifically." His voice goes hoarse, his eyes glassy. "Ronan was the best friend I'd had growing up, and losing him unhinged something in me. When Ciaran won the case, he made it a point to also kill the human father, leaving the kids orphans. Since I couldn't just stand by and do nothing, I sought the bastard out. So, you see, my pride really got in the way there."

"Is that how you got exiled?"

Finn nods, his eyes faraway. "Ciaran left me a choice. To leave of my own accord, and my family and pack would be fine. Or stay, and he would burn them to the ground. I couldn't risk their lives, not after Ronan, so I left."

I'm silent for a long time in his arms. The way he talks about Ireland, about his kin, leaves me the impression he'd return, if it were possible. With this thing started between us, it makes me scared – I don't want to lose him.

You're pathetic, she says.

Go away! I'd been alone in my head for the longest time, and now that she's back, it makes me tense. Finn's arm around me tightens in reassurance.

If you really think he'd stick around for you, when he's obviously got loads elsewhere to live for, you're sadder than I thought.

She goes silent after, but her words have the intended effect. My mind won't shut off, weighing the options – the risks.

"Do you miss it?" *A few tiny questions won't hurt anyone.*

Finn laughs bitterly. "Oh, love, you have no idea. That country is in my blood, my very soul. Every breath away is agony." Then he meets my eyes. "But so is every breath away from you."

His meaning is clear – he wouldn't leave me. But I'm unable to keep my mouth shut, my heart hammering against my chest. "What if you had a chance to go back?"

Finn doesn't give me an easy answer, for which I'm grateful. "I love Ireland, darling. But much as I feel torn being away, I couldn't leave you here, either. You saw what that week apart did to us." He pauses, frowning. "Did Tytus tell you...?"

I blush. "Yeah, he mentioned something about us being more tied than we originally thought, or realized. How did you figure it out?"

"Ileana told me."

"Ah." Makes sense Dom's godmother would intervene again. "Why do you think she's so interested in us?"

He shrugs. "Who knows? She seems to have taken a liking to us, maybe because we're Dom's pack, maybe because she feels our loneliness. We each gave up something in order to end up where we are now, and that kind of thing leaves a mark."

"That makes sense, I guess." Chewing on my bottom lip for a bit, I debate on saying more, but Finn moves his head towards me, silently asking me to continue. "Don't you think it's weird, this whole...thing, between us?"

Can I tell him about the mating process, and the fire?

She's way too quick to offer her opinion. *Oh, I'd love to see his face.*

"Naw, love." One hand lifts to cup my cheek, thumb caressing my skin. "I think we're right where we are meant to be – with each other." He lifts up then enough to brush his lips against mine, before dropping back to the couch pillows with a groan. "Now come here, I need to rest some."

I snuggle deeper into him, and we fall asleep.

Finn

Morning comes too damn soon, and thankfully Dom drives over to pick us up. As I wait for Elle to shower and get ready, my buddy meets my gaze. "Did you tell her about your exile?"

"Yeah."

"What about what the púca told you, about Ciaran?"

I sigh. "It's all conjecture at this point, and I've got no way to sort it. Not until this púca gobshite is done and over with. What's the point in worrying her more?"

"You sure that's the best option?"

"Aye," I glance up the stairs. "I need to get this deal with the púca out of the way, it's like a damn sword hanging above my head. Once it's over, we'll be able to talk more. I'm thankful at least the creature came after me, and not my family."

"Why do you think that is?"

I frown at him, not having thought about it. Dom shrugs. "I only mean, when those vrykolakas killings were happening here, I had a sense there was something more happening. Turns out, Radu was behind it all and targeted me on purpose. What if there's more to this than you understand?"

I run a hand over my face. "I don't know, mate, but it's making me damn knackered just thinking about it."

Elle shows up then, and they help me in the car. I'm still bruised and sore and full of cuts under my shirt, but at least I can move. The drive over is silent, broken only by Dom constantly revving the engine. By the time we get out, I'm thankful to still be in one piece.

They help me inside, where Lucas is already with Lucrezia. A heavy duffel bag peeks out from behind her desk – it must be the púca's payment.

One look at me, and we move to his office, leaving Luz at the front. I may be injured, but these damn senses of mine catch the first whiff of trouble. Trying to move my arm from around Dom's shoulders only leads to almost falling on my face.

"What are you doing, man? Stand still," he mutters, then turns to Lucas.

At the same time, the back door to Lucas' office opens and Tristan and Dani run through, panting. Lucas stands to attention, frowning. He opens his mouth, but Dani beats him to it.

"They're coming!"

"Who?"

"The Reapers." Her gaze goes past Lucas, to Dom. "Where's Luz?"

I taste Dom's panic, and he shrugs me off. "Tristan, take over." Then he's off, bellowing through the hallway for his beloved. We stand in tense silence, waiting to see if he'll return with her – he does. Not that it helps his antsy mood.

Lucas waits until Luz is settled in a chair, Dominic standing behind her, to speak. "Enough waiting. What's this about the Reapers?"

Tristan steps forward. "We were patrolling all night through the woods, hoping to catch their scent again. Tytus was helping with the skies. When we got his signal that he'd spotted some, Dani camouflaged us and we managed to get pretty damn close."

Pulling her dirty blonde hair in a ponytail, Dani says, "Cade wasn't around, presumably with the Fiona. But the other two were talking about their plan. They intend to destroy us, wipe us out."

"It'll mean no more competition for this town," Tristan says. "And then they intend to bring back someone who can have their back. But they need Elle to do so." His somber chocolate eyes settle on my girlfriend, and soon enough everyone's staring at her.

A slight tremor goes through Elle, under my other arm. "Why me? Who are they bringing back?"

"Declan. And they need you, because of your blood tie to him, same as Tytus." Dani gives her a look filled with sympathy, then she takes a step towards Lucas. "We can't hesitate about this. It's time to mobilize our efforts. I can place a spell around Luz, and–"

"I'm not leaving Dom."

"Lucrezia..." Elle whispers her name, and I taste her fear. I'd be scared, too.

Dani shakes her head. "You can't be here when they come, you'll be their first victim! Then Dom will lose his head, and that'll be the beginning of our unravelling. Dom, *tell her*!"

He clenches his jaw, then kneels in front of Lucrezia. As they speak in whispered tones, Dani moves to me. She draws a rune in the air and its cooling effect washes over me. One by one, my wounds start healing. Though my clothes are a mess, I can breathe easier, and move accordingly. I stop leaning on Elle and Tristan, and instead wrap my arm around my girl.

"Lucas, I have a better proposition," I say. "Let's meet the Reapers head–on, all four of us. Send the girls into protection first."

He narrows his eyes, considering my suggestion. Dani steps in front of him, already clenching her fists, frustration coating the air around her. "Like hell you're going to leave us behind! You need my magic to fight them."

Lucas' eyes glitter, and I know he's not appreciating the hit to his ego. "*Need* you? Highly doubtful, cara. This pack prevailed without magic quite well before you joined it."

Dani scowls. Before she can talk, Tristan moves by her side, meeting his alpha's gaze. "She's right, though. And before you say anything else, listen to the rest of what we saw. The witch with them... She gave the Reapers magical powers. They were fooling around with them all through the night. Same like Dani's family used to have."

"And is there a reason you didn't wake me up in the middle of the night to tell me, and instead waited until the last minute?"

Dani growls low. "We were trying to find out when they'll attack, Lucas! Would you quit being so stubborn already?"

Lucas is quiet, his features darkening. Dani chooses to press on. "Our only advantage is the Reapers don't fully know how to use the magic, and Fiona didn't get a chance to tell them before Cade was all up in arms and high on the power. But we have to press the advantage by moving now, else they'll come here and too many innocents can get injured."

Deadly silence reigns on the room, until Lucas looks towards Dom and Luz. They're both standing now. I can tell he's thinking, gathering all the facts, but knowing him, he'll do exactly as he wishes – nothing more, nothing else. When he speaks, it's not what I expect at all.

"I will go meet the Reapers...with Lucrezia."

Dom's anger flares, permeating the air. My gaze locks with Tristan. *Watch him. He's on a tight leash with Lucas.* He nods, and I'm glad he grasped my warning.

"Me?" Lucrezia whispers. Then she clears her throat, and glances up at Dom. Whatever she sees in his face makes her soften in response, trying to appear braver than she's feeling. "I'll be okay."

"No," he says through gritted teeth. "Lucas is doing this to prove a point. And I'm not about to let you get in the middle of this!"

"Think what you will," Lucas says, "but I'm not speaking out of pride. Lucrezia has to come with me, because she alone can pause the Reapers in their tracks."

"And how, pray tell, will she do that?" They're about to get to punches, I can taste it. But then the real reason behind Lucas' idea hits me.

"You want to use her as bait, don't you?"

He looks over his shoulder, eyes narrowed. "Not bait, as I don't intend to let them harm a single hair on her head. I do, however, know that her presence alone will unfocus them. And while they'll be busy hurling insults and being distracted with the tasty morsel in front of them, the rest of you can close in from behind. They won't feel you coming, not with a dose of Dani's camouflage. They'll have too much magic running through their veins."

His glare settles on Dani. "Tell him that's true."

She meets Dominic's eye, and nods – not that it calms him down. A low snarl escapes him, and he takes a step forward. "And how do you propose to protect my mate from any magical attacks while she's by your side?"

Lucas is silent at that.

"He can't," Dani answers for him. "If they try something and fail because of a barrier I put in place, they'll know something's up."

"And they won't think the same if the alpha and a human go meet them, without a pack?"

"Not if they believe she's my mate," Lucas smirks.

Luz practically pales at the suggestion, and Dominic growls loud enough to shake the walls.

"Enough of this crap, Lucas!" Tristan intervenes. "While we debate this senseless idea, they're getting closer. We need to move, now!"

"I'm not letting her in danger!"

While Dom is busy arguing with Tristan, so inflamed he's ready to snap, Lucrezia sneaks past them, to me. "Watch over him, please," she whispers. Then she walks the remaining steps to Lucas. "I'll come with you."

Her voice, though barely above a whisper, stops Dom and Tristan's squabbling.

"Lucrezia!" Dom's roar makes her glance back, and her lower lip trembles. But she still stands strong.

"If it's the least I can do to protect you guys, then so be it."

Dani's gaze is filled with respect, and Elle's tears fall on my chest. None of them try to stop her, because they've been in the same situation – with Tristan, and me. So I narrow my eyes on Lucas, hoping he reads my warning instead. "Watch over her."

"You focus on ending your business with the púca, Irish. I've got this." Then he offers his hand to Lucrezia and leaves through the same door Dani and Tristan had entered. Dominic's curses follow them out, and I turn my attention to him.

Elisandra

"Poor Dom," I whisper, watching Dani and Tristan walk away with Dom. It took both of them to hold him back from chasing after Luz, then they walked him away to cool off. So it's just me and my boyfriend left, trying to make sense of it all.

Finn snaps out of his thoughts, shaking his head. "Lucas shouldn't have done this. I have a bad feeling about the whole thing." He meets my gaze. "And I think it's high time we call Tytus."

He hands me his phone, and I dial the number pre-programmed in. After what Dani and Tristan just told us, I expect him to be eager to join us for the fight. Instead, what I get is his usual indifferent drawl.

"Yes?"

"The Reapers are on the move. Lucas just went to meet them now, and we're going to try to corner them in. I think it might help if you provide aerial support."

Tytus snorts in the phone. "And are you planning to accept your magic, and join me, while I'm at it?"

My gaze falls to my hands, and I clench them in fists. "Maybe next time. I don't want to be another distraction."

His voice is odd when he speaks again. "What do you mean, another?"

"Lucrezia went with Lucas. She wanted to help and he thought she'd be a good distraction for the Reapers.... Tytus?"

There's a slamming of something, a roar, and then the line goes eerily quiet. I meet Finn's gaze. "I don't think he liked that last part."

Finn nods. "Good. We need him in this, and I don't care what motivates him to join."

He kisses me quick, pulling me against him, and for a moment I lose myself. His lips are too damn sinful, and the power in his grip has me feeling all kinds of things.

When he pulls away, it takes me a moment of dazed blinking to gather my thoughts. "Something just struck me... Finn, how will they get Luz out of there once the battle starts?"

He's closing up shop, but stops in his movements as if struck by lightning. "I have an idea, and we only need to make one quick pit stop. Wait here."

He sneaks back in, and comes out with a heavy duffel bag, which he throws in the backseat of his truck. I follow inside, Finn takes the driver's seat, and soon we're back on the road.

"Is that the púca's payment?"

Finn grins. "Aye, it is. With this, I may be able to convince it to give me something in return."

I bite my lip, recalling how just the day before the creature had trampled him to death. "What makes you think he'd be willing to negotiate?"

"Because, it's a trickster. Plus, if I'm right about this, it won't be able to deny me."

"Why not?"

"Something Dom said earlier. That maybe this is happening for more of a reason than just money."

"But isn't it a risk?"

"It is, and if it fails, you're going to keep the keys to the truck and get Luz out of there as soon as the fight starts. Take her to their house, and wait for me there."

I nod, hoping my friend will still be in one piece. But more than that, my heartbeat quickens at the thought of Finn in danger – again.

∞ ♦ ∞

It doesn't take much to call the púca, apparently. Once we're parked somewhere on the side of a dirt road, Finn gets out of the car, duffel bag in hand, and heads into the woods. I follow him at a distance, so I don't intervene with whatever he's got to do.

He comes to an abrupt stop, and whistles low. "Thought you were eager for your cut, púca. Or have you gone into hiding?" His voice is low, close to a growl.

Something shifts in the forest, fast as the wind, and then everything comes to an eerie standstill. Majestic as always, the púca walks out of the darkened woods.

Finn lifts the duffel back, unzips it to show the cash, then throws it at its feet. "Your payment."

The púca snorts. "How kind of you." Then it pauses. "I suppose this finishes our business."

"Good. Because I have a favor to ask."

"That is not how this works, foolish wolf." The creature digs its nose in the bag, and huffs out puffs of breath. As they envelop the money, something weird happens. It crinkles and... vanished into thin air.

"What just happened?" I bite my lip the moment after the question escapes me, not having meant to draw attention.

The púca lifts its red, glowing eyes, assessing me. I recall what Finn told me, about how I was able to push it away last time. Gulping, I hope that won't be necessary again.

I'm more than happy to take over, she offers.

Ignoring her, I refuse to blink, and the púca finally straightens up.

"I accept the payment. You may consider your debt erased."

He turns to leave, and I hear Finn mutter, "You asked for the hard way."

Then he runs past me and hops on the horse's back.

This wasn't part of the plan!

I'm torn between going after him, and keeping my distance, but the choice is made for me.

The púca rears its head, bucking and trying to throw him off. "You think you can tame me?" Its voice vibrates with rage, and it makes me back away, further into the comfort of the woods.

Undaunted, Finn bends his upper body over it, and grabs onto its mane, his fists white–knuckled from the force he's exerting holding it. "Enough!"

"This earns you no favors with me!" The creature keeps going, angrily trying to get Finn off its back. If it succeeds, I have no doubt he'll be flying into a tree and cracking his skull open.

Undaunted, Finn bends over it, completely stretched out over its back. Then he unclenches one hand from the mane, and puts it around on the side of its massive neck. He breathes in and out, impossibly calm when my heart is beating so wildly for his life.

The púca bunches, kicks, neighs like crazy. But still Finn holds on, closing his eyes and concentrating. Then something happens – the hairs at the back of my neck stand to attention, and it seems like mist itself creeps in the meadow.

The creature stills, tilting its head further to the side, as though listening. Finn murmurs something, his lips moving, but I'm too far to hear what he says. Then, to my bemused gaze, the púca freezes completely.

Finn

Éist liom, is mise do thiarna agus do mháistir.

You will listen to me, I am your lord and master.

The púca freezes under my clenched muscles, breathing heavily. One eye I can see is rolling heavily. "How....did you find out?"

I smirk, but don't relinquish my grip. "A good friend of mine pointed out that coincidences don't just happen around us. And they don't, do they?"

A soft neigh escapes it, a shake of the head, but it no longer tries to throw me off. "The money is not the only reason you followed me here. Whether you're using it for yourself – or whatever the story is – I know it's not about that, or the debt that I owe you. Rather, because it's what you've always done, keeping an eye on the alpha of the last faoladh clan." I pause, my heartbeat quickening. "Isn't that right?"

The púca tries to glare at me, but when I don't flinch, it tilts its head to the side in silent acquiescence. "Aye, it is."

"And the reason you have done so, is because of our mark. The half-crescent moon on my shoulder I've had since birth. It brands me as, what, exactly? Because whatever it is, it was enough to get you to cross oceans."

"The mark is your past – your ancestor's past."

I blink, and it's my turn to tilt my head to the side. "What are you going on about?"

"The High King of Ireland, who tamed me eons ago..."

I snort. "If you're about to tell me some story about my royal lineage, forget it."

"Not royal," the púca says. "Because in truth, it was not the king himself who tamed me, but his knight. It is his lineage you have inherited, wolf."

The news makes my jaw grow slack in surprise. "I suppose I should not be surprised at the history books getting it wrong."

A snort escapes the creature, then its mucled body still underneath me. "Indeed. For what it is worth, you...are alone in your gifts, faoladh."

"I am," I whisper back. "You chose the wrong wolf to mess with."

I slide off its back, and face it with my back ramrod straight. Lucas doesn't have to know I went back on my promise never to use my alpha lineage.

The púca relents, kneeling to the ground and bowing its head. I feel its honesty in the gesture, and Elle's surprise. I had almost forgotten she was there. And then the púca says, "Very well, my liege. What is it you command?"

A slow grin tugs at my lips as I watch it. "You had a hand in making it harder for us to find the Reapers, and put this to an end earlier. So, you will help us now." I move closer, whispering instructions in its ear.

The púca steps backwards and nods, then it leaves in a trot. Elle inches closer to me, slides her hand in mine and looks at me with new eyes. "'What was that?"

"That, my precious, was the púca submitting to me."

One day, maybe I'll explain to her exactly what I mean. If ever I fully understand it, too. Meanwhile, we head back to the car and drive out to meet the Reapers.

∞ ∞ ∞

∞ Cailleadh Cara ∞

"The <u>loss of a friend</u> is like that of a limb; time may heal the anguish of the wound, but the loss cannot be repaired."

–Robert Southey–

Finn

By the time we park and run to where I sense the rest of my pack, it's late afternoon again. I stop us under a rather large tree, and peek around it. Lucas is in the middle of a valley, Lucrezia by his side. They've got their fingers interlaced, and opposite them is Cade with his pack of Reapers.

"Shite."

"What is it?" Elle asks.

"Cade brought everyone." This'll be a problem, given we're still outnumbered.

Elle's soft gasp tells me she also just noticed their numbers. "How are you going to fight against them all, Finn?"

"With a wee bit of help, hopefully." I look up at the skies, but thick clouds cover them. Then I look closer – just earlier this morning it had been crazy sunny. And do I taste anger in the air?

Yeah, we're definitely not alone.

The affirmation reassures my wolf, and I wrap my arm around Elle's waist, pulling her closer to me. "I need you to be really careful," I whisper, so the words don't get carried by the wind. "Don't forget the Reapers want you – need *you*, in order to raise Declan."

"Maybe it should've been me down there as bait, then."

My breath steals at the idea, as I picture her in so much danger. *No wonder Dominic lost it.*

"Absolutely not," I say. "I'm going to be pulled away from you as soon as this starts, so I need your promise that you'll get out of here, with Lucrezia, as soon as you can."

Elle looks up at me then, and nods. "I swear it." One hand lifts to cup my cheek, and she pushes up on her tiptoes to brush her lips against mine. "Come back safe to me, please."

I bury my head in her neck one last time, inhaling her scent – something to keep me grounded. Then I release her, and crouch low. I look within for the wolf, allowing him passage through me. My body changes, hands morphing to paws, limbs to back legs, and before long I'm standing in wolf form next to my girl.

Elle's soft hand pets my head, and I nibble at it with affection. *I'm not a dog, love.*

She chuckles softly, catching my meaning. "Sorry. Force of habit."

Rolling my eyes, I focus back on the scene unfurling below. Cade splits from his pack with two men, and heads closer to Lucas. From our vantage point, we can hear – too well.

"Got yourself a human whore, Lucas?"

My alpha's growl is loud. "Watch yourself."

"What?" Cade's eyes widen in fake innocence. "Wasn't she with that blondie of yours? Or is it that you like to share?"

"Fuck you!" Luz spits, and I see Lucas trying to jerk her hand, to hold her back. But my redhead friend never did have a filter. And judging by Cade's narrowing eyes, the distraction is working. I just don't know what Lucas is waiting for.

We've got them here.... What the hell is he waiting for? I can sense Dominic, barely restrained, in the area, as are Tristan and Dani. *What's the holdup?*

I get my answer soon enough, and wish I hadn't. Lucas takes a step forward, one hand held up in a gesture of peace. "Can we quit the childish behavior, and talk like men?"

Cade shrugs, then crosses his arms over his bare chest. "I suppose I can afford to humor you."

"You've always had your own agenda," Lucas says. "And God knows I've tried to keep the peace between our packs. But it's obviously not working, and given we live in the periphery of the same town, we need to compromise."

I'm going to fucking kill him.

That threat comes from Dom, and I look around, half-afraid to see him pop out of the woodworks and tackle Lucas to the ground. Elle sees me scanning the area, and kneels next to me. "Go, if you have to. I'll stay here until I see an opportunity to drag Luz away."

I can't leave you.

Elle seems to get my meaning, as she drops her forehead to my furry one. "I'll be okay, I promise."

Dom's anger is getting way out of hand, permeating the air everywhere. It won't be long before a Reaper catches his scent. At a loss, I look up to the skies, hoping Elle catches my drift.

She nods. "Tytus is up there, I got it. Now, go."

I nuzzle her hand one more time, then take off. With each step further from her, I'm praying she'll stay put, as she promised.

∞ ♦ ∞

It doesn't take me long to find Dom. Dani and Tristan are fighting him off, trying to stop him from going after Lucas.

He wants a fucking truce!

Dom, quit it, Tristan says, butting him with his head. *You'll blow this whole thing.*

That's my mate down there!

I step in, trying to calm him down. *And he's our alpha. Give him a minute, and if it doesn't work, we'll step in.*

Dominic bows his head, and I think he's ready to listen. But the moment after, he shoves Tristan away, jumps over Dani, and he's gone down the slope to Luz.

Well, bollocks. I look at Dani and Tristan. *We might as well start the attack.*

Elisandra

Sticking around would have been nice. That is, if she hadn't taken over my body the minute Finn walked away. One moment I'm crouched behind the tree, the next I'm standing and moving forward. *What the hell?*

Move your ass, already! Her impatience makes me even more wary about what she's got planned.

How many times do I have to tell you I'm not trying to hurt you?

No, you just want to take over my body. In an effort to push her back, I focus on the ground, refusing to move. It works. For a bit.

Now you're just being stubborn.

Luckily I'm still hidden from view. I glance up at the sky, noticing the darkening clouds. As Finn pointed out, someone's up there. *Tytus!* I open my mouth to scream, then realize I can't – not unless I want the Reapers to catch me. *Fudge fudge fudge!*

Wow, you can't even swear properly.

Shut up!

Then she's moving us again. At least I'm even closer to Lucas and Lucrezia. Cade's eyes are narrowed on them, and he's got a palm held up.

I don't realize why at first. In fact, I'm too damn slow on the uptake for my own good.

"Lucrezia, duck!" Lucas shouts and pushes her to the ground.

The two Reapers behind Cade attack in unison with runes. Jets of light hit Lucas, and he curls into himself, as if absorbing them. I'm afraid they've killed him when he freezes, going completely immobile.

Cade and his men share a look, and Lucrezia doesn't move from her spot. She glances up though and sees me, her eyes widening. Luckily, she's the only one.

Then Lucas straightens, and somehow seems even larger than before. He snarls, and some birds take flight at his rage. "You fucking *coward*!"

The next moment, he's lunging in the air, morphing into a gorgeous russet wolf with grey, ashy and black stripes, and lands on Cade. Another zap of magic hits him, but Lucas seems immune. Lucrezia is staring, stunned, at the spectacle, then manages to get herself to her feet.

Stumbling, she heads in my direction. I look to the forest behind me, doing as Finn did – a low whistle, praying the púca will answer to me, as it did my boyfriend. Nothing happens, and I turn back to Lucrezia, motioning for her to hurry.

"We need to go!"

She looks behind, hesitating. Lucas is grappling with Cade, two more wolves jumping on his back. He throws his head back and howls, a rippling sound, and more wolves emerge from the woods – ours.

I recognize Finn's ashy coat, and the others in black and dark charcoal I assume are Dom and Tristan. This really makes Lucrezia stop, especially when she notices her mate.

Grabbing her hand in mine, I tug at her. "There's nothing we can do! Dani will help them."

Luz turns to me then, and her eyes widen. "Watch out!"

Before she can drag me out of the way, a stabbing agony ripples through my arm. I stumble towards her, but the pain comes with. One look behind shows me a Reaper, in human form, stabbing my shoulder with some kind of elaborate knife. Behind him are three more wolves, having snuck up behind us while we've been busy arguing.

Darn, darn, dammit!

Luz moves to my side and side-kicks the Reaper with the knife, sending him stumbling backwards. The movement rips the knife out of my shoulder, drawing an agonized groan out of me.

The guy tackles Lucrezia, but she's giving back as good as she's getting. Meanwhile, one angry wolf lunges on me, sending me flying back.

Rolling over, I notice Luz has incapacitated the guy, and is trying to come to my aid. But another wolf steps in her way, separating her. Then the one who'd tackled me comes closer, forcing me to back away – right into the field of war.

I look at my bleeding hand – and the world around me narrows. The wolves' snarls, yips, clashing of bodies on bodies, none of that exists anymore. My heartbeat is the only sound, growing louder and louder in my head. I'm vaguely aware of magic – and then more, and more aware. It's permeating these wolves, but also in the forest.

Dani.

Her jabs of light keep the wolves safe, including my wolf. *My Finn.*

I inhale sharply, and the scent of burning fur and blood is strong in my nose. My neck cracks from side to side, as though weighed by an impossible barrier. Above us, the skies open, and down flies Tytus – drawing closer, and closer.

Fire. Blazes. Flames.

Burning hot, and hotter around me... The wolf threatening me crumbles to ashes. Flames erupt from the ground, but they don't come near me, shying away instead of hurting me.

What the hell are you doing? Her voice, for once, is panicked.

And I think I know why. *You don't want me using magic.*

That's absurd, she says. *You* can't *use magic.*

And maybe I can't. But the feeling coursing in my veins, the rumble in the pit of my stomach... Everything slows. My bloody hand digs in the ground. I try to hold on –

More. More. More. Use the power, use it all...

The voice is male. Unknown. But I cannot deny him, the impulse stronger. Teeth gritted, I clench the earth, then throw my head back and look at the skies. Dark clouds gather round, right above my head, and then the rain starts.

Euphoria fills me, like I've never felt before.

Finn

It's a bloody freaking mess.

The moment we emerge on the battlefield is the moment Lucas howls, calling us to his aid. Dominic shifts course, trying to get to Lucrezia – whose scent is on the borderline, now. But a group of Reapers blocks his way, enticing his growl.

Tristan, on my right, equally meets his match. The Reapers are soon burned down, courtesy of Dani watching over us in the woods.

Good thing for your mate, I tell him.

I know, but it looks like Cade's been busy turning humans.

One glance around confirms he's right, given the number of Reapers increased since last time. I take this moment to see where Elle is, and catch sight of her way too close to the battlefield for my comfort.

Lucas then jumps in front of us, startling me. *Negotiations are over,* he says. *Kill everything that moves.*

I share a look with Tristan, the same thing going through both our minds. *About damn time!*

We rip and claw our way through the throng of Reapers, trying to get to Cade – who's conveniently always in the middle of a group of them. Lucas seems to be filled by an insane desire to rip everything apart, as he's making more of a mess than all of us combined.

On my way to ripping a wolf's throat out, I catch something in the air – fear. Then another – panic. I finish the wolf and pivot on my paws, trying to see where the danger is coming from.

Dom is close to the edge of the woods now – single–mindedly trying to get to Lucrezia. I don't blame him, she should be out of here already, not facing Reapers. *Where the hell is the púca?*

I throw my head back and howl, demanding its presence, focusing all my thoughts on it. The shadows in the forest shift, and it's finally here, its mystical scent easy to catch. *Get the human out of here!*

A wolf jumps on my back. I grow too distracted, and Dani can't keep all of us safe. I roll on my back, tossing all my weight on him. When I get back up, I notice Lucas disposing of three more. Tristan has increased his bulk to three times its original size, and he's stomping and exploding heads wherever he steps.

I turn my attention back to the púca. Elle. *Where's Elle?* She's no longer with Lucrezia, who's now fighting a Reaper. I know my girl wouldn't have left her alone, unless ––

Feckin' hell, did her alter get to her?

Then the skies open above, and Tytus swoops down. I glare up at him. Why the hell did he wait this long?

The answer comes soon enough. A vibration in the earth, a crackling in the sky... Reapers move aside, also trying to see the reason for the change in the air. It's Elle – on the battlefield now, bleeding from her shoulder.

I run towards her, killing Reapers on the way. Tytus throws fire to surround her, protecting her from anyone not looking to get themselves scorched. It's definitely Elle, and not her alter. Even this far away. I can see her eyes are still hazel.

Then midway, Tytus changes his course – his head is pointing in the wrong direction, to the woods.

NO!

Tytus' roar, Lucas' shout, none are as loud as what I hear next. A howl that tears through the forest, and stops everything in its track.

Tytus swoops down, burning half the Reapers with one blow of smoke. Lucas is running across the field, desperately trying to get somewhere.

But it's Dominic – Dominic's pain, his agony, his desperation – that I taste closest. And it's to him I turn – in vain.

He's frozen, staring at the gory picture in front of him.

Elisandra

The buzz of everything fades away, replaced by the sounds of the fight again. Then, cutting over everything else, something that makes my breath catch in my throat.

I hear an impossible howl, and look behind me. Lucrezia's impaled by a Reaper's claws, gasping for breath. It's the same wolf she'd been fighting with, the same one she'd rendered unconscious. But he's now standing facing her, one hand turned into a claw, the rest of him completely human.

Dominic, in the distance, snarls again, and slams into the Reaper trying to block his way. Then he tears two more, ripping their throats as he makes his way to Lucrezia. I stand immobile, protected by Tytus' fire.

The Reapers takes a step back from burning fire, and I notice its source. Dani is behind Dominic, panting, tears streaming down her cheeks. She catches Lucrezia as she falls, and Dominic joins them, shifting to human form as he runs over.

With a cry of agony, he pulls Lucrezia into his arms, holding onto her, refusing Dani's help. She crawls away from them, resting against a tree. Sobbing, she lifts her hand and draws a single rune, clothing Dominic with a pair of jeans.

I become aware of the scent of burning ground – Tytus has drawn a line of fire behind us, stopping any Reapers from breaching it. Lucas and Finn have crossed over, Tristan now by Dani's side, whimpering. They're still in wolf form, jaws bloody, heads bowed in grief.

Tears clog my throat with each step I take. Luz smiling, her help, she'd been a friend... I gasp at the sight of her wound, half her organs missing. Unable to stand, I drop to my knees, holding my bleeding shoulder.

"Iubirea mea, no...no, don't do this!" Dom's sobbing, rocking her body. "You cannot be taken from me."

"Dom..." Luz's eyes open, and she lifts her hand to his cheek. "I.... I'm sorry. I meant forever, please believe me. But I love you, always will. Remember that."

When she closes her eyes, I feel my own heart bleeding. But Dom's roar... He looks up, blindly, and his eyes settle on me. I think he's about to berate me for leaving her, for being the cause of her death, but all he says is, "Protect her with your life."

I'm afraid to agree, afraid of what he'll do once I take her body off his hands... But I don't have it in me to stand in his way. So I move closer, putting my bleeding hands on her stomach, in a stupid effort to stop the blood flow.

Out of the corner of my eye, I see Dominic leap through the flames. It's only then I realize Lucas was no longer with us, having gone back to the fight. I assume Dom goes to help him...

But when I look up, through the flames, it's not what I see. Without thought for his life, Dom attacks his alpha from behind. Lucas throws his head back, shouting in pain as scratches show on his back. Then he turns to Dom, panting.

Dom jumps him again. Lucas tries to evade, but he has no choice but to protect himself. A gust of wind draws my attention away from them. Tytus crushes the forest behind us, landing over trees without a care in the world.

Then he's human again, running towards us. His features are filled with pain, an anguish I'm not used to seeing on him. He drops to his knees beside me, and pulls me away from Lucrezia.

"No... Dom said to... protect her..." The sobs clogging my throat erupt, and I can't stop it. Tytus draws me to his chest, and I swear I feel his tears on my bleeding shoulder.

I lose sight of the battle then, until Finn comes to me, pulling me from Tytus' embrace and taking me away from the scent of loss and death.

Finn

"What happened to Lucas? To the fight?"

I glance at Elle, curled up in the passenger seat, tears streaking down her beautiful face. My own anguish is raw, my chest clenching. I feel everyone's pain, unable to separate it from my own. So it's with a thick voice I say, "Cade took off with the remaining Reapers he had. Presumably back to his witch, and intending to turn more humans. Me and Tristan managed to separate Dom and Lucas. Tristan went to take him home, and Dani was trying to heal Lucas, last I saw."

She gulps, and her grief is also palpable. "Why did Dominic attack Lucas? Why not me? I was the one who left Lucrezia alone."

"No, love." I reach for her hand blindly, desperately needing to feel something. "Dominic saw everything – saw you being pushed away. From the moment we entered the battlefield, the Reapers didn't matter to him. He was trying to get to Lucrezia." I pause, clear my throat, "And Lucas, he blames him because he's the one who brought Luz there in the first place."

We arrive at my house, and I go to open her door. Her steps are tiny, her hand clenching mine as we head towards it.

I open the door and lead her inside. She's apprehensive, I can taste that much in the air. But when I touch her lower back, a zing of electricity goes through both of us. Elle stops moving, turning her head over her shoulder to me.

And that invitation, I can't resist. Not after this battle, not after being so close to losing her, too. Not anymore.

I drop my mouth to hers, and end up pushing her against the wall. She moans, arching her back, pressing into me. My breathing speeds up, and blood rushes to one part of my body. It presses into her, insistent.

My hand goes to hers, placing it on the wall beside her head. I glance at our interlaced fingers, panting, trying to find a semblance of peace of mind.

This isn't right. Not now. Not when we've lost one of our own.

"Elle..."

"No talking," she says, and turns in my arms. "Not tonight. Not after what I saw with Luz and Dom. I want to enjoy this – you – while I can. No more hesitations, not when life is this short."

A rumble of laughter runs through me, so at odds considering what we both witnessed. I don't know what we'll face tomorrow, but I'll be damned if I let this slip through my hands.

So I dig my hands into her mane, releasing it from her ponytail. Then I angle her head up, and drop my mouth to hers. Elle surrenders, and I taste its sweet taste, fueling me on.

Picking her up in my arms, I walk us both to the living room. The couch is the nearest place, and I drop on it with her straddling me. Heaven is Elle in my arms, her mouth on mine, her body so close. Torture is the slips of clothing separating us, which I start taking off.

Elle helps me with her shirt, and mine, revealing her beautiful goddess body. My breath stutters when I lay eyes on her, for the first time wishing I was taking my time with this, with her.

"There's time for slow later," she whispers, as though reading my mind. Then her hands go into my hair, tugging on it. "Right now, it's you I want, Finn."

Her eyes are darkened by desire, but they're still the sweet color I know. No grey in sight. No alter, no second thoughts, it's just us. For this, I'm thankful as I take off the remnants of her clothing and push my jeans down my hips.

Elle then drops her mouth to mine again. It's like we can't get enough of the other, of feeling this connection, of breathing each other in. When I finally thrust into her, I stop, looking into her face, memorizing her features as she takes me deep.

She smiles, a flush staining her cheeks, and rocks against me. Pleasure shoots to my core, and I grit my teeth so this doesn't end faster than it began. Then Elle drops her forehead to mine, her hair a curtain around us.

"I can't live without you," I whisper, and pull her mouth back to mine.

I'm drowning, drowning so bad...

∞ ∞ ∞

CHAPTER THIRTEEN

∞ Grá ∞

"<u>Love</u> will make men dare to die for their beloved – love alone; and women as well as men."

–Plato–

Finn

Someone's shaking me. I open my eyes, meeting Elle's sweet hazel ones. A grin escapes me as I remember last night, and I reach for her. But rather than melt in my embrace, Elle pulls away, shaking her head.

Then I notice she's holding my phone out, and after a few blinking attempts I make out Tristan's name on the screen. Rubbing a hand over my face to shake the sleep off, I grab the phone.

"Dani, don't! They're going to tear each other apart–"

"Tristan?"

"Finn!" Relief spreads in his voice, replacing the panic from before. "Meu amigo, you need to get here, now!"

"Here, where? What time is it?"

"Lucas' place! Dominic's about to tear him apart."

The line goes dead, and I stare at Elle in the darkness. "It's only past midnight," she whispers, and I hesitate. Yes, my duty is to my pack, but after what we just shared –

Elle smiles, and bends over to kiss me quickly. I only taste acceptance and support in the air, which reassures me. Then she snaps off the bed and throws me some clothes. "You have to go, I get it. I'll be here when you come back, I promise."

When I still hesitate, she adds, "Tristan said they were keeping an eye on Dom... They helped bring Lucrezia's body to his place, because he wouldn't let go of it. After he went through a bottle of Romanian țuică, he got up and started shouting about Lucas."

"Shite," I mutter, and finally get out of bed. "They're not on good terms in regular times, there's no way in hell they're going to survive this."

One more kiss, and I'm out the door. Too knackered from the fight to morph, I grab my car and drive over. When I park, Dani's outside the house, moving her hands and drawing runes. I don't understand why, at first. The area is quiet – almost too quiet, given Tristan's phone call.

Keeping my eyes on Dani, I get out of the car and walk over. Once I pass her, it's like someone cranked up the sound on the radio. Crashes and curses erupt from Lucas' house, and I stop in stupefaction.

"Took you long enough," Dani mutters. "They've been going at it for the last hour. I managed to get a sound protection on the area, before some humans hear the ruckus and try to call the *policiais*."

Not sure what to expect, I walk up the steps and inside the house. Tristan is by the door, his dark expression settled on what's left of Lucas' living room. I've been here only a few times, but I remember a baroque-style decorated hall and living room, with gorgeous antique furniture and leather everywhere. The place had screamed money – at the time.

Now, it was in shambles. Holes in the walls, mirrors broken, pieces of furniture lying about. And in the middle, panting, Lucas and Dom in human form. They've each got cuts and bruises on every part of their body I can see, and their clothes are ripped. Lucas' one arm is bleeding rather profusely, and Dom's got something piercing his leg.

Not that it matters to either of them. I taste their rage, their desperation – their grief. It clogs my throat, reminding me of what I lost long ago.

"Why haven't they morphed to wolf?" I ask.

Tristan speaks out of the corner of his mouth. "Dani put something on them to stop it. She said there's less chance of them killing each other like this." A pause, and he adds, "Though, they've come pretty close to it."

"And you haven't intervened?"

Tristan gestures to the living room. "What, and become part of this lovely decor? No, thanks. It's better they get it out of their system."

"I reckon there isn't a way to get it out of their system," I whisper and move closer.

Lucas glances over. "Stay the fuck away, Irish."

"And let you kill each other? I don't think so."

With a growl, Dominic lunges and head butts Lucas, sending him flying in the wall. His hands are coated with bruises and blood – his own or Lucas', I can't tell. But I sense a shift in his attacks this time – he's determined to kill.

And that, I can't allow.

Lucas may have made mistakes, but Lucrezia's death was not all his fault. We all could have done more – protected her better. And while the loss is hardest on them two, me and Tristan are also feeling it. And I'm not about to let someone else join her in the great beyond.

Tristan catches drift of what I'm doing and steps next to me. One nod, and we both jump on Dom – grabbing one of his arms each. He struggles, rages against us – and holy shite, he's strong. My vârcolac friend has been blessed with extra strength, but I never counted on having it used against us.

The first time, he throws us off and goes for my alpha's neck. Lucas evades it and lands a punch, giving us the moment of distraction needed to try again. This time, I'm prepared. So when Dom struggles again, I touch the side of my hand to his temple and pull some of his rage inside me.

It's not enough to calm Dom down – but it's enough to get him to stop struggling. His emotions are all over the place, until, like a deflated balloon, he falls to his knees. Tristan and me share a look, and kneel next to him in solidarity – and to make sure he's not about to jump up.

But no, Dom is definitely down for the ride. He won't cry in front of Lucas, but he's done fighting.

"Grazie," Lucas whispers.

I glance up at my alpha, and the words are out before I can stop them. "I didn't do this for you. Lucrezia wouldn't have wanted him to go down killing you, is all."

Then I grab Dom up, and Tristan helps me get him to my car. I bring him home with me, but as soon as I turn the corner, I know we're not alone. A faint glow by the side of the house drawas my gaze, and as we get closer I recognize Ileana.

With a trembling hand, Dom opens his side door and drag himself out of the car. He stumbles towards his godmother, whose expression is wrought with sadness.

"Dragul meu," she whispers, and it's all it takes.

Dominic freezes in his tracks, his entire body shaking. It's pain, rage, and grief all mixed into one, coursing through him. Yet he's holding it down, refusing to let the emotions out. Ileana glides to him and wraps her arms around his shoulders as if he were a babe.

"I know your pain," she says as I stare at them.

I'm both infringing on their moment, and afraid of leaving them alone in case he goes back after Lucas. Ileana glances at me and gives a slight nod, so I step to the side where I can give them privacy, but still be there if I need to intervene.

Dominic says nothing as she holds him, just seems to soak up her embrace. Eventually, after long moments, he pulls back. His eyes are red-rimmed, his jaw tight with fury. "I will get vengeance for this."

Ileana lifts a hand to his cheek. "Nu, dragul meu... My darling godson, vengeance will only taint your soul."

Dom grabs her hand, and I see his knuckles tighten over it. "I. Don't. *Care.*"

Ileana grimaces as if in pain, but when I try to move closer, she holds out her palm in a silent gesture meant to stop me.

"My soul is the least of my worries right now," Dominic growls. "I have lost my fucking mate, Ileana, and someone needs to pay."

She only stares at him with her sunny gaze, until he drops her hand and steps back. He runs a hand over his face. "I didn't mean to hurt you."

I figure it's as good a time as any to intervene. "Why don't you come inside, mate? Get some sleep."

Dominic looks at me, but doesn't really see me as he shakes his head. "I can't let Luz sleep alone. I never have, and I won't start now."

Before I can stop him, he morphs to wolf form and takes off at a gallop.

Ileana turns her sorrowful gaze to me. "Watch over him. He is not in his right mind, and will not be for a while."

With my next breath, she's gone in a whirlwind of flowers. Elle opens the door then, her expression filled with understanding.

"Was that Dom?"

I hesitate between chasing him down, and going to keep him company. But there's a quality to his pain that I know not even I could soothe.

So when Elle holds out her hand, I take it and bury my head in her neck, inhaling her sweet scent. "I don't know what I would do if I ever lost you."

"You won't," she whispers, wrapping both arms around my shoulders and pulling me inside. "I'm here, and all yours."

I bury my own grief in a kiss, and she seems to understand my need as we kick the door shut behind us.

∞ ♦ ∞

The next morning should be a work day. I wake up to five missed calls from Lucas, and listen to a voicemail saying the shop is closed, and no one's presence is required.

Still nursing his wounds, that one.

Rolling my eyes, I get out of bed and join Elle in the shower. Last night, I dreamed of Ronan for the first time in years – my beta. He died at the hands of the dragan I pissed off in Ireland, and it's something I haven't yet forgiven myself for. Luz's death has made the memory even more present in my head.

Maybe it's our mate bonds getting stronger, but Elle feels it. She lets me wash every inch of her body, melting into me more with each passing second. Unable to resist, I bend my head and take her sweet mouth, enjoying the way she has to stretch to kiss me back – thus pressing her entire body against mine.

"We never quite finished, last night," I whisper, nipping at her ear.

The delighted squeal from her spurs me on, and before long I've got her legs wrapped around me, her back to the wall, and I'm right there – teasing her, teasing both of us. Elle moans under me, trying to shift her hips to take me in, but my hold on her ass grows tighter and she can't move.

Eyes glazed with desire settle on me. "Please, Finn..."

The invitation is too sweet. I drop my mouth to hers, stealing the kiss – and drawing it out. Sucking on her bottom lip only drives her crazier, and I feel the tremble in her body. Elle breaks the kiss, panting, nails digging in my shoulders. She tilts her head to the side, offering me her graceful neck.

My lips trail down her jaw, then her neck, and I nibble on it, enough to leave a mark by the time I stop. Her trembling increases in my arms, as do her moans, her pleasure coating the air around us.

"Finn..." It's more of a growl this time, and I pull back just enough to check her eyes. It's only the hazel that meets my gaze, none of the grey I associate with the alter.

Kissing her nose, I say, "Stay with me."

Then I drive into her, groaning at how tight she is, how feckin' amazing she makes this simple act. I free up one hand to nudge one breast up to my mouth, then the same fingers trail down to her centre. Panting, steam around us, she comes around me and I groan at the sweet sensation.

Dazed from the orgasm, she lifts a limp hand to my lips, tracing them. A slow grin curves her lips. "More?"

"Thought you'd never ask, love," I grin back and pull out, only to slide back home. With each thrust I go deeper, and Elle digs her nails harder into me. The pain is as sweet as the pleasure, and it's not long before I lose myself into oblivion, screaming her name.

∞ ♦ ∞

By the time we're out of the shower, my doorbell is ringing insistently. I pull on a pair of sweatpants and open to find Dani there. There are shadows under her eyes, a stark reminder of what we have all lost.

"Where's Tristan?"

"Nice to see you too," she grumbles and pushes past me. She notices Elle in kitchen, and my sweet, innocent girlfriend blushes crimson at the thought of what we've been doing just minutes earlier.

Dani lets out a weak smile, catching on. "Sorry to interrupt, but this was urgent." She meets my gaze. "Remember the spot your púca showed us?

"Yeah?"

"I was by there earlier this morning." At my look, she rolls her eyes. "Not alone, relax. Tristan was with me."

"Why would you both take the risk?"

"You know why," she growls. "We're not just going to sit by and let Cade's bastardos get away with killing Lucrezia. Anyway, point is, for some stupid reason the Reapers are still camping there. Maybe they think they're safe, não sei. I don't know. But it got me thinking."

I lean against the wall, crossing my arms. "I have a feeling I won't like this."

Her gaze grows pleading. "Listen, that witch gifted me with powers, but she's been used by both my brother and now Cade. If we free her, maybe she'll make a run for it. We can try.... Without her, they can't bring Declan back. And we can't let them do that, not after they took Luz from us."

I glance at Elle, recalling the blood they took off her during the battle. She steps closer to me, interlacing our fingers. "Go. I'll be okay by myself."

"Naw, love. Not by yourself. Call Tytus, see how he's coping about Luz... And don't stay alone."

She squeezes my hand in reassurance, and I steal another kiss from her. It's hard to stop at only one, but I manage to tear myself away.

"Let's go." I follow Dani out the door and into the woods.

We get by the barn in too short a time. Fiona is still strapped to the same wheel we saw her on last time, looking haggard and like she's lost even more pounds. Pity fills me – she didn't deserve this.

In wolf form still, we creep around the area, trying to see if there are Reapers about. I catch no scent, and one look at Dani confirms the same.

They were here before, she warns me, *so keep an eye out.*

With our teeth, we get to pulling at the ropes holding Fiona captive. The witch turns her head to the side, noticing me, then Dani. Recognition flashes in her eyes, as does fear. I wish we could tell her we're not here to hurt her.

We don't have time to morph human and back, Dani says. *Just keep going, she'll figure it out.*

Sure enough, by the time I'm done with one foot, and Dani the other, Fiona's fear has ebbed away. Her eyes are more alert, though her face looks gaunt and haunted. Guilt at what she's done – what she's caused – fills the air.

I focus harder on the wrist I'm trying to unbind, and finally manage it. She lays there for a minute as Dani cuts the remaining wrist, then whispers, "I am sorry."

I nod, trying to tell her I know. Then I turn my head to the side, pointing to the woods.

"You're freeing me?"

Dani nudges her forward, and Fiona manages to get off, but stumbles. Her feet won't hold her up. I share a look with my companion.

Bollocks! We didn't count on this.

Well, we can't take her in the car, either!

I think for a second, then step away and into the woods. The púca still owes me, since it wasn't able to get Luz away from the battle. One howl, and the woods tremble. Something passes by as swift as an arrow, and shadows part to let it through.

The black mustang takes one look at me, then the witch. "So this is your new favor?"

I hold its gaze. *Not new. You couldn't deliver at the battle, so this is what you owe me. Get her away from here, and we are even.*

The púca stares at Fiona again, as though assessing her, and listening to my words. After a few lengthy moments we don't have to waste, it finally drops to its front knees. With much prodding from us, we get Fiona on its back and watch as they ride away.

Then I follow Dani back to the car, morphing back as she clothes us. My thoughts are churning, an odd feeling in the pit of my stomach. "It's odd they would leave her unprotected."

Dani voices what we both dread. "Maybe it's because they already got what they wanted out of her."

A sigh escapes me. "If they did, then God help us all."

By the time I get back home, Elle is asleep. I change into a pair of clean shorts and slide into bed, pulling her in my arms. Whatever the Reapers are after, there's no way I'm letting them touch her again.

Elisandra

Wake up.

I groan, tossing and turning in bed. A warm arm wrapped around my waist succeeds where the voice hadn't. My eyes pop open in the darkness, and it takes me a minute to separate my very vivid dream of flying – and the male voice prodding me to keep at it – from the reality.

Then I remember Finn's hands on me this morning, and smile. Turning in his arms, I try to hold on to sleep, but it escapes me.

Wake UP!

This time, I don't get a choice. My body jerks from under him, and before I can think otherwise, I'm standing. Finn rolls to his back, throwing an arm over his face. It's only a second later I realize he's done so to block the light coming from me.

Or, more specifically, from the fire that my hands are holding.

Move to the bathroom or I throw this on the bed.

Gritting my teeth, I do as she asks, and look in the mirror. Whether it's my imagination or not, I can practically see my reflection moving as she speaks.

You're wasting time. Yeah, he's hot as sin, but you have so much power in you. Use it!

I frown at my reflection. "I thought you didn't want me to."

That's what the zmeu put in your head, not me. Use it! Use it all!

"And if I don't want to?"

Why not? What has you so afraid?

"Nothing!" I hiss at my reflection. "But there is no need to use this. Not when I'm here, safe."

And were you safe when the Reapers cornered you on the field, taking your blood without permission?

"Finn and Tytus protected me!"

After the Reapers had already hurt you.

Tears fill my eyes. "It wasn't me they were after, it was Lucrezia!"

And if you don't listen to me, if you don't use these powers, you will end up as stupidly useless as she was!

"Stop it," I beg.

Look at you. Snivelling like a child.

I glare at my reflection, my voice more assured. "This isn't going to work. I have a good support system around me."

And it will fail you!

"No, it won't."

Declan will come for you... You're not only Tytus' descendant, you're his too.

I remember the male voice on the battlefield, directing me to the magic inside me. It can't be a coincidence that both Declan – if that was him – *and* her are asking me to tap into these powers now, can it? Aloud, I say, "Finn and Tytus will protect me."

Declan will hurt you if you don't join him. He's the stronger one, you shouldn't hesitate!

I wash my face, refusing to listen any more. It enrages her further.

I will make you.

"And I won't let you."

Running out of the bathroom, I crawl back in bed with Finn. My body is trembling, needing his heat – his reassurance. Then my hands become questing, demanding, feeling his naked body underneath my fingertips. His strength ripples through every muscle, and I desperately need that same force inside me.

She's trying to push at the back of my head, to take over, but I focus on the feel of Finn, his scent, his hold on me – on my heart. Resentful, she slouches back to the corner of my mind, and I want nothing more than to forget the poison she's spewing.

So I give in to the only thing that matters. Finn's kiss, his lips, his inexplicable patience... Half–asleep, he still knows my body with a mastery that astounds me. Nuzzling my neck, he pulls off my shorts and t–shirt I slept with, then sighs against my skin.

One hand goes to cup my breast, toying with my nipple, the other moves over my hip, gripping it. In one smooth move, he pulls me on top of him so I'm straddling him, then stares up at me through half-hooded eyes.

His emerald gaze is dark with desire, his expression intense. There's more here, between us, than we shared before. It was grief – the loss of a friend – that made me jump the cliff the first time. Too afraid to lose Finn in this war that's taking place around us, I wanted to at least know we'd been together – shared each other – in every way possible.

No regrets.

Now, my head is clear of everything else, because there is nothing – *nothing* – in this world that grounds me as he does. I cup his cheek, lowering my lips to his. Finn tastes me first, then his free hand sinks in my hair, tugging me closer.

One shift of his hips, and I'm spread over him, and he's nudging my entrance. We sigh in relief when he's finally – *finally*– inside me. I wait for the telltale yaps from my alter, but only blissful silence answers in my head.

With each stroke, with each shared breath, Finn brings me to the stars and back. His hands roam over me, finding spots I didn't know were sensitive, making my body sing to his tune. Stars are nothing compared to the pleasure coursing through me. It's a darned supernova, burning hotter the closer I get to my climax.

And damn him, but he feels it. The expression on his face changes, growing more intense. His thrusts inside me become harder, and I groan, letting my hair fall back.

"Not yet," he whispers, drawing my gaze back to him. "Stay with me."

I couldn't if I tried. The fire inside me burns hotter still, and when the orgasm courses through me, I swear I stop breathing. A moment later, I'm aware Finn's frozen, deep inside me, and I open my eyes.

Finn's staring at me – *through* me. His gaze is hot, intense, his palms scorching me. I shift on him, only to realize it's not his palms that are scorching, but my own. My body's on fire – within, a heat that suffuses my skin, drawing out each breath painfully.

I meet his gaze, Tytus' warning in my head. "I..."

Finn cups both my cheeks this time, and I drop my forehead to his. "We'll stop if you want," he whispers. "This isn't just another session in the sack, my love – *mo grá*. It's a hell of a lot more."

I stare at him, at this guy who's been in my life for the past year, who I stayed away from – and for what? The ties binding us are already thicker than anything I've ever known, and I don't intend to stop.

So I drop my mouth to his, kissing him with all I've got. Then, inch by painfully scorching inch, I lift up, and drop my hips back down, taking him as deep as he'll go. Finn hisses against my kiss, then a low growl builds in his throat.

The second after, he's flipped us over, drawing one leg of mine over his hip, and slams inside me. His mouth is still glued to mine, his free hand going to my centre, and I come undone. Finn drops his head against my chest, panting as his own release overwhelms him.

When I've calmed enough to draw in a shaky breath, Finn's touch alone keeps me grounded.

Every fiber of my body is attuned to his – breathing in sync, feeling in sync. I can't tell where he begins and I end, and the feeling of completion is too much.

It's scary. What's even more scary is the nasty voice at the back of my head warning me that this won't last, that it can't. That it'll evaporate just like the ashes of Grandmama's bakery. But I don't have time to dwell on it. Because as is his usual, my boyfriend is too damn perceptive for his own good.

Finn

I fall back on the bed, panting like I've run a marathon. Every nerve ending is shooting off sparks, and my heart feels like it's been electrocuted. Next to me, Elle is also trying to catch her breath.

My hand crawls over the crumpled bed sheets, seeking hers, and finds it trembling. That gets my attention, and I turn on my side. "What's wrong, love?"

Elle moves her head away from me, and her erratic breathing worries me. I push myself to an elbow, turning her face towards me. It's tear–stained, her nose red, and yet she's the most beautiful creature in the world.

"Elle, talk to me."

"I'm okay," she whispers, and grabs my hand in hers. "Promise. It was just... Intense. I didn't expect it, this connection, the mating, to be...so much."

The clenching around my own heart subsides, and I feel like I can breathe normal again. "Nor did I."

"Tytus only said that... That, because I was tied with you, that my zmeu part, the way we mate it's through fire. I thought... He made it sound like I'd be burning you with magic, or something."

A chuckle escapes me. "Well, it wasn't so far from that now, was it?"

Her cheeks go crimson, and she buries her head in the crook of my neck, forcing me on my back. I wrap an arm around her, pulling her closer still. "If this is what mating with you is, my darling, I'd walk through fire any day."

Elle jerks in my grip, and the air of satisfaction around her solidifies to something else, less pure. "What's going on?"

"Nothing." And yet she pulls back from my embrace, scooting to the edge of the bed, blanket wrapped around her naked form.

I can taste her fear now, but she's lying to me. The deception stings after what we just shared, and I sigh. "You're lying, mo grá."

Elle glances over her shoulder, frowning at the endearment. "I am not."

"You are," I repeat, and tug her into my lap. With easy movements, I turn her around so she's sitting between my legs, and start massaging her shoulders. "Why don't you tell me what's really bothering you?"

She says nothing, stuck in an obstinate silence that I want to tear down. "Is it what just happened? Are you afraid of where we're going with this?"

"Maybe," Elle says, but I taste the lie again.

"No, it's not." I continue the massage, unperturbed, and try to think of other options that might have set her off. "Is it Tytus? Did he say something?"

"Maybe," she whispers, but again, I taste the lie. With each question I ask, though, she's closer to telling me the truth, whether she realizes it or not.

"Maybe it's your powers?"

The muscles under my hands tense. "It's got nothing to do with that."

Bingo.

I stop the massage, and turn her to face me again. Elle tries to avoid my look, but I cup her cheek to stop her movements. "It's got everything to do with that. What's the story, love?"

"It's..." She bites her lip, hesitating. And just as she opens her mouth to speak, my cell rings. Her eyes shutter, glancing at the blasted thing.

"I'm not going to get it. What were you saying?"

It's already a lost cause. Elle's looking away, and moving off my lap. "Answer it. You can't keep ignoring your alpha's call."

More frustrated than ever, I pick up. Only it's not Lucas, but Tytus' name flashing on the screen. I debate on ignoring the call, forcing Elle to talk to me instead, but something tells me to take it. So I do.

"Yeah?"

"Get to Dominic's house. Now. Something's happening."

∞ ∞ ∞

∞ Dóchas ∞

"<u>Hope</u> is a waking dream."

–Aristotle–

Finn

I pull up to Dom's house just as Tytus' Hummer parks. Exiting the car, I try to keep my expression schooled, but Tytus immediately narrows his eyes` on me.

Whatever he's about to say gets lost when we hear the sound of something crashing inside. A few steps later, we're both in front of the house.

"What's going on?" I ask him.

His stormy gaze is focused on the bungalow, head tilted to the side as if listening for something. "Be ready to back me up with your friend. He's not going to like this."

I follow him to Dom's door and he knocks on it. After a few minutes, Dom opens it. He looks like shit – bloodshot eyes, hair a mess, unshaved and stinking of alcohol.

"What do you want?"

He sounds angry, but what I really taste around him is a frightening desperation. His blue eyes, once so startling, are dull and lifeless. Whatever joy had been in him, it's now gone, replaced by hatred and bitterness. Those, I feel them in troves around him.

"You shouldn't have been left alone, buddy," I say. "Not after..." We'd tried to give him space, especially after his fight with Lucas, but we were so, so wrong.

"After my mate died, you mean?"

Tytus interrupts. "I need to see Lucrezia."

Dom glares at him. "No." He goes to close the door, but Tytus moves his foot to block it.

"Listen to me, fool. Something's going on here, and it has to do with her body! So let me see her."

Dom wavers, and I admire Tytus for not shoving him aside and stomping his way in, as he's used to – as he could do. It's yet another mark of the respect he had for Lucrezia that he's willing to take her mate's emotions into account.

"Let him in, Dom." My plea seems to get through. He shifts out of the way, and walks into the living room. A half-drunk bottle with a crystal liquid awaits him on the table, and he takes a huge gulp out of it.

Tytus ignores him, eyes narrowed on the bedroom. From the entrance, I can see Lucrezia's body laid out on the bed, still in the clothes she died in. Tytus is moving as if expecting an ambush, so I leave whatever this is to him, and turn my focus to Dominic.

"Have you... thought about funeral arrangements?" It can't be healthy having her cold body here, but at the same time, I realize his need to do so.

Dom shakes his head. Then his entire body shudders, and he reaches for the back of the couch, fingers white–knuckled as though he's using all the force he has to stay upright. Something wet drips on his hands, and I look at him to notice silent tears falling down his face. An inhuman sound escapes his throat, and rips through me.

His arms start shaking, and still he's clenching the damn couch as though alone it could give him the strength to withstand the avalanche of emotions in him. What I taste in the air around him – so close – makes the hair on my skin stand to attention.

This is not the strong beta I've come to know. He's a wolf who just lost the only meaning in his existence – his mate. There is nothing keeping him tied here, or to anyone.

I move to his side, placing an arm over his shoulder. I hope I'll be able to take at least some of this pain away, but the minute I try, Dom looks up.

Eyes glassy, he lets out a hoarse whimper. "Don't. It's the only thing I've got left of her... And it's better than the void."

I only squeeze his shoulder in understanding.

Tytus' exclamation in some foreign language makes us both jump. Dom wipes at his face, then he's running to the bedroom, glaring at him. "What did you *do*!"

Tytus is pale, his grey eyes almost transparent with shock. "Something I didn't realize was still possible."

Before Dom pummels him into the wall, I step between them. "Don't. Let's talk about this like adults."

I didn't need to worry, because Dom stops breathing. He's staring at the wall as though not seeing it, eyes blinking repeatedly. Then his nose lifts in the air, sniffing...

"Ty? Dom? What are you doing?"

We all freeze, and turn in shock to the bed. Lucrezia's struggling to a sitting position, holding onto her head like she's fighting a migraine. The pallor I'd noticed from afar is gone, and instead she's...alive.

Dom moves from my grip, staring at the bed as if entranced by her. Realizing the room is too silent, Lucrezia looks up at us. "Why do you all look like you've seen a ghost?"

In our continued silence, her eyes fall on Dom, and she frowns. "And why are you such a mess?"

He's close to the bed now, and as if all strength has left him, he drops to his knees. Grasping her hand, he bends his head over it and murmurs in Romanian, as if in prayer.

Luz glances at us. Tytus manages a small, "I need air," and leaves the room. I'm in too much shock to do anything other than observe.

Then Lucrezia focuses her attention on Dom, and she runs her free hand through his messy hair. "Dom, talk to me. What happened?"

His body breaks into sobs, heart wrenching and body wrecking, and it's too much to witness. I tiptoe away, leaving them to their moment.

Elisandra

After Finn takes off, it doesn't take her long to show up.

He's already bored of you, huh?

I stare at the ceiling, unwilling to give her the attention she seeks. Ignorance is never bliss though, as she insists.

Come now, that's more than a couple times he leaves in the middle of the night!

"His pack needs him," I mutter.

Sure they do. And you're all good with that?

"Yeah, because I'm not psycho." *Not like you.*

She laughs at that, and suddenly I don't have my hand anymore. She's ordering it around, swishing runes in the air and I panic. The walls rattle as I try to get ahold of whatever she's trying to release, getting weaker by the minute.

Then there's a knock on the door, and I'm snapped out of my darkness. She retreats to the back, as though spooked by whoever's coming in. Panting, I drag myself to Finn's living room and open the front door.

Dani breaks away from Tristan's embrace, her eyes taking me in. "That was you with the magic?"

"Um..." I glance at her boyfriend, and Tristan smiles.

"I don't bite, beleza. We're about to head to Dom's, Finn called us. Couldn't reach Lucas, so he told us to come pick you up, too."

"Protection, and all," Dani adds. "But it doesn't look like you'll need it."

Her speculative looks makes me uneasy, and I shake my head. "I'm okay to wait here."

"Not a good idea, given the Reapers."

"I don't have house keys."

Dani smirks. "Finn's place is in the middle of nowhere. Doubt anyone will try to break in."

With a sigh, I grab one of Finn's sweaters off the clothes rack, slip it on, and step out of the house. "Fine. But if they do, you can explain to him what's what."

Tristan's massive SUV fits us in without a hitch, and then we're back on the road. Dani turns in the passenger seat to look at me. "So in the time you were with Tytus, did he not teach you how to control your magic?"

I look away. "It's not the magic I need to control. It's the other one, inside me."

Tristan's eyes snap to mine in the rearview mirror, and he frowns. "The what, now?"

"Apparently, as a female zmeu, if I don't learn to control my powers from when I'm young, they eat me up from the inside. Luckily, I don't have full zmeu powers, but what I do have was enough that my human mind couldn't cope with it. So it split, and there's an alter inside my head that occasionally gets control over my body. That's why I went after Cade."

"Told you she didn't go after them alone," Tristan throws to Dani.

She doesn't say anything at first, as though choosing her words. I wish I had Finn's extrasensory perceptions so I could figure out what she's thinking.

"And does this alter know how to use the magic?"

"Unfortunately."

She taps her chin. "Then technically once she and you become one, you'd have all her knowledge, too."

"One would suppose."

"You don't sound too excited by the prospect," Tristan points out.

"I..." A sigh escapes me. I don't, it's true. Have to admit as much to myself. But how could I, faced with the possibility of losing who I am?

"You're afraid of who you'll become," Dani says, a wistful tone in her voice.

I snap my gaze to hers, mouth gaping. "Can you read thoughts like Finn, too?"

She laughs. "No, I wish! It's because I had much the same identity crisis, not too long ago."

Tristan reaches over the space between them and takes her hand in his, squeezing it. The gesture is sweet, supportive and I have a feeling it means a hell of a lot more than what I can guess.

Then Dani says, "When the witch, Fiona, forced these magical powers onto my pack, I didn't want them. I didn't know who I was anymore. Was I a witch, or a wolf? When I first met Tytus, he called me wolf–witch – I hated him for it. But then he explained to me that I had to reconcile both aspects, otherwise I would never truly be me."

"And did you?"

"In a way, *sim*. I learned to use my magic when I had to, my wolf otherwise. It's all useful in battle, but outside of it, I'm still a bit of a mess." Her gaze softens on Tristan. "He helps me through most of it."

"As you do with my nightmares, querida," he grins and kisses her open palm.

A moment later, we're pulling in front of a bungalow. The door opens and out steps Finn, followed by Tytus. Their somber expressions cause a deafening silence to settle on us.

Finn

I'm glad Tristan and Dani brought her over, but I don't know how much more craziness I'm ready to dump on Elle. At least not without finishing the conversation we didn't get a chance to.

So I rush to the backseat door and open it, tugging her into my arms. Elle sighs and reaches out to kiss me, whispering, "I'm sorry for earlier."

"And I, love." I search her eyes, seeing those same haunted shadows in their depths. The air around her is not quite clear, either. Everyone's feeling so many things, including me, that I'm having a hard time pinpointing Elle's emotions.

"What's going on, Tytus?" Dani asks.

I glance over at him and nod, then pull Elle to the side. With each step away, the air becomes more clear, and I can read her better. Curiosity sparks the air around her, but I need her focus on something else.

"Why aren't we with them? What's going on?"

I meet her gaze then, cupping her cheeks. "First off, what happened this morning?"

Her eyes cloud. "Is that really so important?"

"You're the most important thing here, regardless of what else is going on. So, aye."

She still won't meet my gaze, and dread grows thick and heavy in the air between us. "Was it her?"

Elle looks at me then, and I know. "She made you do something."

She nods. "I woke up, and she was able to conjure magic in my hands. Threatened to throw it on the bed – burning you – if I didn't do as she said."

"And what was that?"

"To talk… About me leaving you, the pack, and going to Declan."

I try to keep a rein on my temper. How can I help Elle, if I'm fighting the invisible?

Then Dani squeals, and Tristan gasps loudly, and the moment is broken. "Luz!" They rush inside the house, and I let Elle join Tytus.

Face impassable, he says, "Lucrezia is alive."

Elisandra

I glance between Finn and Tytus, trying to understand. "What do you mean she's alive? How is this possible?"

Tytus speaks, though each sentence is halting, as if he's half-talking to himself, and trying to make sense of the mess. "It's not... I'm not very clear on it, either."

Elle arches an eyebrow his way. "You must know something, you just told Tristan and Dani!"

"I'll tell you what I told them. When I first met Lucrezia, she ran into a pack of rogue Reapers in the city. I protected her, warned them off... It was an instinctual thing, I didn't think anything of it. But she always calmed me down, always spoke to me... Loyalty begets loyalty, and I would have laid down my life for her, but I was too late when she died."

His gaze meets mine. "But you were there. My direct descendant, my blood link. And you were hurt. She was hurt." He shakes his head in amazement. "When your blood mixed..."

"But it was only a drop!"

Tytus shrugs. "It was enough."

I'm no longer so sure I want to know the answer, but I ask nonetheless. "So... What happened when our blood mixed?"

"The protection was sealed. The process was started when I saved her from the Reapers, and finally circled to its ultimate ending when she died. Luz became a member of my zmeu tribe from the moment I put my own safety in jeopardy to protect her, without even knowing who she was. This meant she was entitled to protection of her body *and* soul. It's... an ancient, ancient rule of my kind. Zmei live and exist to protect each other, and if one of us dies, the soul may still be salvaged and put into another body. It's... what would have happened to Declan, had he been worthy."

"I don't get it. The zmei, then... Why did this kind of protection not work on the rest of your race?"

"Because their souls were destroyed alongside their bodies. A zmeu's natural form is as a human, meaning if that is destroyed, then everything is gone." He shakes his head. "I know it's a lot to take in, but since Lucrezia's body was not fully destroyed, her soul was only displaced – kicked out of her body. But it remained in the abyss, disconnected. And it took my coming here to awaken her – to form the connection. To pull her back."

I stare between him and Finn. "Are you saying Lucrezia's alive because you threw some protection over her, without even knowing you were doing it?"

Tytus hesitates, then nods.

"That's amazing!" I try to push past him. "Can I see her?"

Finn grasps my arm. "No, wait. There's more."

"How can there be more?"

"Tell her the rest, Tytus."

"I saw what happened in the fight, that high you felt... That's you reaching your zmeu potential. You need to accept your full self now, there's no more delaying."

"I already have."

Liar.

It's like Finn's agreeing with her, when I look at him. He doesn't believe me and, worse, he appears hurt by my lie. Our recent conversation is heavy in the air between us, causing Tytus to frown.

"Elisandra, there is no choice left. What Ileana warned you about, what I did, it's coming closer now, especially since you have wrapped up the *legătură* between you two, and started heading towards the *împerecheare* stage."

"The joining..." Finn whispers, and narrows his eyes. "We're not fully mated, then?"

Tytus snorts. "You wish, but no. It is not something that happens overnight, or through one very good romp in the sack." Dismissing Finn, he focuses that stormy gaze on me again. "Elisandra, you must to start using the magic – I can show you how. The more you do, the less control she'll have and –"

"I'm not the topic here. Lucrezia is." His words have sparked panic in me. *Does this mean I really would have to burn Finn?* I choose to focus away from that, and on my friend instead. "And she's *alive*!"

Finn's stare is heavy on me, then he catches on and helps me redirect the conversation. "Unless this is temporary?"

My ancestor shakes his head. "It's permanent, I swear it. Magic as old as time, from the beginning of my clan's history. She will be fine. In so far as her human status, however, it may not be exactly true that she's fully normal."

"What do you mean?" I ask. A part of me wishes she's been endowed with these powers I have, so I won't feel so alone.

Tytus breaks that hope with his next words. "She'll always be able to call on me, for one. The connection between us, it entitles her to my protection until she – or I – are no more. And fire will no longer harm her... She may even be able to protect herself with it."

"So she'll be a witch?" Finn asks.

"Not...quite." Tytus glances towards the house. "She'll be a Solomonar."

"A *what*?" The word alone makes me shiver.

Tytus grins. "It's a type of witch who can ride a zmeu, and control weather. They used to only exist in Romania, recruited by zmei from the common folk and taught to use magic. Then, those that succeeded were permitted to ride my kind – to win battles."

"So how did all the zmei die then, if they owned the sky and had witches protecting them?"

Tytus sighs. "A longer story for another day.... But the short answer is our own greed. Humans fear of the unknown led to an inquisition that killed all the Solomonari, and fights with encroaching dragon clans, as well as human persecution, were our downfall."

He really has a gift for summarizing eons of history into a few sentences. It takes me a hell of a lot more than a moment to absorb all that, and silence lengthens between us.

Then Finn snorts. "Lucrezia's going to love this."

"Dominic may not." Tytus looks at me. "I trust you can explain this to him, as I need time to...process it all."

I shake my head, still at a loss on everything that happened. But even as Tytus turns to leave, we have yet another surprise waiting for us. The white–haired witch of the Reapers appears seemingly out of nowhere, soaked with rain and in torn clothes.

Considering the last time me and Finn saw her, she was on the púca, it's a shock to both of us. But we don't get a chance to ask her what she's doing back here.

Teeth chattering, Fiona says, "You have to...stop them. They're raising...Declan..." With a rather dramatic swoon, she falls into Tytus' arms.

CHAPTER FIFTEEN

∞ **Briste** ∞

"The chains of habit are generally too small to be felt until they are too strong to be <u>broken</u>."

–Samuel Johnson–

Elisandra

Tytus couldn't look more shocked if he tried. With Fiona fallen into his arms, he freezes like he doesn't know what to do. Finn sounds like he's trying to stifle a laugh.

The moment after seemingly warring with himself, Tytus bends and scoops her up completely in his arms, then turns to Dom's house once more.

"A little help? She's no feather."

Granted, Fiona's a bit on the curvy side, but considering my ancestor's gigantic size, I wouldn't have pegged him for someone who complains. *Wow, he must really have a bone to pick with her.*

Finn touches the side of my hand, then sprints ahead to open the door. By the time I jump out of my thoughts and follow, they've got Fiona installed on Dom's couch, and are whispering by the kitchen, casting furtive glances to her.

She's interesting. Go closer.

Of course she picks this moment to pop up. *No,* I say in my head. *And this isn't the time for it.*

Why not? Finn was right. So was Tytus. You haven't done anything you promised them.

Would you quit lecturing me?

I'll stop if you go nearer her.

Why?

Just do it.

More out of wanting her to shut up than anything else, I head towards Fiona. It's only once I get closer that I realize Finn and Tytus have bound her hands in thick rope – glowing, thick rope.

Must be a spell so she can't use her magic.

They're afraid, she whispers in my ear.

With good reason. She's the one who gave the Reapers so much power.

And what's so horrible about that?

I ignore her taunts, instead checking out the witch. Her white hair is streaked with more mud than violet, and her face is gaunt, making her cheekbones stand out more. Olive skin that's tanned, long fingers.... When I glance back at her, those insane violet eyes are open and watching me.

We stare at each other for a beat, and I check her hands to make sure the spell is still in effect.

"Your ancestor made sure I cannot use my magic," she says in a whisper. "But it won't stop what's coming. It's too late for that."

Stunned by the veracity of her words, I head to the kitchen. On the way there, I glance towards the closed bedroom door – Dani and Tristan come out looking stunned, and I catch a glimpse of red hair behind them as Luz shuts the door again.

The only one missing from our merry band is Lucas. Biting my lip, I reach Finn and Tytus. "Did anyone call Lucas?"

Tytus glances at the closed bedroom door. "Not a good idea to have the hothead here. He'll more than likely try and use the witch to trade with Cade, so he can keep his precious peace."

Something about the steel in his voice warns me I don't want the answer, but I ask nonetheless. "And what do you plan to do with her?"

Tytus doesn't even blink. "Kill her, of course."

Finn

Elle's surprise coats the air around me – and she's not the only one. Thing is, I get Tytus' stance, and would fully support it if not for a wee bit of an issue: he's not my alpha.

Dani folds her arms across her chest. "Isn't that a tad harsh?"

"Harsh?" Tytus' features turn to marble. "She gave the Reapers powers. She forced magic upon you and your pack, too. Magic that drove your brother out of his mind, and caused you to lose everything you once held dear." He stops for a heavy pause. "Is that not enough reason?"

Dani's amber eyes flash. "No, it's not! Fiona's a victim, much as I was. And she's only gotten passed around from Thiago to Cade, without mercy."

Tytus sneers. "Really? Was it not you who freed her last time? And yet she still ends up in the hands of the enemy. A bit convenient, if you ask me."

Tristan intervenes, taking a step to block Dani. I don't know which of them he's trying to keep away from the other, given both their emotions are out of control. "Come on, Tytus, you know as well as we do the Reapers were waiting for Fiona. They captured her before she had a chance to escape."

Elle glances at me, begging with her eyes not to say anything, but I can't let this unravel without full disclosure. Still, I have to try. "We should not be having this conversation without Lucas here," I say.

Tristan arches an eyebrow. "Do you really think it's a good idea, given last time?"

"Last time?" Tytus frowns.

"Lucas and Dominic, er, after Lucrezia died, or we thought she did, they went at it."

"Destroyed Lucas' house," Dani mutters. "He's been pretty quiet since."

I stare at her and Tristan. "Have either of you seen him since?"

They shrug, and Tristan says, "I did once and he kicked me out. Didn't want help cleaning up, and seemed to be halfway between a mood and drunk out of his mind. Thought I'd give him some time before I head back."

"We don't have a few days," Tytus growls. "In the absence of the alpha, the beta can make the call."

"And the beta is stuck in personal drama," I point out, "so we can give him a minute. There's no rush to this."

Tytus narrows his eyes on me. "You cannot stand in my way, faoladh. I will get this witch to tell me everything she wants, prove she's here a spy, and then get rid of her."

He makes a move, but I side-step him, tossing my chin up. "Fiona isn't here as a spy."

"And how do you know that?"

"Because, me and Elle released her not so long ago. I used the favor the púca owed me and sent her out of here. Why would she return on her own, when she could have gotten free?"

That seems to mollify him – but it's too late.

Elle's anger rises like a tidal wave, and I try to reach for her hand. Angry at me disclosing what we did, she pulls it out of my grip. "How about we ask her, then? Rather than make all these assumptions?"

Elisandra

Ignoring their wide eyes, I stride to Fiona and cock my hip to the side. "Well? Are you a spy?"

She opens her eyes and blinks as though something's hurting her vision. Her violet eyes fall on me, so unnerving. Then she pulls herself to a sitting position on the couch, and looks at the rest of the gang.

Between the three guys each more intimidating than the last, I'm not surprised when she pales even more. But her voice is firm, without a trace of fear when she speaks. "I am no spy. And I did not intend harm to any of you, though I was forced to do so."

Her gaze falls to her hands, and she goes quiet. Not for the first time, seeing her so bedraggled, I wonder what the hell she had to endure at Thiago and Cade's hands. Whatever it was didn't break her, because there's a strong resilience that still lingers in her eyes.

Finn seems to pick up on that as well and kneels in front of her, forcing her chin up. A jolt of white hot jealousy goes through me as he touches her, but I stifle it down.

"Hear me when I speak, because I will not hesitate to let the zmeu have his way with you – killing you. That is what he wishes. If possible, I would like to spare you."

"There is no sparing me, not after what I have done."

A lone tear falls down her cheek, and Finn wipes it away with his thumb. Fiona inhales sharply, like she hasn't been used to kindness in a while. My heart goes out to her, at the same time as my inner bitch surfaces.

You're going to let him touch her like that?

Shut up.

He's your wolf, isn't he?

Finn glances over his shoulder at me, frowning. He feels her. Again. A wave of shame floods me at my irrational behavior, at being unable to keep her at bay, and I look away from his gaze. He turns to Fiona and says, "Are you here of your own volition?"

She nods. "Yes."

"And are you here to hurt us or help us?"

"Help."

He nods and stands, turning to Tytus. "You cannot kill her, not unless Lucas decides it. Especially not when she's willing to help us."

Tytus sneers, and glowers at her. "And how do you plan to help?"

"I know where the Reapers are trying to break out Declan from his prison."

Her declaration causes another jolt to run through everyone. Finn and Tytus immediately start arguing over what to do, while Dani heads to the Dom's bedroom and Tristan tries to keep them from going at each other's throats.

The conversation fades to a muted whisper in my ears. It's another's voice I'm hearing... The same one from the battle, and my dream.

Come to me, little one...

I glance up, looking around. No one noticed I dazed out. Except for her – the violet eyes are glittering on me with something akin to pity.

Something pulls me to this witch. It's only too late I realize the chaos surrounding her mirrors my own. When those violet eyes meet mine, it's like she can see right through me. With Tytus and Finn arguing in the background, and Dom and Luz not yet emerging from the room, she motions for me to come near her.

"Don't give in to it," she whispers.

"Give in to what?"

"His call."

I've no idea what she means, but I want to understand.

Then Finn is there, pulling me away. "Keep your distance until we know why she's really here."

I yank my arm out of his grasp. "I can think for myself."

He narrows his eyes. "Really? When you refuse to listen to reason? You'll have to excuse me for not believing you."

"I'm not some hopeless case you can fix!" The rage suffusing my voice isn't normal, and I feel it as much as he does.

Rather than back away, Finn tries to get closer, reaching for my arms. I backtrack from him, shaking my head. "Don't touch me right now."

"Let's not do this here, mo grá."

"*Stop* calling me that! I'm not your love, I'm not even your damned mate!"

Finn frowns, taking a step closer to me, hands facing upwards. "That's not true. You heard what Tytus said, we've already started the process. Let's talk about this, Elle. Stay with me."

I want to calm down, I really do. But she's been pushing at the back of my head, and coupled with my anger, it quickly results in something going loose inside me.

One moment, I'm shaking my head, telling Finn to stay away – the next, she's front and center, tossing the hair back over our shoulder. "For the record, baby, this is the perfect time to do this." Our gaze sweeps the room, stopping on Tytus' glare. "And this party kinda sucks."

"Bring Elle back," Finn growls. He seems calm on the outside, but his eyes give away his desperation. Locked inside my own head, my heart gives way for the hurt I'm causing him.

But *she* only sneers. "Not likely. You think that just because you've started mating her, it's going to mean anything? No, no, dearie. I've got other plans for us."

She whirls around, but Finn rushes to stop her from moving. "Where are you going?"

"Away from you."

Finn tries to reach for us again, but she draws a rune so quick in the air he has no way to stop it and gets blasted backwards.

Stop it! I don't want to hurt him!

Shut up, weakling. I'm doing what's best for us.

One last sweep of the living room shows the shocked expressions of everyone we leave behind, including Tytus, who looks ready to strangle us. Not that she cares.

Instead, she makes *my* body march through the door, draws another rune in the air, and we disappear.

Finn

Feckin' hell!

I get up from the ground and run a hand through my hair, turning to the witch. "What the hell did you say to her?"

Fiona shakes her head. "It's not my fault. I told her not to give in to the call."

"To *whose* call!?"

Tytus steps between us, stopping me from throttling her. He also answers my question. "My brother, Declan. I felt it, too." His gaze is speculative on the witch. "You did, as well."

"As did your great-granddaughter." To my surprise, Fiona doesn't stop there. Instead, she drops to her knees, bowing her head to Tytus. "Declan has arisen, zmeu. I have been his to control for too long, and wish nothing more than to break that link. Let me help, and make up for all the wrongs I have been forced to commit."

Tytus stares at her a moment longer, and I taste his eagerness in the air. Finally, he seems to make up his mind. "Very well." He meets my gaze. "This is beyond your abilities, wolf. I and the witch will handle Declan."

"Like hell you will alone!"

His expression grows dangerous. "Do not think that because you are Elle's chosen mate, you can outmatch Declan. I know my brother, and he will only take one bite out of you."

"You don't understand." I step closer, lowering my voice. "I need to be involved. If anything happens to Elle–"

Tytus bares his teeth. "Nothing will happen to her on my watch. Now step aside, and let me handle this."

"You can't," I say, but he pushes me out of the way. Some of his zmeu strength is seeping into his human form, which means he's ready to morph.

He glances over his shoulder at Fiona, and she stands up, nodding. Her resignation fills the air, and the ropes fall away from her hands.

As they walk away, I yell at his back, "You know she's expecting to die!"

Tytus looks down at Fiona, his gaze inscrutable. "Whatever price is required, she'll pay willingly."

I run out the door to stop them again, but they're already gone. Only a faint wind is left behind, enough for me to know they took the aerial route rather than magic, as Elle had.

I run a hand through my hair, leaning against the wall. Lucas is going to have our hide over this – mine especially. The door to the bedroom opens and Luz emerges, dragging a subdued Dom behind her, with Dani and Tristan following.

"What's with all the shouting?" Luz's gaze sweeps the empty living room. "Where's Tytus?"

Sighing, I run them through everything.

Luz walks to me when I'm done and hugs me. It's still a shock to my system to see her up and about, as if she survived nothing more than a scratch. Her hug is warm, and it's definitely all Luz.

A bloody miracle.

"We'll get her back," she whispers against my chest, then turns to everyone else. "So, do any of you know how I'm supposed to tap into my so-called new powers?"

Heads shake all around, except for Dom. He's still staring at Luz through bleary eyes, as if expecting her to vanish. Noticing this, she goes back to him and interlaces their fingers.

My heart clenches, already feeling the pain of being away from Elle. "If we don't know where they all went, there's only one other thing to do."

"What's that?" Dani asks.

"We need to get Lucas... Set up perimeters around town. We've been out of touch for days, and the town is probably overrun by the Reapers."

I glance at Dom, waiting to see if he'll stop Luz. When he doesn't, Tristan says, "Only one problem with that, Red."

"What's that?"

"Lucas and Dom, they don't exactly see eye to eye anymore."

She rolls her eyes, and squeezes her mate's hand further. "We'll see about that. Can you bring him over?"

Tristan takes off, but Dani sticks behind. "I may have an idea for trying to track Tytus... But I'm not sure how valid it is."

"What is it?"

Dani points to the ropes the witch left behind. "Think you could pick up her scent, Finn? Her emotions, I mean?"

I shrug. "Golden retriever, I am not. But I'm willing to give it a shot."

"So don't waste time," Luz adds. "I'll wait here for Lucas. Should be able to handle him and Dom, with Tristan's help."

Dani nods, and the minute after we're both morphing. Grabbing the ropes in my mouth, I follow her out the door and into the forest beyond.

Elisandra

We emerge somewhere – some part of the mountains where the moon shines brightly. She makes us walk a good ten minutes, then the dense trees part to showcase a crater, with wolves on the edge. The darker one – Cade – looks too damn pleased with himself.

My feet step on a branch, and the sound of it breaking into two grabs the wolves' attention. Cade is the first to turn. His eyes glitter oddly in the moonlight – or maybe it's the magic he can now wield.

Either way, when he notices me, I see recognition in his eyes. So does she.

"Nice party of furballs," she says. "Can I join?"

Growls answer from the pack of Reapers – and holy shit, there's a lot of them. *Has he been turning more people, in order to fill the ranks of those that were killed in the last battle?* The thought makes my skin crawl, but not hers.

Cade walks towards us, head tilted to his side. When he's close enough, he takes one whiff, then glances to his wolves. They part at his command, revealing the man in their midst.

He's completely naked, but holds himself with the composure of a king. Hair light as corn, a body built of muscle, he's Adonis personified. A small growl of satisfaction purrs from my throat – her doing.

As if hearing it, the man turns little by little, giving us time to take him all in.

His eyes, when they meet our gaze, are an unreal shade of golden, like someone took pieces of molten gold and crafted them for him alone. The smirk on his face is cold, and his voice is deep and vibrating. "Darling, I thought I'd have to hunt you down."

My alter shrugs. "Well, we're here."

He arches an eyebrow. "*We?*"

She stares at him, and the smirks widens. "Ah, I see." He holds a hand out to us. "This... Is a welcome surprise. Come join me, draga mea."

And without me being able to do anything to stop it, I watch as my hand is gripped into his much larger one. Fiona's warning rings in my head, but it's too late to do anything about it.

The previous anger fuelling me is gone, replaced by a growing dread. My alter's eagerness overlaps it, and I wonder how long it will take her to fully claim me, now that I'm at her complete mercy.

∞ ∞ ∞

∞ Créachtaithe ∞

"A <u>wounded</u> deer leaps highest."

–Emily Dickinson–

Elisandra

"You're... Declan." My mouth is dry, and she seems to have eased up at the back. Or maybe I took control. Either way, my hand is still in Declan's and he's looking at me like I'm the most curious thing he has come across.

"Guilty as charged." The grin is blinding in the moonlight, but it doesn't warm up his eyes. Nothing could, my heart tells me.

"What... Why did you call me here?"

Declan tilts his head to the side. Again, that feeling like he's a cat and I'm its prey. "Why did you come?"

I can't answer that, so I don't. Instead, I take in the crater, his still naked self – a blush creeps on my cheeks – and the Reapers around. For the second time, I notice their eyes, much like Cade's. I'd originally thought it was the moon reflecting on them, but no – it's something else. Their stillness clues me in. They're *too* obedient.

"What did you do to them?"

Declan shrugs. "The fools thought that because they brought me back, it meant I was indebted to them."

"What did they want with you? Why raise... All this?' I gesture to the crater, at a loss for words.

"Because humans are greedy." Declan stretches again, and then in a wash of runes, he's wearing some loose breeches like I've seen in medieval TV shows, and a shirt that comes to his elbows. He remains bare feet, which on another man would have looked hot as sin. On Declan, it's plain dangerous.

"Besides which," he adds, "their greed has suited me nicely. It feels good being back after so long imprisoned."

I can only stare at Declan, mesmerized by the power emanating off him. Part of it is her fascination, but I can't deny there's a big portion that also comes from me. Here stands another ancestor of mine, as different from Tytus as day and night are. It's a chance to learn, maybe, or at least find out more about everything that being *me* entails.

A deep breath, and I try to speak. "Tytus said..."

"My brother is here?" His eyes narrow, and a change goes over his features. They contort in rage, and in two fell swoops he's in my face, grabbing me by the throat. "*Where* is he?"

Panic flares through me, but I keep my mouth shut. His eyes narrow even further and he says, "You are not the one. I want *her* back."

His touch on my skin burns a second, then she's back front and centre, grinning at him. "Me, lover?"

Declan eases then, letting go of our neck. "Perfect. Now do me a favor and *stay* here."

"She keeps trying to take control. Damn morals."

"Then don't let her." Even my alter knows not to reply anything to that tone. "Now, where is my brother?"

"Some house in the woods, last I saw him. He's surrounded by wolves and the witch who brought you back. And, unless I'm mistaken, he planned to come looking for you."

Declan smirks at that, flexing his fists. "Let him try."

His gaze drifts around the surroundings, on the forest, and he closes his eyes as if sensing something. It oddly reminds me of what happened to Tytus in the car – the vision, he called it.

When Declan opens his eyes, I see the remnants of white leave his gaze. His dark glare settles on the wolves, and with a swoop of his hand they snap out of their obedient state.

"Go stop the mutts heading here. Their scent is on the wind, and I need my skies clear for what comes next."

Mutts? He must mean Lucas and the pack – and Finn! Despite my outburst, he's coming for me.

She relishes his words, taking a step closer to Declan. "And what's that?"

"The fight of a lifetime."

Finn

We're swerving in and off the scent. I don't know what's causing it, unless it's some weird magic, but it's hard to find a trail and stick to it. I pull to the side, motioning Dani to join me.

Panting in her wolf form, she meets my gaze with her amber one. *What is it?*

This is going nowhere. I haven't gotten anything more than the faintness of the witch's trace.

Dani shakes her head. *We have to keep trying, Finn. No way we're letting those bastardos get away with what they did, or Elle be taken. And Fiona's scent will lead us to them.*

My throat constricts, out of nowhere. Air is hard to take into my lungs. Dani panics, I can hear her whimpers, but there's nothing she can do. My vision blurs, my breathing nonexistent – then I'm released once more.

Panting, I get up on my feet, and I realize what it was. *Elle is in danger.*

How do you know that?

Because that – what I felt – was happening to her.

Dani's eyes widen. Before she stops me, I'm back on the run. I can't let anything happen to Elle – nothing, and no one, can stop me.

Elisandra

With the Reapers gone, it's quiet in the crater. Declan keeps pacing, but there's nothing stressed about it. More like he's eager for the fight coming to him. Then he stops, and an odd smile spreads on his lips.

"Always the dramatic entrance, brother," he whispers.

Slowly, his gaze goes up, up into the darkening clouds. Like an avenging warrior comes Tytus, in full zmeu form. I'm so stunned – as is my alter – by the ferocious look about him, it takes us a minute to realize he's got someone on his back.

He swoops in and I think he's only going to take one bite out of Declan. But then Declan rears his head back and turns into fire in front of my eyes.

There is no other way to explain it. Flames engulf him, burning away the human, and in its place is a massive dragon. Or what looks like a dragon, given what I've learned.

I'm left staring at not one, but two zmei. Unlike Tytus' red scales, Declan is all black. With a single push on his powerful back legs, he's in the air, stretching his wings and blowing a gust of wind towards Tytus.

He rears back, roaring and spitting fire. In so doing, he turns a little to the side and I see the most unexpected person riding him – Fiona. The witch looks like she's got a hard time clinging onto him. Tytus seems to notice as well and backs off Declan, trying to turn in an attempt – I'm guessing – to drop her closer to the ground.

But Declan's on his tail, reaching with his talons and blocking his escape. His head bumps Tytus in the chest, and they clash in the sky. Declan swipes at Tytus as a cat would, and blood whooshes in the air, falling like rain droplets in front of me. Unable to decide, unable to move, I can only stare as Declan then digs his claws into Tytus' thigh – he roars in agony.

Fiona turns on Tytus' back, gathering magic. My own hands lift up of their own accord. No, not their own accord. *She's* controlling them, trying to retaliate before the witch can hurt Declan. But I can't let her.

It's bad enough she made me turn my back on Finn and the others. Bad enough I haven't been able to get rid of her, and all she's done is feed me to Declan on a silver platter.

I can't miss this chance to set things right. So I focus all my mental energy on taking control of my hands, visualizing the muscles, clenching them, trying to pry them from her control...

She growls aloud. "Let me go!"

No. Way. In. Hell.

By the time we're done struggling, it's too late. Fiona's taken aim, a crown of runes around her head. Bursts of magic shoot from them and hit Declan's muzzle, sending him toppling into a downward spiral.

He doesn't fall, though. At the last possible moment, he rights himself up and beats his wings – away from us, disappearing into the clouds.

"Where the hell is he going?"

I'm hoping he's forgotten all about us.

But, no. Declan only meant to show exactly who we're dealing with. As Tytus swoops close to the ground, Fiona jumps off him and lands in the grass. My alter wants nothing more than to throttle her, but we're both searching the skies for Declan.

"No..."

Her pained moan draws both our attention. Fiona is clutching her head, as if in physical pain. Then I smell smoke.

I glance up to see a blaze in the distance – it's the town! *Declan's burned it.*

Bile rises up my throat, but *she* takes over again, and clears it. "Grow a pair, would you?" Then her gaze narrows on Fiona. "As for you..."

I force my feet to stay rooted in the ground, no matter how she tries to yank out of my mental grip. Then Declan's back, drawing her attention away from Fiona. Tytus roars up in the sky, and comes out of clouds with his talons pointed towards Declan's chest. They roll in the air, until they both land with the heaviest thud on the ground.

It sends me flying up in the air, and I land hard enough to rattle my teeth.

By the time I look up, Declan's going at Tytus, trying to nick him in the wings, but Tytus pulls out of way in time. Fiona's still crumpled on the ground, unable to help him as she moans in pain. The thought crosses my mind that she's somehow able to sense the agony of humans miles away, but then it's wiped away by *her*.

"Shut up about the damn witch already," she says with my voice, "and look at this majestic one."

In tune with her words, Tytus flies above Declan, and kicks out his back feet, hitting him in the line of his spine. This sends Declan spiralling again, and I'm afraid he's about to pull another disappearing act and burn the town some more.

Tytus is there though, blocking his exit. He roars a gust of fire in his brother's face, which gets blown away by wind. Seeing them go at each other, a clash of red and black scales, is straight out of a fantasy movie. Clouds gather round even more, turning the landscape black as if night was here. Talons, scales flying, flames thrown around – neither gives up, always coming back for more.

Seeing he can't win, Declan switches strategy mid–flight and pulls his worst move to date.

He feints to the side, and goes under Tytus, heading straight for Fiona – who's still on the ground, clenching her head in pain, and oblivious to the danger. Tytus roars his rage and ducks in the air after Declan. At the last possible moment, he grabs his brother by the tail, pulling him back.

Declan, however, is no fool – he curls his wings around his body, letting himself go with the pull. When he's a foot away, he unfurls the wings and digs his talons into Tytus' chest, then reaches out with one back leg and rips into his wing.

Tytus wrestles against him, and they're circling, falling, each clinging to the other – then Declan disengages, letting Tytus drop alone.

Like a bulldozer, he hits the ground with a velocity out of this world. For the second time, I go flying, only this time my alter is prepared for it and makes us land on our feet. Then she stands, smirking, and takes a few steps towards Tytus.

I sense her intent to hurt him and struggle against her hold, enough to make us pause in our steps and freeze. While we mentally fight for control, Tytus lifts himself up and drags his body to Fiona, placing his bulk in front of her.

It takes me a second to realize what he's doing – protecting her with his bulk, as though a last stand. But Declan is still in the sky, circling above us, which means there's only one threat he's trying to protect her from – me.

I told you so, she says smugly. *You were only good until he found someone way better, stupid one.*

"You're a liar," I whisper, my words carrying across.

Tytus, breathing heavily, looks up. His stormy grey eyes land on me with all the warmth of the North Pole, and I shiver. Only then do I realize my hands had been raised this entire time, as though ready to attack him.

I drop them by my side, shaking. I want to tell him I'm sorry, that I –

Grow a pair already, would you? You've picked a side, now it's time to stick with it.

As though hearing her, Declan touches ground by my side. In comparison to Tytus' fumble, his landing is as gracious as a swan's. When I try to take a step towards Tytus, he drops one wing in front of me, effectively blocking me from doing so.

My gaze lands on Tytus again. On shaking knees, Fiona gets up and places her palm to his bleeding wing, which now covers her in a cocoon of protection. I realize she's trying to heal him as fast as she can, in anticipation of another fight.

One I'm not sure he'll survive.

Besides his torn wing, Tytus is a mess. Scales are missing all over his body, ripped away by Declan. Where they once provided protection, there are now only gashes and wounds, bleeding heavily and infusing the ground with his blood.

His eyes are half-mast, as though he's having a hard time standing up. My trembling intensifies, afraid for him – afraid of what else Declan will do.

A line of fire shoots out, and I look up at Declan in surprise. He's burning the ground between Tytus and us, barring him from moving further. Declan stares at his brother for a beat. Then he moves closer to me, nudging me with his head.

"I'm not—" She cuts me off, taking over me swifter than I thought possible. "Lead the way, handsome."

The second after, we're back in the air, leaving the world I've always known behind. I keep hoping someone will follow, yearning for that elusive rescue, but no one does.

Not even Tytus.

Finn

As we run through the woods, the air changes. Smoke fills it, and me and Dani stop to sniff it properly. *It smells like...*

Charred flesh, Dani finishes.

Declan?

Must be.

We pick up speed, hoping to get to them before he does anything major. When we get closer to the scent, wolves pop out of the woods.

Just feckin' amazing, their timing!

That looks like the entire Reaper clan, Dani says, and steps closer to me. *Got a plan?*

Elle and Tytus are past these bastards, you know it as well as I. Declan must have sent them to stop us.

She throws me a nervous glance. *But we don't have the force to fight them off, Finn.*

We do if you use your magic.

Dani hesitates. She's been hinting at this for a while, to get her skills more and more used, but even she must know this is a suicide mission. My desperation makes me reckless. I'll risk anything – any*one* – if it means I can get to Elle before it's too late.

She senses this, and nods. *I know what I'm getting into with this and risking, but be warned. If I end up dead, Tristan will kill you.*

Noted, I say dryly.

As she morphs to human, the wolves attack. Dani ducks one attack, blasts another with a rune, and whistles as she straightens up. I catch the sound of leaves moving fast – then ravens pop out of the woods, spreading like a swarm over the Reapers.

The birds listen to her because of her magic, but I know it's taking her concentration to keep them bound to her will *and* use magic. So I focus my efforts on watching her back, while at the same time trying to force a path through the Reapers for us.

With the ravens blinding the Reapers – more than one loses an eye – and Dani's spells, I'm almost positive we can cut through. Then more wolves come out, this time led by Cade. He keeps himself in their midst, but it's hard to miss his dark glare.

Bollocks!

Truth is, we're outnumbered. And even with Dani using runes as fast as possible, there's no way we can get out of this without help.

Ask, and you shall receive.

The woods part and out comes a rusty colored wolf, followed by a very pissed–off looking dark grey one.

"*Finalmente!*" Dani breathes, and shifts back to wolf.

With Lucas and Tristan, it's not exactly a fair fight, but we manage. At least until Cade jumps out of the shadows, and takes control of the pack. *It's about damn time you paid for all the trouble you've caused me, don't you think?*

Lucas, who until now has done his utmost to preserve the peace in this town, growls. He slams a paw on the ground and the vibration shakes under all of us. Even Cade's wolves stop moving, tilting their heads to listen.

Then Lucas speaks, only not in our way. His mouth moves, and actual words come out of him. "Payment? Sure. Let's talk payment."

The second after, he's lunging in the air, toppling over Cade, his claws dug into his neck hard enough that they pull blood. "You have pushed my last buttons, trash. Now get the *fuck* off my territory."

This is... Reaper....territo––

He doesn't finish as Lucas presses heavier on his neck. "This. Is. *My*. Territory. All of it, including the pieces you think belong to you. Learn to recognize who you're speaking to, and get the fuck away before I tear you to shreds."

Cade scrambles away, but the minute Lucas turns his back one of the Reapers tries to catch him from behind. Lucas whirls with his paw up in the air and tears his throat off, not even blinking. Leaving the carcass behind, he resumes walking towards us.

"There is nothing for you here," he says with a glare to me. "Elle left with Declan."

That's not...possible.

Lucas doesn't answer, instead walks away. Dani follows him, seemingly in a shock over his display of power. When Tristan comes in front of me, it only takes me a second to realize it's definitely not surprise he's feeling – but anger.

It's possible, alright. We were on the edge of the woods and saw the fight. Tytus is hurt, and Elle was trying to help Declan. Maybe she has been all along. Either way, we need to go see Dom now. He gets closer to me, his muzzle an inch from mine, and bares his teeth. *And for the record, meu amigo, next time you put my mate in danger for the sake of your own, I'm going to have your hide.*

Dejected, I follow in his footsteps. And while Elle is predominantly on my mind, there's another thing that drags my attention more. *What the hell is going on with Lucas?*

Elisandra

At some point as we fly, I doze off, yet manage not to fall off Declan. I don't know how, really, it's almost like my body instinctively knows what to do. Either way, by the time the sun's rays poke through the clouds and blind me, we emerge into the world again....

And we're no longer in Rockland Creek, I'm pretty sure. The mountains are too high up, and too damn cold. I've seen this kind of landscape – in books, on TV, but never in real life. So I can't help my jaw dropping as we fly over majestics places.

"Is it okay for you to fly under the clouds now? Will no one see us?" Declan snorts, which I take it to mean *no*.

Much, much later, we swoop in between two mountains on a seemingly regular plateau. I dismount my zmeu, and stand there shivering in the coolness of the air.

When he shifts to human, Declan is naked once more, and seems completely unbothered by the cold.

"Would you put on some clothes?"

He throws me an amused look over his shoulder. "For your modesty, of course."

I look around as he dons another pair of old–school breeches and one of those fluid, creamy shirts. "Where are we?"

"My home. And yours, for that matter."

"What?" I take in the emptiness surrounding us, trying to make sense of it all.

Declan grins then, and he looks impossibly beautiful – and ruthless. The golden eyes shine with the thrill of being free, and he extends a hand to me, palm towards the sky. "Come here and touch my hand."

I wait for *her* to show up, but she's not in my head – yet. So when I follow his instructions, I do so freed from her influence, and fully aware I'm humoring the enemy. The minute our palms join, a pulsating beat releases, and the fog around us dissipates. From its misty depths, a castle is revealed, and my jaw drops.

If this were a fairytale, I still wouldn't believe the image in front of me. White walls, a pont–levis across clear water, mountains in the background, the glare of the sun on windows made out of crystal. Rainbows dance off them, adding a unique quality to the whole landscape. With two towers on each side, the place looks like Camelot – or some mythical kingdom not meant for this world.

"What the..."

"Welcome home, Elisandra. Your *real* home."

Declan struts across the bridge, while I'm still staring at the impossible building.

∞ ♦ ∞

It takes me a long time to snap out of my stupor – an hour, or close to. It's the chilly wind, more than anything, which forces me to move.

A cobblestone path leads to the pont–levis, but once I step on it and glance back, I notice the path disappears. Recalling the fog that had surrounded this place, I realize they probably hadn't meant it to be discovered by regular humans.

Whoever *they* are, that is.

My eyes take in the castle, which seems even more imposing the closer I get to it. Large oak doors painted white are open, handles made out of gold. I hesitate on the step, wondering whether to take it, or not.

A bit late for second–guessing yourself, no?

Her voice in my head draws out my hesitation. I've left my mate, all that I was used to, and come here... Why? *What's Declan's angle, bringing me here?*

"Step in, don't be shy."

Said the wolf to the sheep, I think to myself. She only laughs in my head, not offering any other help.

Gulping, I take a step closer, then another. I cross the threshold, and blink at the inside. So much light comes from the outside, dancing through the crystal windows into rainbows. It almost looks like there are disco balls everywhere.

The marble floors are dark, filled with the occasional golden lightning bolt. The end result is astounding, too much for my eyes.

"Why would you bring me here?"

Declan steps out from behind a column, and smiles. "To show you what you can really do. Everything you can be, and more, micuță. Welcome to my childhood home, and your training ground."

∞ ∞ ∞

CHAPTER SEVENTEEN

∞ Coimhlint ∞

"The harder the <u>conflict</u>, the greater the triumph."

–George Washington–

Finn

We've been making our way into town in silence, Dani and Tristan lagging behind. Not surprising, given they've been running around more than most of us. I don't even know how much longer I can keep this up, and the fight hasn't even started.

It's because I'm so focused on Lucas, trying to see what's going on with him, that I miss it at first. Then smoke smoke fills my nostrils completely, and I slow down my stride. *What the feckin' hell did Declan do?*

"Burned half the town," Lucas says in a voice devoid of emotion. "They'll attribute it to some human freak accident, but I am done bowing down to being morally good just so I can save my soul."

I share a look with Dani and Tristan. *What does that mean?* They seem as confused as I am.

Nothing about Lucas gives way to his thoughts, except maybe the rigidity in his back indicating he's close to snapping. He doesn't even look at us, but keeps moving. "Nothing."

Then how is it you can speak out loud right now?

"I've always been able to," Lucas mutters. "It's part of my heritage."

Cryptic answer, Tristan mutters. *You going to elaborate, chefe?*

"No. Less talking, more following, shall we? We're wasting time going at a snail's pace." His words have a stronger effect than normal. As our alpha, we have to listen to him, but this time it's impossible to fight the pressure in my head, ordering me to move.

I'm the first to match Lucas' pace, so I hazard one last question. *Where, exactly, are we going?*

"To inspect the damage."

The thought hits me that had Declan wanted to burn down the entire town, he easily could have. But, he didn't.

Why? Dani asks, when I voice my thoughts in the middle of rubble upon rubble.

It was bad when Dani blew up that building, Tristan adds, *but this is... Chaos.*

Hidden in the shadows of the tree line, we've been watching as humans throw water over the remaining flames, in an attempt to salvage the few still-standing buildings. The fire turned to ashes whatever was left of Elle's bakery, as well as the pub we used to spend every weekend at, and a couple of other store.

Is our shop safe?

Lucas shakes his head. "No, but I don't care. I will rebuild it." His gaze surveys the area, then stops, frozen, on someone a few feet away. A flash of red catches our eye, followed by blonde.

Uh oh, Dani says.

I glance between her and Tristan, and move closer to my friend. *Did you not tell him?*

Tristan throws me a look. *I didn't really get a chance to, in between running after your ass, saving it, and chewing you out for putting Dani in danger.*

I said I was sorry for that!

He takes a step closer. *Matter of fact, you didn't.*

Guys, we don't have time for this! Dani moves between us, nudging me towards our alpha. *Go do your thing before shit really blows up in our faces.*

I move in front of Lucas, unsure how much he heard of our exchange, but already it's too late. He morphs to human and rushes out of our hiding spot. Luckily, Dani snaps out of her daze fast and morphs too, using her magic to throw clothes over him.

Meeting our grateful gazes, she says, *The last thing we need right now is to attract human attention by running around naked.*

Agreed, I whisper. Then I follow suit with Tristan and morph, shooting Dani a quick, "Thank you," when she clothes us both.

From a distance, we approach Lucas. He stopped a few feet away from Lucrezia, staring at her and completely unaware of the fact Dom's about to go crazy on him again. She's frozen in the middle of the street, and Dom's practically blowing smoke through his nostrils.

There are too many humans around, I try to tell my friend, but neither he nor my alpha seem to hear me. Then Lucas takes a step forward, and engulfs Lucrezia in the tightest hug I've seen him give. He buries his head in her hair, and I see his shoulders shake.

His relief is palpable – even Dom feels it, but it's not enough to stop him. He lunges at Lucas, ripping him away from

Lucrezia and baring his teeth at him. "Stay the *fuck* away from her!"

"Dom!" Luz tries to grasp his hand, but he shakes her off and places himself square in front of her.

"You don't get to touch my mate, dumbfuck. Not after she died because of you!"

Of muted understanding, Tristan and I step between them. "The humans are staring," Tristan says. "Let's take this back to the shop."

"Claws Auto is ruined, Lucas," Lucrezia whispers, tears shining in her eyes. The sound of her voice seems to snap my alpha out of his daze, as he inhales sharply.

"Mio Dio, how are you alive?" His voice is hoarse. "*How* is this possible?"

Luz scans our surroundings, noticing the curious – and suspicious – looks from the town people. They may be around to pick up debris, but we stand out like a sore thumb with our little gang.

"Lucas, let's go back to your place," she says. "We need to talk, but not here."

Dominic's nostrils flare, and his glare intensifies on Lucas. "You're not going anywhere with him."

Luz stares up at her mate and smiles. "You can come, but don't try to kill him. That's my one rule. Deal?"

I have a feeling it's only her soft, questing touch to his hand that makes Dom nod tightly. Then he engulfs her hand in his, and walks away. In complete silence, we follow them to the car.

Dani quickens her pace and taps my shoulder. "Is it really a good idea, cramming us all in Dom's pick–up truck?"

"You've got a point. Hop in the back, at least this way the inside won't be suffused with testosterone."

She nods at my suggestion and goes back to let Tristan know.

On the way to the house, Lucrezia fills us in on hearing the roar, and getting Dom to drive them into town and see what was happening. That's when they'd seen Claws Auto burnt, but according to them it was only the back of the building that suffered, and the rest survived.

"Damn miracle," Tristan mutters through the open window of the backseat.

I nod, but say nothing. Luz looks at me, biting her lip. "Where's Elle? And Tytus?"

My heart clenches, and I dig my fingers in my thighs to grasp some semblance of control. "I don't know about him, but Lucas says she left with Declan."

"Of her own will?" Luz frowns. "Elle wouldn't do that."

"Tell it to the evidence," Lucas mutters and jerks his head ahead.

Dom slams on the breaks just in time to avoid running over the two bedraggled looking people in the middle of the road. One look at the white hair, and I know we fell upon Fiona, and a half–conscious Tytus she's hosting up.

Before Lucas can say anything, I jump out of the car, Lucrezia and Dani on my heels. We get to them just as Fiona collapses on the ground, and catch Tytus' bulk before he topples over her.

Elisandra

Declan wasn't lying when he said this was his home. He moves around like he was born here. I'm too stunned by the amount of opulence to care much for him, to be honest.

There is gold *everywhere*. Threads in the old tapestries on the walls. Metal intertwined around the chandeliers in the walls. Antique furniture in every room, of various shades and colors – all vibrant, though a tad dusty. Basically, the entire place looks like it was decorated for a tzar, or something.

Mesmerized, I don't immediately realize Declan is watching me. Then he clears his throat, and I face him. There's something unsettling in that stormy gaze, so like Tytus' – and so not, at the same time.

"You would do well to stop comparing me to my brother," Declan says. There's a hint of a warning in there, which I choose I ignore.

Instead, I lift my chin and glare at him. "If you brought me here to intimidate me–"

"Intimidate?" Declan laughs. "You are here to train."

"For what? I don't have full zmeu powers. I can't ever be what you and Tytus are. It's bad enough I'm not normal, I don't need crap like magic in my life, too."

"Should have thought of that before following me here, then."

"I didn't! *She* did!"

He circles me, arms crossed. "She *is* you. Lie as much as you want to yourself, but you cannot to me."

I narrow my eyes on him. "I don't know what your goal is here, but I won't help you hurt my friends."

"You already have."

"No, that was *her*."

"In *your* body."

It's like arguing with a very immovable wall. I've got nothing to say to that, because it's true. And the thought they're all thinking – that Finn thinks – I betrayed them... Air escapes me, and somehow I can't get it back.

Declan narrows his eyes on me, looking more than a little annoyed. "What did you go doing something so foolish for?"

Still hyperventilating, I shake my head. "Don't...know...what you mean."

Declan strides towards me, a muscle in his jaw ticking. "Starting the legătură with a wolf, *really*? Is that what my lineage has come to?"

Then he grasps my hand in his, squeezing it – hard. A shudder runs through me, then I'm being pushed to the back again. She's in the driver's seat, grinning up at him.

"That's better," Declan praises. "Now show me what you can do."

Finn

With Dani and Fiona's help, we make it back to Lucas' in one piece. He goes in first, followed by us with Tytus, and finally Dom, Tristan and Lucrezia. Her soft gasp when she sees the state of the living room makes me turn and grin.

"You should see the rest of it."

Her distress is clear as we advance, and she looks between Dom and Lucas. "You two nearly killed each other!"

They share a look, neither saying anything. Tytus groans in pain, so I set him on what's left of a couch. I don't see any injuries at first glance, but his sweaty forehead and clammy body tell me otherwise.

"Just what do we know about a zmeu and healing?" Tristan asks by my side, then glances at Dani.

"I..." She's at a loss, I can taste it in the air. She's not used to seeing Tytus in such a weakened position – none of us are. And it's a rough wake–up call, showing us how badly outmaneuvered we are.

"His wounds can only be healed while in zmeu form," Fiona whispers from behind us. She's been so silent, pale as a ghost, and leaning against the darkest corner. Even now, as she speaks, her eyes are closed, her voice faint.

"Can we get him to morph?" Tristan asks. "He's not looking so good."

Fiona shakes her head, and the movement seems to get the most of her. "He needs rest. Once his human form recovers, we can attempt it. But for now....he....rest..."

I'm closest to her and catch her just as she passes out. Looking at Lucas, I ask, "Is there another spot I can place her, so she can sleep?"

"Over here," Luz waves me over. She's got some blankets and pillows, and is pointing to a corner behind Tytus' couch. Once she sets everything down, I lower Fiona to the ground, and pull the covers over her.

"She doesn't look so good." When Luz doesn't answer, I look up to see her staring at Lucas and Dom. They're on opposite sides of the living room, glaring daggers at each other.

Tension is thick in the air, and getting worse. I quickly finish tucking the witch in, knowing I'll need my hands ready in case they go back at it.

As if catching my train of thought, Lucrezia shakes her head and straightens up, marching so she's standing between them. "No more. You can't be at odds because of me, I won't accept it."

"How..." Lucas clears his throat, then clenches his jaw. He's having a hard time keeping control of himself, and I can guess why. His wolf's agitation permeates the air – as does his need to make Dom submit.

"Basta. Enough avoiding the topic, Lucrezia. How are you alive? I saw you die with my own eyes."

Something in Lucas' tone must clue her in that he's serious, as Luz looks to the floor, biting her lip. "And I was. Dead, I mean. But Tytus, he protected me."

Lucas' nostrils flare, and I figure now's as good a time as any to step in before he loses it completely. "What she means is, way before Luz became part of our pack, she had already been afforded protection by Tytus, though not willingly."

"Not willingly?"

"Aye," I nod, holding his gaze with mine and hoping Lucas hears the warning in my tone. "Tytus didn't know he was doing it when he threatened some Reapers away from her. There's some old zmeu magic involved, but the story is, that action provided Lucrezia with protection of her body and soul. When she died, her soul lingered around – Tytus accidentally called it back last night."

Lucas turns the full effect of his burning stare to Lucrezia. "È vero? Is this true?"

"Yes," Luz says. "All of it."

At her confirmation, Lucas turns his back on her and walks to the wall. His shoulders radiate tension once more, and he puts up a palm on the wall, then breathes in deeply. After a few moments, he faces us once more.

"It is... I'm glad you are well, Lucrezia," Lucas says. "There is much to be thankful for, but unfortunately we also have a new set of problems on our hands."

"All thanks to you," Dom mutters.

A low growl escapes from Lucas, and his gaze pins Dom. I taste their rising tension in the air, and I fear another incident. Only this time, I doubt Lucas' house would survive.

Dom opens his mouth to speak, but Luz turns to him, lifting a hand to his chest. "I know you're mad, I feel it off you, my love. But if you care for me, I need you to stop fighting. Please. At least try."

The desperation in her voice gets him, and he grits his teeth. "I will if he does."

"I promise," says Lucas, surprising us all. Me, most of all, because there's nothing I taste around him that would give me the impression he's so easily subdued.

Tytus' groan interrupts further conversations. He blinks, regaining conscience for a moment. "Declan... Underestimated his strength. He got away with Elle."

My gut churns more painfully, and this time I drop to the ground, panting. "It's happening again," I whisper.

"What is?"

"They're... Whatever's happening to Elle when they're apart, he feels," Dani explains, because I can't. All I see is darkness, and I shout in pain.

Elisandra

When I wake up, it's with the sun's rays on my face. The unfamiliar bed quickly shakes me wide alert – I don't recall ever owning such luxurious sheets. They're like feathers where they touch me, tickling my skin...

Skin!

I jump up. I don't remember getting in bed – but luckily I'm alone, and dressed. At least in something that covers mid-thigh, which explains why I felt the covers on my skin.

Snippets of the day before – hours before? – run through my mind. After taking over my body again, she showed Declan the magic she knows. I recall him being impressed at some, and disappointed at other parts, but it's like putting together pieces of a puzzle, and not seeing the bigger picture.

And she kept *flirting* with him. It scares me, their connection. But not as much as the realization she took to being bad super easy. What if that's who I am, deep down?

The idea is too much to linger on, so I try to think back to what else happened. Nothing comes to mind, other than stumbling here to rest – I think. My body feels like it's been run over by a train, so I step into the bathroom.

It's not a twentieth century place, that's for sure. But there is a large tub and a knob that presumably is connected to some type of plumbing system, so I let it run. Water spills out and I let it fill the tub, amazed at its clarity.

Surprised it still works after all this time.

Declan fixed it for us, she says. *Enjoy it while you can. I'm going to rest a bit longer.*

I ignore her, hoping she'll go away for good. She does – but she'll be back, I've no doubt about it.

After I finish with the bath, I get up and clothes are waiting for me. A simple royal blue gown, held up by two brooches on the shoulder, with some sort of bustier keeping my breasts afloat. The fabric is silky – I blush just touching it.

What the hell is Declan playing at?

She doesn't answer.

I drop my dirty clothes in the tub to soak, hoping I can return and wash them by hand. At least, after whatever

Declan's got planned for this morning finishes. And if it's anything other than magic training, he's got another thing coming.

Now would be the perfect time to escape, I think as I'm braiding my hair to keep it out of my face. But I know it would be futile. I have no magic, no way to get back home, and there's no phone in this damn place – I looked.

The only thing I can do is try and figure out the magic. If I do what Finn and Tytus have been begging me to try since the beginning, then I may have a chance to get my body back.

Resolved, I head down the stairs. After stumbling in numerous places, enough to make my head dizzy, I find Declan.

He's standing in the impossibly tall living room, staring at the sunrise. "For eons, I was robbed of this," he whispers, and for the first time there is no malice in his voice. Rather, it's soft and whimsical, completely at odds with the man I've seen so far.

Desperate to keep him in a good mood, I keep my voice low as well, hoping it will continue whatever trance he is in. "It wasn't fair."

Declan freezes at the tone of my voice and turns with a smirk. It freezes on his lips when he sees what I'm wearing, and a different glint burns in his eyes. "Ready to continue your training?"

"I..."

He narrows his eyes. "Where is she?"

It's uncanny how he knows the difference between us. Instead of cowering away like I have so far, I lift my chin up and say, "I'm here for now. Stop trying to push me away, this is *my* body and *my* choices! Now what the hell did you mean yesterday about whatever I did with the wolf? And when will you return me home!"

Declan watches me for a moment, as if waiting to see if I'm done. Once I fall quiet, he shrugs. "You are no good to me tied to a wolf. And since the mating you have begun is impossible to break, I have only one choice. Dispose of you in favor of your alter, who did not mate."

"But she did....We both did..." *Didn't we?*

She doesn't answer.

Declan grins. "Perhaps my brother neglected to mention that in order for a mating to be complete, your mate has to travel through fire for you."

I gulp. "He mentioned that, yeah."

"But given there are two of you, and only one with magic...."

Realization dawns on me. "Only *she* can complete the mating?"

"As humans say, bingo. Now, I do love answering idiotic questions, but I need your other half here."

He grabs my hand and once more I'm pushed at the back. She comes to the front, smug as always. And flirting. Always damn flirting with him.

"Like the outfit?"

"It suits you," he says, then puts a distance between us. "Now, show me you remember what I taught you last night."

She draws a rune in the air, and it looks more complicated than most. Declan nods, a faint smile on his lips. "Good. Again."

I don't know what it's supposed to do, but whatever it is, the rune is important to both of them – at least judging by their focus. I try to imprint it in my memory, but her questions distract me.

"Why the rush?"

Declan touches a strand of hair – *my* hair – and twirls it around a finger. His voice is soft again, though deadly. "My brother has a pendant with my blood in his possession. If the witch does the counter spell before the new moon phase ends, everything will be undone. I need to retrieve and destroy it, breaking all ties with my past."

"And how do you plan to do that?"

Declan grins. "With your help, draga mea."

Finn

"You know they can't continue like this."

I snap out of my dark thoughts and look up. It's only then I realize how aching my muscles have become. So I stand, towering over Luz.

"Who?"

She nods towards the corner, where Lucas and Dom are at a standoff – again. Our alpha sent Tristan and Dani to try and track Elle or Declan, and Dom didn't agree with splitting us off. Obviously.

A sigh escapes me. "I don't have the energy to deal with this."

I glance at Tytus and Fiona, still asleep in the opposite side of the living room. I need to find out how to get to Elle, and they're the only two people who can help me.

Luz reaches for me, then seems to think better of it and stops herself. "I know. I get how hard it is to be away from the one you love." Her gaze slides to Dom, and something tells me there's more to her story, and what she saw when she was dead.

Then Luz shrugs, and smiles at me. Weak as it is, it's still blinding. "But you have to help, Finn. We need to fix them, at least to get them to fight on the same side, else we're screwed. Who knows what the Reapers are planning now? *Please.*"

Her plea is what gets me, and I nod. Then turn to my two superiors. "Oy, you two! Are you done fighting it out yet?"

Lucas faces me first, his expression tight and ready to snap. Dom's still busy glaring daggers at him, so Luz moves closer to him, straight in his line of vision. Dom's expression softens and he reaches for her, pulling her into his side as if he can't be apart from her for even a second.

I get that, mate. Boy, do I get that now.

The familiar burning is back in my veins, and I wish I was by Elle's side, regardless of where she is. Instead, I meet Lucas' gaze. "The time for fighting is over. We need to put our heads together and see what we can do to stop the Reapers."

"Hard to do, without information," Lucas bites.

"And whose fault is that?" Dom snaps.

Luz moves between them again. "Enough! Please, both of you. I know why you're at odds, but it's not right."

"Not right? What's not right is that *you died* because of him!"

"I died because of a Reaper, Dom!"

"Because *he* put you there!"

"He's right."

Luz whirls around, facing Lucas. I'm just as shocked. My alpha's shoulders drop, and he shakes his head, running a hand over his face. "Lucrezia, I... Mi scuzi, bella. It's my fault. All of it."

She takes a step closer, grabbing his hand in hers. "I'm alive, aren't I?"

"But you could have been dead for good."

"She *was* dead!" Dom growls.

"Enough! I'm alive, that's what matters. And maybe we can use this to our advantage."

Lucas tilts his head to the side. "How so?"

"The Reapers don't know I'm alive, nor that I've been...enhanced, so to speak. I can help–"

"Absolutely not!"

The shout comes from both of them, and I grin. "Well, at least you agree on something."

∞ ♦ ∞

After an hour of negotiation, we finally get Lucas and Dominic to sit down and talk through options – under our supervision, of course. I wish there was some way to just shake some sense into them, but given they're both at the top of the hierarchy, I doubt that's possible.

"Do you think it'll last?" Luz joins me on the floor, resting her head on her knees, and looking ready to fall asleep.

I shrug. "Hell if I know, Red. I guess we'll have to wait and see."

My gaze runs to the blood–red sky. What am I going to do if they're right, and Elle is with this guy? How am I supposed to fight my mate?

CHAPTER EIGHTEEN

∞ Straitéis ∞

**"<u>Strategy</u> without tactics is the slowest route to victory.
Tactics without strategy is the noise before defeat."**

–Sun Tzu–

Elisandra

I wake up to darkness, and the glint of metal. Stormy eyes are stare at me, searing a path to my consciousness. "Tytus?"

"The better brother, darling." Declan laughs, and I realize it was the moon's reflection that made his otherwise golden eyes seem stormy. He holds out his hand. "I think it's time we finish your training, and then you can help me get my revenge."

Hiding my gulp, I shift in bed to an upright position. I've barely had control of my body, and am completely unaware of how much time has gone by. My alter has taken great pleasure in pushing me aside, so for me to feel like myself upon waking up is new.

I just need to keep being me for a bit. Obviously, trying to learn magic isn't working since she's the only one profiting from it, so it's high time I get the heck out of here.

Declan clears his throat, and I catch his impatient expression.

"Sure," I say, trying to mimic her smug tone.

Declan steps away and I get out of bed. I go to follow him out the door, but at the entrance he turns, catching me by surprise. His hand is on my throat again. "I know you're not *her*, darling. And it's all right. You can enjoy your last few hours of freedom."

Gulping and fighting my trembling, I follow him outside.

Majestic mountains rise up to the cloudless sky. Cold stars watch down upon us like judging ancestors. My bare hands catch the drift of the cold, and I shiver. Something about tonight feels...eternal.

Declan takes no notice, instead marching ahead. It's a choice between the darkness or following him, so I force my feet to move. We contour the castle to the backyard behind, and I wonder why we didn't just go through the house.

My zmeu ancestor snorts, as if hearing me. "I thought you might appreciate the walk, given the long hours of training

I put you through." I could've believed him – if not for the sight awaiting me around the last corner.

A massive bonfire burns in the middle of the courtyard, and I can sense the magic radiating from it. The flames go higher and higher, as if reaching for the stars and begging me to join them.

Declan watches me closely, waiting for my reaction. "Take your time," he says.

I gulp, wondering which part of this plan of his will end with me still alive. "My time for what, exactly?"

"To make peace with it, of course. See, it is high time you live to your full potential, which of course is your other half – your *better* half. I am doing you a favor, ending the chaos inside you painlessly." His voice is toneless, as if he's offering me drinks. "Once you feel ready, you can step into the fire."

"Wait, what now?" I turn to ask him what the hell he's thinking, and Declan laughs.

"Or, we can do it now."

With one push of his hand, he hits me in the chest and knocks me straight into the bonfire. His golden eyes stare at me unfeeling, and I open my mouth on a scream.

Too soon, the flames engulf me, wrapping around my ankles, my wrists, my entire body. I expect agony where they touch – instead, all I feel is calm.

Time for this body to be mine, and mine alone, she says.

What?

Declan has figured out a way to have me always in charge. Now let yourself go, my lesser self, so that I may take over.

That's not possible! Arguing is futile at this point, but I have to try.

Sure it is, dearie. Same as had you mated Finn completely, it would have snuffed out my existence. I've simply beat you to the finish line.

All I feel is a mental push, the same as when Declan brings her forth. It's followed by a sense of disconnect, like a string has been cut, and I lose sight of everything.

My last thought is of Finn. *I never got a chance to tell him I love him.*

Finn

I jerk awake, nearly hitting Lucas with the force of my movement. Last night I slept on his couch, too tired to go back home. Dom and Tristan took their mates away, but the thought of being in my house alone with Elle's scent everywhere was too much to bear.

In the darkness, I stare at my alpha. He's tense, and his outstretched hand looks like he'd been about to shake me awake.

"What is it?"

He shushes me, then motions to the other corner. Tytus and the witch are asleep on the floor, but something glows between them.

Lucas points to it and I nod, getting up and following him on tiptoes. As he bends over to reach for whatever it is, I lose my balance. Or, not quite. More like the rug is pulled out from under me, only there is no rug.

My alpha is oblivious and gets back up with some sort of necklace in his hand. I can't breathe. It's like I've lost – my soul. There's no other way to describe the cold filling me, numbing me, stealing away my vision and making my teeth chatter as if I've been submerged in icy water.

A voice whispers close to my ear, *I never got a chance to tell him I love him.*

"Elle!"

My agonized groan draws Lucas' attention – and wakes Tytus up. His eyes glow in the darkness, taking me in, and Lucas' hand holding the pendant.

"That belongs to me."

"I'll give it back," Lucas says, all nonchalant. "Soon as you tell me what it is."

Tytus glares at him, but his gaze flickers to me when another groan escapes me.

"It's a portion of Declan's blood," Fiona whispers. All the ruckus must have woken her up, too.

Tytus throws her a look over his shoulder. "Did anyone ask you, witch?"

"Get over yourself," she mutters and stands. Then she inches closer to me, pressing her cold hand to my forehead. I don't even jerk.

"What's wrong with him?" Lucas asks.

"It's the legătură." She speaks at the same time as Tytus. "Because of his close bond with Elisandra, your wolf feels her distance strongly, and it's tearing at him. But...."

Fiona trails off and glances at Tytus. "Have you ever seen this before?"

He joins her by my side and Lucas pulls out his phone, shining a flashlight that blinds me. They're pointing it at my chest and, when I look down, I see why. Dark veins are spreading underneath the muscle like a spider's web – then they disappear, as if absorbed within me.

My heartbeat thuds louder and I gulp past my dry throat. Everything else narrows on one question. "Is Elle alright?"

Tytus seems stunned. "I....don't know."

His lie – I taste it in the air, and force him to meet my gaze. "Tell the truth."

"I'm not sure the Elisandra you reunite with will be the same one you knew."

"But we can get her back, right?" If we don't, whatever happened to her is about to happen to me, because those veins on my chest won't release me – not if my mate is in danger.

Tytus only stares at me, and his silence speaks volumes.

Elisandra

After the initial darkness, I drift into fog, like I'm atop of the clouds and floating. Tied to nothing, no one, I still exist. Only I no longer have a body, nor a purpose.

Light replaces mist – so blinding, so stunning. It makes my eyes hurt, and the thought of pain and parts of my body wrenches me back from the unknown.

There is fog, and darkness, and then light – again.

Then I'm falling...

Falling...

And I land with a jerk, back in a familiar place.

Something went wrong. I don't know what, but it did, because I'm back as an observer in my own body. It's kind of like before, except I can't get past this wall in my own head, like I'm stumbling around in the dark.

"Well?" Declan says as my alter steps out of the fire, fully in control.

She grins. "Gone. It's just us, dearie."

He grins wider and pulls her – me – by the waist, dropping his mouth onto ours. "Good. Because once we defeat my brother, I fully intend to come back and celebrate."

There is nothing I can do as she kisses him back, answering his promise with one of her own.

Like Finn would say, bollocks!

Finn

Everyone's gathered back as soon as the sun rises. Dom looks he like he hasn't slept a wink – I wouldn't have either, if I'd just gotten my mate back from the dead. Lucas, too, keeps glancing at Luz out of the corner of his eyes. His guilt fills the air, but I try to ignore it and focus on his words.

"We are in a reckoning phase, amici. The Reapers have taken advantage of this chaos and hidden into the forest. Luckily, they're scared shitless of crossing my wrath to try and step into town. But this doesn't mean we are safe. We need to get rid of them, once and for all."

"Why now?" Dominic asks. "You've been all about kiddie gloves."

"Things change," Lucas says through gritted teeth, but his eyes betray him as they shift to Lucrezia.

"You just want to get rid of your own fucking guilt," Dom snorts. "Some alpha you've turned into."

Lucas takes a deep breath as though trying not to strangle him. Lucrezia intervenes before he can say anything, but it's not with the words I expect. "Dom's right, Lucas. If you're doing this for me – because of my death – it's not right. I don't want to be the cause of their execution, no matter how well deserved it might be."

Our alpha looks around at us, then takes a step closer to Lucrezia. In a move completely unlike him, he smiles and tugs on a lock of her hair. "Cara, believe me when I say that it's not all about you. Some, yes. But the rest is simply me having lost my patience, and refusing to put any more of my pack in danger for the sake of my own morals."

When Dom's growl turns into a snarl, Lucas lets go of her hair and steps back. "And, we have no choice. If we ever want peace in this town, it is high time to go full offensive."

"What about Declan? I'm not that eager to put my mate in danger," Tristan says.

"Nor I," Dominic adds.

"Fair points," says another, softer voice. We all turn around to see Ileana glide into the room. Her usual light expression is sober, and for the first time she doesn't look like a young woman, but like the powerful immortal she is.

Her sun–filled gaze lands on Dominic and Lucrezia, and a faint smile touches her lips. "I am happy to see you returned, my dear. His soul was lost without you."

"And mine without his," Luz says and inches closer to Dom, interlacing her fingers with his. Their connection makes every breath harder, reminding of me of what I had – and lost.

Tytus is quiet in his spot, but Fiona is staring at Ileana with both wariness and awe. Noticing this, Dom's godmother says, "You have suffered much at the hands of many. Are you ready to break those chains, and truly regain your freedom?"

"I am," Fiona whispers. "Whatever the cost."

"Good. There is a way to defeat Declan, but it involves a lot of pieces falling into place at the exact right time." Her tone is hard, less of twinkling fairy bells and more of rock. "Zmeu, do you still have the necklace?"

Tytus jerks his head to Lucas. "He's got it."

"Very well. Declan was imprisoned in the bowels of Earth itself, through powerful magic from the Council of zmei and dragons. Unfortunately, the zmei are gone, and what's left of dragons won't be of much use to us. To put it mildly, there is no Council, thus no power to use."

Silence answers her, as we all try to figure out what the magical solution might be.

"We can't let Declan continue to kill humans," I say. "It's bad enough he burned our town down, and the Reapers have recruited a lot of the remaining citizens for their own needs."

"Yes, there has been much bloodshed," Ileana admits. "And there will be more before the sun rises tomorrow."

She floats closer, and her flower scent fills the air. "You will need to bait Declan back here, from the fortress he has locked himself in. His greed will help, as he will more than likely come for the one piece you still have of him – the necklace."

Lucas opens his palm and tosses the piece to Tytus, who catches it mid–air. "There, necklace secured. Then what?"

I'm surprised at his openness to Ileana, given the last time they ran into each other. There's something really changed about him – like he's willing to clean up our territory once and for all, at any cost.

"Once you draw Declan back here, bait him with the necklace and lead him back to the crater he came out of."

"Seems simple enough," Tristan says, nodding to Dani. "But what about after?"

"He's right," Dom adds. "We don't have nearly enough power together to imprison him. What are we supposed to do, dig a hole and bury him?"

"We can kill him," Lucas says in a quiet voice.

Ileana shakes her head. "Let us not be hasty in upsetting the balance. There is good in the world, and so there must be bad. As the last two of their race, Tytus and Declan maintain that."

Lucas takes a step closer to her, clenching his fists. "Do I sound like I give a shit about the balance?"

Ileana tilts her head, an odd smile on her lips. "You, above all, should care, *lordul morții*."

Dominic jerks like he's been stung, and I know that whatever Ileana just called Lucas, it's not something simple. Our alpha only narrows his eyes.

Undeterred, Ileana says, "So no, killing Declan is not the solution. Once you corner him in the crater, I will need lightning and blood of his future kin, then we can imprison him somewhere he cannot escape."

"Blood of his future kin?"

Ileana looks at me, her gaze gentle. "Elisandra's. But do not worry, she does not have to be harmed for it. A drop or two will do." From the folds of her dress, Ileana produces a dagger. It's only slightly larger than her palm, with a curved blade and intricate leaf designs on the ivory handle.

She hands it to me. "Your task, my faoladh friend." Once I take knife and tuck it in the waistband of my jeans, she looks at the rest of us, lingering on Dominic. "I wish you all good luck." The moment after, she vanishes in a whirlwind of flowers.

Silence reigns again in the room, then Dani breaks it. "Do we know how we're going to bait Declan?"

Lucas smirks, a cold expression on his face. "By doing what I mentioned earlier – ridding this town of the Reapers, once and for all."

"So, who's going to be responsible for bringing Declan to the crater?" Tristan looks between us.

Lucas nods to Tytus. "The zmeu and the witch can handle Declan."

"Like they did last time?"

"They'll have me," Luz adds. "I can help now."

Dom pales at her suggestion, throwing a pleading glance to Tytus. He shakes his head ever so, a promise that he'll take care of her. It doesn't seem to do the trick, as Dominic walks out in an agitated frenzy. Luz watches him go, then says, "Go on, Lucas. He just needs a minute."

I think it's more than a minute he needs. There's something emanating from Dom I feel, even inside this house. Unsure of what it is I'm sensing, I let it go, and focus instead on Lucas.

"Tristan, you go back up Dani. Her magic and skill can protect us, while me, Dominic and Finn attack the Reapers."

"You think it'll be a fair fight?" I point out. "Every time we run into them, more have joined their numbers."

"Do you have a better idea?"

I shrug and sit back down, gesturing for him to continue. It'll be a suicide mission, for sure, but what other option do we have, when our home is at stake?

By the time Lucas is done outlining our attack, Dominic walks back, seemingly more at ease. He grasps Luz's hand in his and nods to our alpha. "Might as well get on with it now, no?"

Lucas narrows his eyes on him, not quite sure what to make of the change of attitude, then nods. I stop him before he leaves, my hand on his shoulder.

"Promise me something."

"You've got some balls, Irish, after everything you pulled." He snorts. "Very well. What is it you wish, amico?"

"Elisandra safe. Once I get what we need for this, I want your promise she will be unharmed."

Nothing in his expression tells me what he's thinking, and unlike before, his emotions are hard to taste in the air as well. "That all depends on how much trouble she'll make for us in this last fight. I cannot allow her to escape unscathed if she is helping Declan."

I gulp, and step back. "Noted." *Guess I'll just have to be quick about it.*

We all head out the broken door, but I linger behind to catch Tytus and Fiona. He seems better, more color in his face and an angry look in his eyes. "Will you really be alright fighting?"

He nods. "I've healed enough. My brother won't get the best of me again."

I can only hope the lie I taste in the air won't get us all killed.

Elisandra

I've lost it – myself – somehow. Watching her, in my body, preparing to hurt my friends and mate is unbearable. Over the next hours, I go into some sort of comatose state. Seeing, but not quite registering anything. What's the point when I won't be able to do anything to stop them?

I never should have left Finn. That last fight plays on a loop in my head. How I'd let her bait me, allowed myself to be persuaded... Maybe if I'd fought harder against her mental overbearingness, I would have been able to resist Declan, too.

It's too late now. Way too darn late. I think of my grandmama, who'll be alone and heartbroken. Maybe Tytus will lie to her, tell her I died saving the town, rather than contributed to destroying it.

Lost in my thoughts, floating in a fog of my own making, I lose track of time and everything. I'm not sure what really brings me back. Maybe it's the satisfaction coursing through her veins, or some gut feeling that I need to listen in.

Either way, one moment I'm in the fog, the next it's like I'm abruptly pulled back into my body, hearing *her* with utmost clarity.

"They have someone with them," she says in a sickly version of my voice.

Declan looks up from sharpening a dagger. I'm not sure why he'd bother bringing it with him, but again, it's not like I'm actively registering stuff.

"I know about the witch," Declan says.

"Not the witch, the redhead."

He narrows his eyes. "Who?"

"The human who befriended the daft version of me. She died, but came back to life. Tied to Tytus. He called her a Solo...."

"Solomonar." Surprise coats Declan's features. "How in the hell did my weakling brother manage that?"

"Will she be a thorn in our side?"

Declan laughs, nowhere near worried. "No. In fact, she may be key to killing him. You will simply have to deliver the blow."

"Not a problem."

Oh, but there is. Because just like that, my stupor is gone. No way I'm letting them kill Lucrezia, not when I've already seen Dominic without her. Someway, somehow, I need to get control back.

But how?

∞ Bua ∞

"Know yourself and you will <u>win</u> all battles."

–Sun Tzu–

Finn

Finding the Reapers is as easy as hunting down a rabbit. That's to say, all we had to do was morph and get to the edge of the woods, and we ran into the first guards. Lucas takes care of one, while I force the other to tell us where they're all gathering.

The crater, he says.

Convenient for us.

So we follow our fearless leader deep into the forest, but come upon Cade and his people a few miles away from said crater.

Less convenient, but do–able nonetheless.

Half of them are in human form, the rest in wolf. Cade himself is stretching like he's about to go for a run.

"Finally," he says when he notices us. "The zmeu left us a task to take care of. It's about time you make it easy for me."

Lucas glares, and I wait for him to give the signal. After his outburst at our strategy meeting, I know he's planning no mercy for them. As a result, neither are we.

You know your orders, he reminds us. *Kill.*

Dani steps out of formation, morphing to human. Within moments, I hear the caw of ravens nearby. Tristan is in massive lobisomem form by her side, and looking like he'll rip apart anyone that comes too near. Dominic moves to Lucas' shoulder, taking his spot as the rightful beta, but I sense him edgy, as if waiting for something.

His eyes scan the surroundings, presumably searching for his mate. I don't blame him for not wanting Lucrezia here – wherever she's hidden.

To give the illusion we're less powerful than we are, we all follow Lucas' lead and morph to human, as well. On edge, we survey the Reapers, waiting for their first strike. This standoff was imminent, but even now, with Dani and her magic, I'm still not feeling this fight. Even more concerning, I'm wondering where the hell Declan is.

Then Tytus tilts his chin to the skies, eyes narrowed on the darkening clouds. "Welcome to the war you always wanted, brother," he growls.

I throw him a look, and am surprised by the pity in his eyes as he says, "He's not alone."

Cade chooses that moment to attack, his wolves jumping on us, and magic flying from everywhere. Tytus and Fiona are already heading to the side of the battle, trying to use the Reapers as camouflage so they can attack Declan unbidden. He's still circling above, at least momentarily, while we defend ourselves – still in human form.

It's only when the black zmeu lands, making the entire meadow rumble, that I realize what Tytus meant. Declan roars once and the Reapers pull back, then he moves his head to the side and reveals the person perched on his neck.

"Elle!"

I take a step forward, prepared to drag her off Declan, if I have to. Lucas grabs my forearm in his strong grip, jerking me a stop. "Don't be a fool!"

"Let me go, Lucas!" No amount of yanking will release his hold on me, so I settle for glaring at him. "You swore I'd have a chance to talk to her."

"And I will keep my promise, Irish. But is that really your mate up there? Look closer."

Clenching my jaw, I do as he says. I want to dispute his quick assessment, but the truth of the matter is Elle doesn't even acknowledge me. Instead, she's petting Declan's scales with a completely enamored expression.

"She... I... No, it's not." Lucas finally releases me. "But I *can* get through to her, I swear. Just let me try."

"Not while she's atop that zmeu, you don't."

"So let's match her."

The suggestion comes from the witch. Taking advantage of the lull in the fight, her and Tytus shifted closer to us.

Lucas throws her a bored look. "Excuse me?"

"You have a zmeu at your disposal, alpha. Use him."

Tytus snorts, and I taste his amusement at her audacity. "And what makes you think I'd let you ride me, witch?"

"Besides the fact you already did?"

"That was pure necessity."

Her violet eyes glint menacingly. "It wasn't me I was referring to."

Tytus' eyes widen as he realizes she means Lucrezia. Since she's off to the side with Dani, he glances to Dom for permission. "Well?"

To everyone's surprise, Dom nods. "Fine, but on one condition. Take Finn on as well."

"Why me?"

Dom grabs my forearm with his. "Because you're right. You can get through to Elle, just like Luz did with me. And in the meantime, we'll have your back."

There's something smug in his tone of voice, an assurance I taste in the air. I don't understand his meaning and he steps away from the pack, facing the Reapers. Cade snorts. "You really have a death wish, now that your insect mate is dead?"

"Maybe." Dom growls low. "Or maybe not." Then he throws his head back and lets loose a howl so loud, the hairs at the back of my neck raise.

"Sonofabitch!" Tristan mutters.

Even Dani's at a loss, but no more than me. What we're staring at is not one, but dozens of creatures stepping out of the shadows. Golden eyes rimmed with gold, wolf bodies larger than ours, claws leaving marks in the ground, I recognize them immediately – they're vrykolakas.

In muted disbelief, I turn to Lucas. The anger in his eyes tells me had no idea this was coming.

"Leave it for later," I whisper. "We're already outnumbered, and whether you like it or not, you know we need them."

He throws me a dark glare, but nods and faces the Reapers.

Cade stops dead in his tracks, staring. I catch his stupefaction in the air, and finish off the wolf in my path, then look around. Lucrezia has stepped in the midst of the battle, Dominic by her side, and they're surrounded by a few vrykolakas.

Not even the coward leader of the Reapers can mask his surprise. *How is this possible?*

Lucrezia grins and lifts a hand. The clouds above darken, drawing Declan's gaze, too. A shot of lightning strikes one wolf, then moves through the others like an arrow. When it's done, Luz grins and looks in my direction.

"You were right. This *is* fun."

She's close enough I can hear the amusement in her voice. Rolling my eyes, I motion for her to follow, and take off with Tytus in the direction of the woods. Lucrezia meets us halfway, eyes wide. "What's going on?"

"You're going to ride me, Solomonar."

"I.... what?" She looks up at the sky, her eyes wide. "That's not a good idea."

"My brother has managed to enchant Elisandra's alter side to take over, and I cannot kill him *and* save her. Finn can interject with her, but not protect me while she attacks, so you have no choice. Hop on."

Luz clears her throat, shifting from foot to foot. "What about training? You promised me training, and a five minute breakdown of how to reach for this magic is *not* training."

"You seemed to be doing just fine back there. Besides, no time like the present. Ever heard of trial by fire?" Tytus grins, and morphs into his zmeu form. Flames engulf him, and then he's standing in front of us in all his true power, burgundy scales glinting, wings spread, head thrown back and roaring.

Shaking himself as though to stretch out his muscles, he then bends lower to the ground and extends a paw towards us. Still stunned, Lucrezia climbs over the extended limb, and I follow at his signal.

Let's hope we don't regret this.

Elisandra

Flying is amazing. If only I could actually enjoy it. She's at the forefront again, and somehow knows more than I do about the magic in *my* veins. Not that Declan minds.

His entire speech about me being so much better, and needing training, was obviously fluff. It was my alter he wanted all along – *her* energy he answered to. And whether I want to admit it or not, they make a great team.

We circle above another battleground, oddly reminiscent of last time. Lucas and the pack are facing off against Reapers. In the distance, I see Tytus, the rest of the pack, and Finn. My heart clenches.

So you're still here, are you? Her acknowledgment of me takes me by surprise. I thought she couldn't feel me anymore.

She snorts at my thoughts. *You're like one of those pests I can't get rid of.* A sigh, then, *Just try not to get in the way, would you? We've got a battle to fight.*

Don't hurt Finn! Don't hurt any of them!

As if you could stop me.

She's right. There's nothing I can do, not when she's fully taken over like this. My chance to assert authority over my own body was a while back, and I failed at it. Had I listened to Finn, to Tytus...

We lose altitude pretty fast, and it's then I realize Declan is about to land next to his wolves. That stops any thoughts of regret, as I focus on the fight. If there's even a small chance I could take my body back, I'll have to take it when it comes.

The Reapers pull back from attacking Lucas – and a new pack that seems to be helping him, though they look....odd. I've never seen wolves their size, with eyes the color of blood and gold combined.

Declan lowers his head to Cade, and his thought runs through both of us. *They have something I need you to retrieve for me – a necklace.*

Cade smirks. "I'll get it for you. Soon as you help us barbeque them."

Rage runs through Declan, but before he can say – or do – anything, a blast of fire hits his left flank. It sends him stumbling away, and he growls, turning his head to the side of the battlefield, where Tytus and Fiona are moving about.

"Are you going to fight, or what?" Cade sniggers.

Declan's massive head turns its full ferocity to the Reaper leader. Smooth like a cat, he draws back, arching his neck as if to stretch, but I know better. I watch from afar as realization of his fate dawns on Cade – a second too late.

With one reach of his sharp talons, Declan swipes at Cade's throat, ripping it out. Trembling hands reach out to stop the flow of blood, but already he's falling to his knees, staring up in shock.

Bile rises to my throat, made all the worse when Declan snorts and throws a ball of fire on him, effectively erasing him from existence. The smell of charred flesh makes my skin crawl.

Oh, grow up!

Unaware of my presence, Declan glances to the side of the forest, where flames envelop Tytus as he morphs into his zmeu form. "Brother... Finally showing your true face."

Only, he doesn't see what I do. As Tytus pushes off the ground, I notice a flash of red hair above him – Lucrezia. And behind her...

Finn!

Declan takes off with a powerful push of his back legs, leaving the wolves to fight amongst themselves. I feel *her* intention – to warn him about me – and I do my best to force her to be quiet. When it works, I hold hope that maybe all is not lost for me.

Finn

Flying is bloody awful. I feel sick to my stomach, but I'm sure Tytus wouldn't appreciate me throwing up all over his shiny scales. I try to focus on what matters. *Elle.*

"You have to get through to her somehow," Luz whispers. She clenches onto Tytus, but there's a thrill I taste in the air I recognize as all hers.

Ready for this? Tytus asks. Another great zmeu ability – to reach into our minds without permission.

While I clench my teeth, Luz nods. Then she lifts her hand to the skies, and the darkening clouds that had been at bay rush over our heads. Soon, rain's pouring down, but it's not what Luz is after. She's calling lightning.

You're a natural, Red.

Before she can strike, Declan swoops up and opens his jaws wide. Not going to lie, seeing those massive canines headed for us, I'm pretty sure we're nearing the end of our lives. Then Tytus moves his massive body with surprising agility out of the way, and picks up speed.

I glance behind us. "He's on us!"

Good. Now we just need him to follow us back to the crater.

Elle, on Declan's back, is grinning madly – I'm hoping there's some way to get through to her, that Dom was right. Luz also glances backwards, and bites her lip.

"Tytus, we're going to need more speed." When he doesn't immediately listen, she peers around his side and gasps. I see what she does then, too. A massive gash on the end of his wing has reopened from the earlier elusive manoeuvre, and it's slowing him down.

"How badly does it hurt?"

One eye rolls towards us, as if to say, *Seriously?*

A bump underneath sends us catapulting in the clouds, and Luz bends over him, me over her, desperately trying to hold on to an incoming train wreck. Spinning in midair, knowing the ground is nowhere close, has a way of straightening one's priorities.

By the time Tytus rights himself up, my mind is spinning with ideas. Declan is here for something, Tytus was right.

"Do you have the necklace?" I whisper to Luz.

She nods, frowning at the skies below and trying to find Declan's trace.

"We can lure Declan with it, if he knows we have it. He'll be more focused in trying to get to us, than destabilizing Tytus."

I pause, another thought occurring. "You *can* keep us safe, right?"

Luz grins and holds out her palm, the necklace dangling. I grasp it, and let it swing in the air. "Oy, Declan! Looking for this?"

It's like playing catch with a very large shark. Looming out of dark clouds, Declan makes his appearance, Elle's eyes narrowed on us. Only this time, rather than try to hit from underneath – where Tytus is already sensitive – they go for above.

I push Luz over Tytus, and bend down just in time before feeling talons graze the top of my head. We straighten ourselves up, and I say, "Alrighty then. Some speed would be nice, Red."

Luz holds out her palm to gather air, and blows it under Tytus' wings. As he picks up speed, I see her do something else – catch lightning, and take aim. I've no idea how she's doing it, but her focus and the intent, I have no trouble tasting.

When the bolt releases and heads towards Declan, I can't help my shout. "Elle, watch out!"

She swings Declan away in time, then grins up at me. "Thanks, sweetums!"

Her alter's fully in charge. *Shite!*

"You have to let us bring them down," Luz says over her shoulder. "*Then* you can talk to Elle."

One glance below confirms we're above the crater area now. And I still need to somehow get Elle's blood. My hand goes to my hip, where the dagger is sheathed.

I glance at the distance between us and Declan, and a crazy idea pops in my head. "I've got a better plan. Fly over Declan."

Tytus' one eye glances at me, then he swoops down. When he's parallel to Declan, I hop off – and land, hard, behind Elle. Gripping her waist for leverage, I almost drag her down with me when I slip, but she holds on.

"What the hell are you doing?" She shouts, turning to me. Her hair's plastered to her face, and her eyes are more grey than usual. Not that it stops me from reaching for her neck, and smashing my lips against hers.

Elle tries to push me off, but I hold strong – enough that she risks throwing both of us off Declan if she doesn't stop wriggling about. Intensifying the kiss, I move the hand on her nape to her waist, and the other interlaces our fingers.

Instead of tasting the air around her, I focus on everywhere I'm touching her. Essence of the Elle I know flutters in the air, like a shy butterfly. A whisp of kindness, a faint trace of light, a shimmer of laughter – my attention turns to it.

My grip on her helps to target my abilities, and thus pull her out of her shell, and into the open. Much like I did with

Tytus, only instead of absorbing her anger – or any emotion – it's my mate I try to release.

When her body melts against mine, and she starting kissing back, I know I've got my Elle back.

There's only one way that makes sense to cement this, and it has to be done now. My wolf pushes me to it, encouraging the crazy idea forming in my head.

Pulling back, I cup her cheek instead and whisper, "I need you to trust me, mo grá."

Her wide eyes latch on to me. "Okay."

I pull out the dagger, and prick her index quickly. A few drops pour over the blade, gathering near the hilt. I sheathe the thing again and glance above. "Oy!"

Luz flies Tytus nearby, and I toss the dagger her way. One perfectly placed wind gust, and it lands safely in her palm. Satisfied I've done my piece for this fight, I focus back on my mate.

"Thank you. Now, I absolutely need you to *not* fight off your magic."

Declan chooses that moment to veer to the side, evidently not liking what I'm doing with the one he chose as pawn. *Too feckin' bad, she's mine.*

Refusing to let him take us away from the battle, I grab Elle's waist tighter, pulling her flush against me. Elle thinks I'm about to kiss her again, as she leans forward. And I do – how could I resist those lips?

But when she's fully invested in it, I let myself fall backwards, dragging her with me and into the abyss below.

Declan's all yours, I tell Tytus.

"Finn!" Elle breaks the kiss and screams in my ear, and we're falling, falling...

I cup her cheek despite the wind all around us, and the promise of death we're plummeting towards. "Don't fight your magic, love." Elle's panic fills the air, and I will her to focus. "I believe in you – only you."

She closes her eyes – we've got only a split few seconds left.

Her lips are moving – the ground is getting closer.

Her eyes snap open – and we stop, midair.

A woosh of air goes around us, holding us up and blowing into both our faces. Elle looks around. We're suspended among fog, completely hidden, only us. She peeks below, to the battle taking place underneath us.

Finally, she sets her gaze on me. "How am I doing this?"

"It only stands to reason that with Declan and Tytus being able to fly, you'd have some of that in your blood. Nothing else has worked to get you to accept your true nature, so I figured the chance of imminent death might do it." I squeeze her hands, and smile. "You may not have wings, love, but you've underestimated yourself."

"And...am I..."

"She's gone." I knew it the moment we leaped, and searching her eyes only confirms it. "Do you feel it?"

I do. There's no more dual essence about my Elle. Her alter is truly gone, all trace erased, except for one thing – her eyes are no longer hazel, but rather hazel with a clear grey outline. That part, I don't tell her just yet.

"How do we get down, then?"

I squeeze the hand in mine. "Up to you."

Elisandra

It's surreal, feeling my head empty of anything but me. And seeing us suspended in midair, I almost expect us to drop – but no, we have a full view of the battle from up here. Lucas and Dominic are working on two sides of it, but they're at least working towards the same goal.

Above us, Declan and Tytus go back at it – only this time, Tytus has the upper hand. He's lunging, Lucrezia providing backup with lightning and air, wrapping Declan into a cocoon. Then the massive black zmeu topples out of the sky, spinning on his way down – and hits it with all the force of an asteroid.

The ground shakes, wolves go flying, and I'm thankful we're up in midair. Finn is still holding onto me strongly, and I sense his heart beating fast. He's worried for his friends, worried for what will happen.

Then Tytus flies over us, and lands gracefully next to Declan. It's the exact opposite of the previous fight, and I almost feel bad for Declan. He's right back in the crater.

Lucrezia slips off Tytus straight into Dominic's expecting arms, and I can't hover midair anymore. I need to see this concluded to the end. Figuring out how to get there, however, is another thing.

I try to think in practical terms – how do birds fly, and land? The air around me feels lighter, as though sensing my need to get back to the ground. Next thing I know, we're landing softly.

By the time I run over to Tytus, Finn hot on my heels, he's back in human form. Declan is still in his zmeu shape, breathing heavily, one visible eye trained on all of us. Dani and Tristan, Luz and Dom, Fiona and Tytus, me and Finn – we've made a circle, blocking all exits.

Fiona speaks first. "You tied me to you for too long, zmeu."

You wanted it, witch.

It's loud enough for all of us to hear. Fiona inhales sharply and lifts one hand, drawing a rune in the air. Tytus grabs her wrist, locking eyes with her, and shakes his head. "No. His fate is mine, and I have already decided it."

Declan's body is surrounded by flames again, and he shifts back to human. One sweep of his hand, and he's clothed, though muddy from the crater. Still he stands, lifting his chin in the air. "Is that so, brother? And what have you prepared for me this time, more eons of imprisonment?"

Tytus only stares at him for a long moment, before he says, "No, brother."

Declan snorts. "You are so weak, aligning yourself with these fools. You don't even know our home is still standing, its power ready to be basked in." There's a mad glint in his eyes, and not for the first time, I wonder what else happened while I was away from my body.

Tytus shakes his head. "You have lost your wits. Then again, I should not be surprised."

"I am not lying!" Declan bares his teeth, taking a step forward, but Tytus raises his hand in warning with magic. "So that's it, then? You plan to kill me?" He spreads open his palms. "Have at it, then."

"It is not killing I have in mind," Tytus whispers, "but something else."

From behind Declan, Ileana glides out. He freezes, sniffing the air, then turns slightly to glance over a shoulder. His entire body goes taut with tension as he sees her nearing. "What are you doing here, immortal?" Then he laughs, a cold, bitter sound that raises the hair at the back of my neck.

"You think *you* can imprison me? Only one problem – you lack the power to do so."

"She is not alone."

The voice is deep, grave like two rocks rubbing against each other. From behind the woods Ileana appeared through comes another man. His blonde hair is long to his shoulders, wavy and catching the light of the stars. His eyes are the color of the moon, and his features are of a beauty that hurts to look at.

In contrast to Ileana's flowing, vintage dress, he is wearing a modern day suit. His eyes narrow on Declan as he joins Ileana, and interlaces their fingers. "Together, iubirea mea?"

"Together," she whispers back.

Declan stumbles a few steps, as if afraid. A light as blinding as the sunrise envelops the two immortals, then drips into the ground, making its way to Declan. It shines brighter than anything I've ever seen, and we all have to look away.

There's a sound like an explosion, and pressure builds in my head – then silence.

I look back at the crater, to find it empty. No Declan, no Ileana, and no...whoever that other guy was. Finn wraps his arm around my waist then, and I sense his kiss on my temple. "It's over, a stór."

"What does that mean?" I whisper sleepily against his chest, drained by the day's events.

Finn picks me up in his arms and whispers, "My treasure." That's the last thing I hear before everything fades to black.

∞ ∞ ∞

CHAPTER TWENTY

∞ Iontas ∞

"The backbone of <u>surprise</u> is fusing speed with secrecy."

–Carl von Clausewitz–

Elisandra

A happy sigh escapes me, and I lean back against the cool sheets. A glance to Finn confirms he's grinning smugly, and I roll my eyes. "You could be less smug."

"After that? I don't think so. What was it, a record?"

A blush creeps up my neck, to my cheeks. "Maybe."

I duck my head in the crook of his shoulder, burying my burning face. Finn trails his fingers down my spine in a distracting dance.

"What happens now?"

"Now, we enjoy life. The Reapers are subdued, and their powers removed. Their leader is dead, and they've been disbanded. They'll go back to the edge of town, move on from here, and stop causing trouble. We'll rebuilt the auto shop and bakery. I'll go back working to the shop, you to the bakery, and one of these weekends we'll go up to visit your granny, so I can get a proper introduction."

I smile. "That easy, huh?"

"Yep." He gets up on an elbow, sensing some of my uneasiness. "What's causing that frown, love?"

"It seems almost, I dunno, *too* easy."

Finn nuzzles my neck, dropping kisses on my sensitive skin. "You worry too much, Elle. The Big Bad is imprisoned, Ileana is keeping watch over the rest of us, and we are all alive."

He lifts his head then, his gaze intense. "And most importantly, *you* are alone in your head."

"That does feel nice," I admit. "But what about Declan?"

"What about him?" Finn stops trying to distract me, instead standing to guzzle some water from a bottle on the nightstand.

"Well, where was he taken? How do we know he won't come back? Or get another witch that he can brainwash and–"

Finn drops back to the bed, index finger on my lips, body hovering over mine. His emerald gaze dances with laughter. "You really do worry a lot, huh?"

I nibble on his index, and his eyes darken, his expression growing more intense. "Maybe."

"I'll just have to take your mind off it," he whispers against my lips, then steals a kiss from me.

My hands go around his neck, pulling him closer, my body arching against his. Then he pulls back, and I groan in frustration.

"As for Declan," he says, "I trust in Ileana and her companion to have him handled."

"Who was that other guy, though?"

Finn shrugs one shoulder. "Dominic will probably tell us, he seemed to recognize him. Now, any more questions, or can I get back to kissing you?"

There is one more, but can I voice it? After everything we've been through, and considering he dragged me off a damn zmeu and into clouds, I figure I've earned the right to do so.

"Yeah, just one. What about Ireland?"

Finn's expression sobers up. "Tytus told you, then?"

"When I was at his house, yeah. Not much else to focus on since I couldn't do magic back then, you know. So we talked, about a lot of things. And he mentioned that the threat keeping you in exile doesn't exist anymore."

"Aye, it's true," he says, and my heart drops somewhere in my stomach. "But returning home, that all changed the moment we gave this a shot. I'm not going to leave you, Elle, not unless you're coming with me." His grins, eyes alight with joy. "I'd love to show you Ireland one day, though, now that the threat of Ciaran's people is off my back."

"I'd love to see it, too." I lift my head to meet his incredible eyes. "I love you, you know? Have for a while, I think."

His smile grows more dazzling. "And I you, mo grá." When he bends his head for another kiss, I sigh and give in.

Finn

After the battle, we took a few days to relax. Elle needed to recover from using magic on her own for the first time, and I know Dom and Tristan were eager for some much-needed time with their mates, as well. Lucas was oddly silent the entire time, so it's with mixed emotions I drive back into town after the fourth day, Elle in the passenger seat by my side.

We reach the auto shop, which feels oddly full from the outside. I catch various scents in the air, and nod to Elle. "Seems like the entire gang is here."

"Even Tytus?"

Before I can answer, his trepidation fills the air and he walks out of the shop. Seeing my truck pull in, he hesitates and leans against the wall, waiting for us. His emotions are swirling around, too many to distinguish aside from the trepidation.

Elle removes her seatbelt and steps out of the car, frowning at him. "What's going on? Did something happen?"

He shakes his head, and glances between us. "No, not really. Did you two rest well?"

Elle says nothing, so I take the lead. "Aye, we did. Like everyone else, it seems." I peer past his shoulder to the dusty inside. "Are they trying to rebuild already?"

Tytus shrugs. "Lucas got it in his head he's going to do it alone. The back is completely gone, and Luz and Dani were helping to clean up."

I can imagine how, with their magic combined, it was a hell of a lot easier to sweep away dust and debris. Glancing at Elle, I ask, "You want to join them?"

"Yeah, in a bit." Her voice is shaky, as if she feels something I'm not. Then again, he *is* her ancestor. "What's going on, Tytus?"

He shifts from foot to foot, then runs a hand through his dark hair. A wince pulls at his features, and I'm reminded I was not the only one injured in the fights that took place. That thought goes out the window when Tytus finally reveals the reason for his agitation.

"I'm leaving."

Elle's surprise – and panic – coats the air. "What? Why?"

"Temporarily, if nothing else. The fights took a lot out of me, and the only way I heal is through my zmeu form. It works better if I'm around land of my own – you know what I mean, faoladh."

I nod, and wrap and arm around Elle's shoulders. "Aye, I do." Tytus holds my gaze for a second longer, and I sense something else. "There's more, isn't there?"

"Mm. I need to find out if what Declan said about our home is true, if it's really still standing. There are some things there that humans should never find, and it is high time someone ensures it remains so. Plus, being in the area will help with my healing."

"So... you'll come back?" Elle's wiping at her face, trying to hide away tears, but it's hopeless.

Tytus catches her chin in his gentle grip and lifts her gaze to his, grinning. "I can fly, can't I?"

She sniffles and jumps out of my hold, and into his. Burying her head in his chest, practically half his size, she whispers, "I'm going to miss you."

Tytus chuckles, but I taste his sorrow in the air as well. "And I you, micuţă."

Gently, but firmly, he moves Elle out of his arms and back into mine. His gaze is solid on mine, both a warning and a promise. "Take care of her."

I nod, and watch as he walks away. Something tells me there's more to the story, but of one thing I'm sure – we'll be seeing him again, and sooner rather than later.

After a few sniffles, Elle pulls back. "Do you think he said bye to Luz and Dani?"

When we enter the shop, their red–rimmed eyes tell me that he did, indeed. "Tytus leaving?"

Luz nods, and blows her nose. "But he promised to come back, to finish my training."

"All three of us," Dani says, smiling through her own tears.

I glance in the garage, where Dom and Tristan are busy pulling apart an engine. "I thought we were closed?"

Luz shrugs. "There were a few cars lined up when we came in. Tristan and Dani had already taken a few clients. Humans are afraid after what happened..."

"They're calling it a gas explosion," Dani says. "Lots of homes were destroyed, and I've got a feeling this place is about to become a ghost town."

"That wouldn't necessarily be a bad thing," I say. "Especially with a couple rogue Reapers around."

"Lucas said something about that, when he walked in earlier," Dani says.

"What did he say?"

"He wants to hunt the rest of them, and make sure they're officially gone." Her hesitation is apparent, and I nod at what she's leaving unsaid.

"You mean he's planning an execution, pure and simple."

Luz tears her gaze from the garage. "Something's going on with him, Finn."

"Aye, I know." I'd felt it coming a mile away, but will my alpha finally talk to me? I'm not so sure about the answer to that particular question.

"And Dom?" Elle's quiet voice draws our gaze to the inside of the garage, and our other pack problem. Sure enough, something about my friend's stance tells me we're in for another surprise.

"Lucas is at the back," Luz whispers. "They were at it again this morning, within moments of us walking in."

I nod, and kiss Elle's temple. "Better I go fix it, then."

Past the dusty reception, the place is in shambles. Plumbing and wires hang from the ceiling, through the floor, pieces of furniture charred scattered about. At the back, I hear an incessant banging.

There's no door to speak of, so when I turn the corner in the hallway, I have a full view of Lucas' office – or what's left of it. Ashes are scattered on the ground, the previous library burned. Pieces of furniture remain, and half of the place is collapsed.

Lucas, in a dirty shirt and jeans, is lifting massive pieces of rocks and hauling them out of the open hole in the wall. I can see a pile accumulating on the outside, to presumably be used to rebuild.

"Need any help?"

He doesn't stop in his efforts, nor does he speak. I try to taste his emotions, but there's nothing in the air – again. Frowning, I take a step closer, thinking it's just the distance. But nope, there's really nothing.

"Lucas, you have to talk to someone."

He thrusts another rock outside, the veins bulging in his biceps, and turns to me. His features are set in stone, his gaze as dark as I've ever seen it. And is that a red rim around his irises? More than his expression, though, it's his words that chill me.

"You want to talk? Bene. Dominic Konstantin has disobeyed me for the last time. I made the mistake of not running it by you and Tristan the first time, but this time, I fully intend to go through with it. He will be gone from this pack before the sun sets tonight."

"You don't mean that," I tell him. "Dom is as much part of this pack as everyone else. You've already thrown him out once."

"Si, and took him back. Stupid me."

"If you throw him out, Lucrezia will go, too."

Lucas shrugs. "So? It's not like she needs our protection now."

"How can you say that, after she just died on our watch?"

A touch of guilt coats the air, then disappears, once again throwing me off my game. "How are you doing that?"

"Doing what?"

"Controlling your emotions, hiding them from me."

Lucas turns back to the rocks. "No idea what you're talking about."

I take a few steps closer, grabbing his shoulder. He shrugs me off, getting in my face. Yep, that's definitely red in his eyes. "Something's wrong with you, mate. Ever since the fight, and now you want to go execute the last Reapers?"

Lucas backs off, and shrugs. Another massive rock gets tossed out the back. "And so?"

"It's not you." I struggle to find the right words. "You've spent all this time trying to keep peace in town, why go to the other extreme now?"

"Because morals are for weaklings," he hisses, grunting as he tosses another rock. "And I am finally ready to live up to my name."

"What does that mean?"

He says nothing, dismissing me as easily as he would an insect. I scowl at him. "Fine, don't answer me. But, Lucas, think this through, will you?"

He throws me a dark glare.

Then the air changes, and I turn around – just as the sound of heels clattering on stone resounds in the hallway. In walks a leggy, raven–haired girl that could have easily stepped off a magazine cover. One perfect eyebrow arches over an icy blue eye as she takes in the mess of an office. "I'm looking for Luciano Conti."

I turn to my alpha, stunned by what I sense off him – startling anger, and a gust of fear that chills me to the bone. "You found him. But I go by Lucas now."

Finally, some emotions, just not the ones I'd expected. And who is she, that she's able to affect him so? I shake the thought off, instead asking, "Lucas?"

His gaze is cold when he meets mine. "Leave us."

Again, that need to listen to him takes over my wolf, and I walk away. For the first time, I wonder if all of Elle's worries were warranted. And then another question, more insistent, worms its way in my head.

Who the hell is Luciano Conti?

∞ ∞ ∞

EPILOGUE

The cave was suited for a king. Gilded in gold, it was a cage perfect for one person – Declan. The black zmeu was in animal form, curled up in a corner, ignoring the luxury all around him. Sulking at his imprisonment, he preferred to watch the days go by, thinking of revenge.

Then a portal opened in the middle of the cave, and Ileana entered. He did not bother looking her way, instead toying with a chest of gold in his vicinity.

She floated closer, observing him in silence for a few moments. "You will not escape here as easily as before," she finally said.

Declan turned to human form, not bothering to hide his nudity as he sprawled himself on top of more gold. "What makes you think I want to? I've got everything I need, right here. Definitely a move up from the last imprisonment."

A tight smile spread on Ileana's lips. "You will not be happy for long, Declan. You and I both know that."

His expression darkened, his golden eyes warning she was treading on thin ground. "Have you come here to gloat?"

She smiled. "Nu, zmeu, but to deliver a message."

Declan pretended to be engrossed in the jewelry surrounding him. The two thick golden bracelets on his wrists prevented him from doing any magic other than switching forms, which rendered his days incredibly dull.

Ileana glided closer still, her soft voice getting on his nerves. "Your brother bid me to say goodbye. He also said to tell you that whatever you did in your home, he plans to undo it, and ensure nothing comes of it."

Declan snorted. "Always the protector, my brother."

Engrossed in the ground, he didn't realize how close Ileana was until she touched his shoulder. He pulled back, scowling at her. The spot she had touched tingled, like something way too sweet had been poured into him. "What was that? What did you do?"

"Call it a gift."

Then she turned to walk away, laughing and gliding across the floor like she had no worries in the world.

"A gift? What gift?"

When she didn't answer, he shouted, "What *gift*, woman!"

Over her shoulder, Ileana smiled. "You will find a love so pure, it will wipe the evil out of you."

Then she was gone.

Declan looked at his surroundings, then laughed. "And how the hell do you think that'll happen, when I'm rotting in this gilded cage?"

In answer, a twinkling laugh echoed around him.

Preview of Book IV

Last to Love — A Moonlight Rogues Novel

Lucas

Matteo. Francesca. A past as buried as it is painful...

All that flashes in my mind when the spitfire bursts into what's left of my office. I'm no fool, and her scent is too easy to determine. And yet, despite my inner turmoil, I manage to keep my regular neutral expression.

"Leave us."

Finn glances at me, and I don't know how much my faoladh friend has sensed of my reaction. I can only hope he keeps whatever he did feel to himself.

My gaze narrows on the brunette the minute he's gone through the door.

"And who are you?"

"Monica Delucci," she says, swinging her hips as she walks towards me, then looks around. Her icy eyes take in the debris. "Redecorating, I see? I'm afraid that'll have to be put on hold. Your parents sent me."

Coldness sweeps through me at her admission, but I mask my emotions before they get the best of me. "Did they, now?"

Monica

Mio Dio, but they could have warned me about him!

Luciano Conti is nothing I expected. He's gorgeous, and fine as hell, sure. But he's also cold, and unsettling. And in control. I didn't miss the way his wolf responded, nor the pack outside of here. Clearly, I've walked in the middle of a warzone.

The question is, how much more chaos can I cause before Luciano – or Lucas, as he calls himself now – throws me out of here? I bite my lower lip, noticing his gaze drop to it. My instructions were clear. Ruin the life he built here, and force him to come back home. If I do so successfully, I'll be queen to his king, and Alessandro Conti would ensure it.

Only problem is, as I'm standing opposite Luciano, it takes all my will to ignore the hum of electricity between us.

In an effort to distract myself, I take in the barren place once more. "You've done well for yourself, Luciano. Your parents will be proud."

A noise escapes him, and I meet his unnerving gaze just in time to catch a glimpse of amusement. Then he schools his expression once more.

"What was so funny?" He clearly doesn't like my question. But it's his words that unsettle me more.

"Funny you keep mentioning *parents*, as if I have two of them. My mother died years ago. Matter of fact, she committed suicide after my brother died in a failed deal – all thanks to my father. But surely Alessandro Conti told you all this, before sending you in the wolf's den?"

His grin is nothing short of predatory. And that dangerous glint in his onyx eyes causes a low tremor to start in me.

Shit. I've been had, that's for sure. Only question is, how the heck do I get out of this now?

Coming to all retailers November 21st, 2019!

Sign up for an ARC now![1]

---

1. https://www.alexawhitewolf.com/last-to-love

Sign up for my readers' group **at www.alexawhitewolf.com/contact** and receive a copy of *Unconditional Love* for **FREE**, as well as first dibs on cover reveals, discounts, giveaways, prizes **and more!**

Cheers,

Alexa

Did you love *Third to Tumble*? Then you should read
Moonlight Rogues: Origins by Alexa Whitewolf!

***Four wolves. Four alpha males. One town to bring them all
together....***

The lupo mannaro without a family....

Lucas was born to be king, until the price was too high.
Now, he'll have to settle for alpha...if he can escape his past.

The vârcolac without a home...

The mountains of yore call his name louder than his
parents' pleas to stay. But is he ready for what gate has in
store, even if it means giving up his hard-earned freedom?

The faoladh without a purpose...

One case was all it took. One mistake he could never take back. Now, he'll pay the ultimate price - exile.

The lobisomem without peace...

Tristan chose to save his country, not knowing the price was his sanity. Is there really a coming home, for the one who's seen it all, and more?

A Moonlight Rogues novella to give you a taste of four amazing stories, each one filled with unique folkloric add-ons.

Read more at https://www.alexawhitewolf.com.

Also by Alexa Whitewolf

Moonlight Rogues
Moonlight Rogues: Origins
First to Fall
Second to Surrender
Third to Tumble

The Avalon Chronicles
Avalon Dreams
Avalon Wishes
Avalon Nightmares
The Avalon Chronicles - Complete Series

The Sage's Legacy
The Dragon Medallion
The Dragon Manuscript
Relics of the Underworld
The Sage's Legacy - Complete Series

Standalone Novels
Unconditional Love
Blood Ties, Love Binds
Blazing in a Storm of Ashes (Coming Soon)

**Watch for more at
www.alexawhitewolf.com.**

About the Author

Alexa Whitewolf is a dog-loving, caffeine-addicted, all-around traveling enthusiast. Author of three series of fantasy, paranormal and young adult, she spends her nights dreaming up new stories and her days fighting reality. She lives in Ottawa, Canada, with her husband and two mischievous furballs- Zeus and Achilles. Check out her website at www.alexawhitewolf.com !

Read more at https://www.alexawhitewolf.com.